HEXES IN TEXAS

HEXES IN TEXAS
CASE FILES OF AN URBAN DRUID™ BOOK 5

AUBURN TEMPEST
MICHAEL ANDERLE

This book is a work of fiction. All of the characters, organizations, and events portrayed in this novel are either products of the author's imagination or are used fictitiously. Sometimes both.

Copyright © 2022 LMBPN Publishing
Cover by Fantasy Book Design
Cover copyright © LMBPN Publishing
A Michael Anderle Production

LMBPN Publishing supports the right to free expression and the value of copyright. The purpose of copyright is to encourage writers and artists to produce the creative works that enrich our culture.

The distribution of this book without permission is a theft of the author's intellectual property. If you would like permission to use material from the book (other than for review purposes), please contact support@lmbpn.com. Thank you for your support of the author's rights.

LMBPN Publishing
PMB 196, 2540 South Maryland Pkwy
Las Vegas, NV 89109

Version 1.00, December 2022
eBook ISBN: 979-8-88541-178-3
Print ISBN: 979-8-88878-032-9

THE HEXES IN TEXAS TEAM

Thanks to our JIT Team:

Dorothy Lloyd
Dave Hicks
James Caplan
Deb Mader
Diane L. Smith
Jan Hunnicutt
Kelly O'Donnell
John Ashmore

Editor
SkyFyre Editing Team

THE USUAL SUSPECTS

Clan Cumhaill
  Aiden – the oldest of Fi's brothers, druid tank, Toronto police officer, married to Kinu, and father of Jackson, Meg, Ireland, and Carragh.
  Bodhmall – Fionn's paternal aunt who raised him and taught him how to be a druid.
  Brendan – Fi's brother, second in the birth order, formerly deceased, given back to the family after the Culling and restricted to living on the mythical Celtic island Emhain Abhlach with Emmet.
  Calum – Fi's brother, third in the birth order, druid archer, Toronto police officer, and married to Kevin. Together they are foster parents to Bizzy, an otterkie shifter.
  Dillan – Fi's brother, fourth in the birth order, druid rogue, Toronto police officer, and in love with Evangeline, Angel of the Choir, formerly a reaper, and now a guardian angel.
  Dionysus – God of Wine and Fertility, Light Weaver, Hunter-god, guardian of the mythical Celtic island Emhain Abhlach, and honorary Cumhaill.
  Emmet – Fi's brother, fifth in the birth order, druid buffer,

guardian and committed caretaker of the mythical Celtic island Emhain Abhlach.

Fiona – youngest of the six Cumhaill kids, chosen by Fionn to represent the Fianna Warriors in a new generation of urban druids, Hunter-god, Celtic shaman, guardian of the mythical Celtic island Emhain Abhlach, bonded companion to Bruin and Dart.

Fionn, a.k.a. Finn MacCool – Hunter-god, mythical warrior in Irish mythology, guardian of the mythical Celtic island Emhain Abhlach, ancestor of and mentor to Fi and her family.

Kevin – artist, high school sweetheart, and husband to Calum.

Lara – Fi's grandmother, nature druid, and the Snow White of the Druid Order.

Liam – one of Fi's best friends, now her stepbrother, operator/bartender for Shenanigans.

Lugh – Fi's grandfather, druid historian, Keeper of the Shrine, and Elder of the Druid Order.

Niall – Fi's father, retired Toronto police officer, married to Shannon and living in Ireland with his parents.

Nikon Tsambikos – ancient Greek immortal, Light Weaver, guardian of the mythical Celtic island Emhain Abhlach, and honorary Cumhaill.

Shannon – mother of Liam, became the pseudo-mother to the Cumhaill kids after her husband and their mother died when the kids were young. Her husband Mark was Niall's partner and died in the line of duty.

Sloan Mackenzie – Fi's soulmate, druid healer, Keeper of the Toronto Shrine, and guardian of the mythical Celtic island Emhain Abhlach.

Wallace Mackenzie – Sloan's father, master druid healer, Elder of the Druid Order, recently separated from Sloan's mother Janet Mackenzie.

Animal Companions

Aurora – Tad's red-tailed kite.

Bruinior the Brave (Bruin) a.k.a. Killer Clawbearer – Fiona's mythical battle bear and Bear of native myth and legend.

Daisy – Calum's epileptic skunk companion.

Dartamont (Dart) – Fiona's Western dragon, involved with Saxa, and oldest brother to twenty-two other dragons.

Dax – Lara's badger.

Doc Martin (Doc) – Emmet's pine marten followed him home from the Santa Claus Parade.

Nyrora (Rory) – Dillan's Koinonos Dragon. Dark purple with gold webbing for her wings, she bonds with him at rest, creating a living tattoo on his skin.

More Greeks

Andromeda Tsambikos – Nikon's younger sister, ancient Greek immortal, Light Weaver, guardian of the mythical Celtic island Emhain Abhlach, and legal counsel for SITFO.

Nikon Tsambikos Senior – Nikon's grandfather, ancient Greek immortal, Light Weaver, and guardian of the mythical Celtic island Emhain Abhlach.

Politimi Tsambikos – Nikon's younger sister and ancient Greek immortal.

The Moon Called

Anyx – lion shifter, Garnet's beta, and mate to Zuzanna.

Garnet Grant – lion shifter, Alpha of the Toronto Moon Called, Grand Governor of the Lakeshore Guild of Empowered Ones, Fi's friend, mentor, and boss at SITFO, mated to Myra and father of adopted bear shifter Imari.

Myra – ash nymph, Fae Historian, mated to Garnet, owner/operator of Myra's Mystical Emporium, mother of adopted bear shifter Imari.

Thaos – lion shifter, one of Garnet's valued pack enforcers, third in the pack hierarchy.

Zuzanna – lion shifter, mate to Anyx, works with SITFO as a member of the Toronto Special Investigations Unit.

The Vampires

Benjamin – vampire, companion to Laurel.

Xavier – vampire, King of the Toronto Seethes.

The Nine Families of the Druid Order

Lugh and Lara Cumhaill – parents of Niall, grandparents of Aiden, Brendan, Calum, Dillan, Emmet, and Fiona.

James and Caitrona Dempsey – parents of Brian and Reagan.

Evan and Iris Doyle – parents of Ciara.

Connor and Kate Flannigan – parents of Erik.

Wallace Mackenzie – father of Sloan, ex-husband to Janet.

Tad McNiff – recently took his place as a head of the Nine Families after his father, Riordan, gave himself over to Mingin in a quest for ultimate power.

Finley and Elaine O'Malley – parents of Lia.

Brian and Gwyneth Perry – parents of Jarrod, Darcy, and Davin.

Sean and Maude Scott – parents of Seamus.

Friends

Danika – witch from San Francisco, Nikon's ex-lover.

Laurel – ghost, companion to Benjamin, Fi's high school friend.

Merlin/Pan Dora/Emrys – druid and wizard of legend, owner of Queens on Queen drag club and the attached soup kitchen, union bonded to the champagne-colored Western dragon, Empress Cazzienth.

Patty – Man o' Green, union bonded to Cyteira the Queen of Wyrms, a.k.a. the Wyrm Dragon Queen.

Suede Silverbirch – elven representative on Toronto's Lakeshore Guild of Empowered Ones.

Zxata – ash nymph, Myra's brother, nymph representative on Toronto's Lakeshore Guild of Empowered Ones.

More Hunter-gods

Ahren – Hunter-god, shaman, navigates the astral plane as a golden eagle.

Samuel – Hunter-god, shaman, navigates the astral plane as an ebony wolf.

Quon Shen – Hunter-god, shaman, navigates the astral plane as a water dragon.

Team Trouble

Brody – wolf shifter/vampire hybrid, new member-in-training for Team Trouble.

Dantanion Jann (Dan the djinn) – djinn, member of Team Trouble.

Diesel Demarco – goliath, new member-in-training for Team Trouble.

Jenna – siren, new member-in-training for Team Trouble.

John Maxwell – Deputy Commissioner of the Royal Canadian Mounted Police, founder of SITFO, the Special Investigations Task Force for Ontario.

Iceland Dragons – Free Dragons of Tintagel

Bryvanay – black, majestic, and slightly smaller than Utiss.

Cazzienth Empress of the West (Cazzie) – glistening champagne-colored dragon with gold and burnt orange wings, and a strong tail that ends in a treacherous-looking ball-spike.

Saxa – a sunshine yellow dragon with dark gold wings and a blunt snout of the same color.

Utiss – a massive purple dragon and the dominant male of the Free Dragons of Tintagel.

Ireland Dragons
Drakes – Chua.
Westerns – Abeloth, Cadmus, Chezzo, Dart, Esym, Kaida, Scarlett, Torrim.
Wyrms – Scarlett, +6 we haven't met.
Wyverns – 7 we haven't met.

Pronunciations
adelphos – *adelfos* – Greek for "brother" or "my brother."
agapi mou – *ah-gah-pea moo* – Greek for "my love."
Cumhaill – *Cool* – Fiona and the family's last name (modern).
gliko mou – Greek for "my sweet."
mac Cumhaill – *MacCool* – Fiona and the family's last name (traditional).
mo chroi – *muh chree* – Irish for my heart/my love.
a ghra – *uh grawh* – Irish for my love (intimate).
a stór – *uh stohr* – Irish for a treasure.
paidi mou – *peth-ee moo* – Greek for "my child."
Slan! – *slawn* – health be with you.
Slainte mhath – *slawn cha va* – cheers, good health.

Irish Terms
Arragh – a guttural sound for when something bad happens.
Banjaxed – broken, ruined, completely obliterated.
Bogger – those who live in the boggy countryside.
Bollocks – a man's testicles.
Bollix – thrown into disorder, bungled, messed up.
Boyo – boy, lad.
Cock-crow – close enough that you can hear a cock crow.
Craic – gossip, fun, entertainment.
Culchie – those who live in the agricultural countryside.

Donkey's years – a long time.
Dosser – a layabout, lazy person.
Eejit – slightly less severe than idiot.
Fair whack away – far away.
Feck – an exclamation less severe than fuck.
Flute – a man's penis.
Gammie – injured, not working properly.
Hape – a heap.
Howeyah/Howaya/Howya – a greeting not necessarily requiring an answer.
Irish – traditional Irish language (commonly referred to as Irish Gaelic unless you're Irish).
Knackers – a man's testicles.
Mocker – a hex.
Och – used to express agreement or disagreement to something said.
Shite – less offensive than shit.
Gobshite – fool, acting in unwanted behavior.
Wee – small.

PRONUNCIATIONS

Pronunciations
   Adelphos – *adelfos* – Greek for "brother" or "my brother."
   agapi mou – *ah-gah-pea moo* – Greek for "my love."
   Cumhaill – *Cool* – Fiona and the family's last name (modern).
   gliko mou – Greek for "my sweet."
   mac Cumhaill – *MacCool* – Fiona and the family's last name (traditional).
   Mo chroi – *muh chree* – Irish for my heart/my love.
   a ghra – *uh grawh* – Irish for my love (intimate).
   a stór – *uh stohr* – Irish for a treasure.
   paidi mou – *peth-ee moo* – Greek for "my child."
   Slan! – *slawn* – health be with you.
   Slainte mhath – *slawn cha va* – cheers, good health.

Irish Terms
   Arragh – a guttural sound for when something bad happened.
   Banjaxed – broken, ruined, completely obliterated.
   Bogger – those who live in the boggy countryside.
   Bollocks – a man's testicles.

Bollix – thrown into disorder, bungled, messed up.
Boyo – boy, lad.
Cock-crow – close enough that you can hear a cock crow.
Craic – gossip, fun, entertainment.
Culchie – those who live in the agricultural countryside.
Donkey's years – a long time.
Dosser – a layabout, lazy person.
Eejit – slightly less severe than idiot.
Fair whack away – far away.
Feck – an exclamation less severe than fuck.
Flute – a man's penis.
Gammie – injured, not working properly.
Hape – a heap.
Howeyah/Howaya/Howya – a greeting not necessarily requiring an answer.
Irish – traditional Irish language (commonly referred to as Irish Gaelic unless you're Irish).
Knackers – a man's testicles.
Mocker – a hex.
Och – used to express agreement or disagreement to something said.
Shite – less offensive than shit
Gobshite – fool, acting in unwanted behavior.
Wee – small.

CHAPTER ONE

"What about this one, Auntie Fi?"

I examine the crimson maple leaf he's twirling in his fingers for my inspection. "Oh, that's a great one, buddy. Definitely that one. Give it to Uncle Sloan to add to our keeper pile."

My nephew is now an unbelievable seven years old. He is one of my favorite people to spend time with, which is high praise considering the awesomeness of my social circle.

I glance across the leafy path between the trees of our sacred grove and breathe in the fae power snapping in the air.

"What about you, Meggie? Did you find anything you want to add to our end-of-summer celebration bouquet for Uncle Emmet and Brenny?"

Meg runs over to me, her cheeks flushed pink and her hands clutching an array of sticks, fallen acorns, and maple keys. "These good?"

"Wow, you guys really are amazing at this."

Flopsy and Mopsy flutter by, wiggling their little cotton tails and waving their iridescent purple wings. They land over where we set out the sweet and salty Smartfood popcorn for them to munch on as a weekend treat.

Pim came out to hang with us for a while too before heading back into their home tree to tend to baby Lydi.

The warmth of summer is quickly receding. The end of our hot season is over like the flick of a switch. In Toronto, September can go one of three ways. It can still be warm, it can be autumn overnight, or it can cool down and give us one last burst of summer heat as a farewell tribute.

Sadly, this summer, there was no last hurrah.

As the season ended, it took its final bow and hit us with cool nights, turning leaves, and the smell of people firing up their fireplaces instead of their backyard fire tables.

Sloan and I missed the past two months, secluding ourselves in the joy of newlywed bliss. With the wells of our hearts and souls filled, we've pledged to reconnect with our lives and catch up with those we've neglected.

A stiff September breeze whips a loose swath of auburn curls into my face. I straighten, trap it in my fingers, and tuck it back in my ponytail. "What do you say, monkeys? Should we take the twins inside and get some hot chocolate and cinnamon rolls?"

"Hells yeah!" Jackson shouts, fist-pumping the air.

I bite my bottom lip to keep from laughing and try not to react. There's no helping it. Jackson is a Cumhaill through and through. His exclamation could've been much worse, considering all the hot-blooded Irish men in his life.

Gathering the handful of nature bric-a-brac from Meg's clutches, I direct them back to where Dillan and Sloan sit in the rattan basket chairs playing with the twins, Ireland and Carragh. Manx and Bruin act as furry barriers to keep the toddlers from escaping.

"Hello, boys," I say as we join them. "We think it's a good time to head inside to create our masterpiece and enjoy our hot chocolate and treats."

"Aye, that sounds perfect, luv." Sloan stands, tosses Ireland in the air to make her giggle, and nuzzles into her neck with a million kisses to make her squirm.

Not to be outdone, Dillan blows a raspberry kiss on Carragh's belly and hangs her upside down, swinging her along the ground while she squeals.

It doesn't get any better.

"You boys coming in?" I ask Manx and Bruin.

"In a bit," Manxy says. "Bruin's going next door to invite Daisy out for some fresh air. With you two so busy these days, he hasn't spent much time with our little sister."

Aw…sweet. "Okiedoodle, we'll be inside when you're done. Give Daisy our love. If you all want to come inside, we'd love to see her."

"Aye, we'll tell her, Red."

The seven of us make our way inside and take off all our outside clothes to race around the main floor and have our treats. I set all the nature treasures onto the craft pad on the kitchen table and instruct everyone to head toward the powder room to wash up.

"Hotness, can you check the gate?" I shout over my shoulder as I rinse Ireland's hands and set her on the floor next to Jackson. He's got the hand towel and is in charge of drying his sisters off.

"Aye, luv. Locked in place and spelled fer good measure."

I snort. Only he would magically spell a baby gate. "Awesome. Thanks."

When the washup is complete, we rush toward the front of the house like a stampeding horde, and I swing the babies into the pack-and-play for safekeeping.

"What's the word, monkeys?" Dillan has the TV remote and points it at the Disney Plus screen. "Pick something everyone will like."

"The babies don't care, but Meggie's favorite is *Zootopia*," Jackson says.

Dillan calls it up and gets them started.

"Good on ye, sham." Sloan winks at him. "Yer the best kind of big brother."

Jackson grins and stands a little straighter. "After crafts and our snack, can we visit Uncle Emmet and Uncle Brendon in the palace?"

I nod. "For sure we can. Today is family fun day. We can do whatever you want. Name it."

A mischievous smile lights up his face. "Then I want you to take me dragon flying on Dart."

Well damn. Outsmarted by a kid.

Kinu is still giving me the cold shoulder from our wedding weekend. I don't suppose taking her son up on a dragon will earn me any points in the "not putting my kids in danger category," but honestly, I've bent over backward for two months now, and it seems I've been tried and convicted already.

"Sure, buddy. You've been a big help this weekend and deserve a special reward. Yeah, we'll go flying once we get the twins down for their naps and the uncles only have to watch Megs."

"Yes!" Jackson races at me with his hand raised.

I raise my palm to give him a high-five, and he pulls back at the last minute. "Whoa, too slow."

I laugh and point for him to sit on the couch. "You're too tricky for me, buddy."

When the four of them are busy watching Judy Hopps on her first day as a cop in *Zootopia*, I shuffle over to help Sloan and Dillan get the snacks together.

Except neither is getting the snacks.

"What's the look?"

"Ye promised Jackson a dragon ride. Are ye sure ye want to do that, *a ghra*?"

"I'm damned if I do and damned if I don't. Kinu's already made up her mind about me, so why break Jackson's heart? Double jeopardy, amirite?"

Dillan laughs. "I suppose that's one way to look at it."

The kettle has boiled, and we make Jackson and Meg each a hot chocolate and leave plenty of space at the top of their mugs for a few ice cubes to cool things down quickly.

Once that's done, I check the temperature and give each a whipped cream shot on top. "Okay, monkeys, over to the snack table."

Because we have the kids for the whole weekend, Dillan brought over their plastic picnic table. We made a spot for it by moving the couch closer to the front door and putting it on an angle. That way, the bigger two can have their snacks and still watch their cartoons.

When they've settled, Dillan and I get the twins locked down in their highchairs and give them their snacks. They get baby cookies and extremely watered-down apple juice.

When everyone is settled and quietly munching away, I sit at the kitchen breakfast bar.

Sloan's already plated our cinnamon rolls and is prepping our hot chocolates. "Fer my lovely bride, extra chocolate, a long pour of Bailey's, and a shot of whipped cream and chocolate sprinkles to top it off."

I accept the chocolatey perfection and sigh. "I heart you hard, hotness."

He winks at me. "Right back at ye, Mrs. Mackenzie."

Dillan snorts. "You realize there are other people in the room trying to eat, right?"

I bite the soft cinnamon goodness and groan. "Please, you have put me through way worse."

He grins. "That was B.E.D., not W.E.D."

Sloan looks confused so I help him out. "That was Before Eva Dillan, not With Eva Dillan."

Sloan laughs. "Yer family really should come with an instruction manual at times. Ye speak yer own language."

True story.

After we consume our snacks and the babies start to droop,

we get the kids wiped off and grab Jackson's shoes and jacket. Meg and the twins won't be going outside, so they're good with what they've got in the diaper bag.

Dillan goes outside to check on Bruin, Manx, and Daisy and returns with all three. "Are you coming with us to the island, baby girl?"

"I miss Doc," she says.

I glance at Dillan. "Do Kev and Calum know we're stealing their girl?"

Dillan nods. "Kev tossed me some of Daisy's medicine over the fence in case we stay past dinner."

"Excellent. Then I guess we're all set." Bruin merges with me for the trip through the portal gate, and I get a better grip on the wriggle monster I have in my arms.

"All set?" Dillan asks the older two. He's got one on each side and reaches down for their hands. "You remember the rules, right?"

Jackson and Meg both nod but it's Jackson who answers. "We walk straight through the portal, ignore the butterfly tinglies, and come out at the island. No stopping. No fussing."

Dillan grins. "That's right. If you forgot anything, we'll come back for it after. Got it?"

They nod.

We don't think there's any danger involved with the kids passing through the portal, but we're not taking chances. They've got Cumhaill DNA and should have no issues, but it's still new, and we tend to be overprotective with our kids.

Sloan has the diaper bag over his shoulder and Carragh in his arms, and I've got Ireland on my hip and our nature bouquet in my free hand.

"All righty then, into the magical pantry we go."

After Sloan and I got back from our honeymoon and settled into our new lives, Merlin set up our direct portal door into a storage room on the palace's second floor. Accessing Emmet's and Brendan's lives is now as easy as walking through the kitchen pantry and finding ourselves here.

I love everything about it, and it's helped a lot to soothe my broken heart about living so far from my brothers, my father, Shannon, and my grandparents.

After releasing Bruin, he lumbers off with Manx and Daisy in search of their missing forest friend—Doc Martin.

"Hello the house!" I call as we step into the main corridor of the second floor. "Where is everyone?"

"We're in the Great Hall, Jane." I smile and continue to join up with Dionysus and the others.

The Great Hall of the golden dildo is our usual meeting place and where we spend most of our indoor time when visiting the enchanted city of Isilon.

As the three of us bring the kids through the door, Gran is the first one we see. She's got her arms out wide and is bending over, waiting for Jackson and Meg to run and give her hugs and kisses.

"Och, I think ye've grown a foot since last weekend." Gran looks them over, her eyes alight. "Ye must stop. I don't want ye growin' up so fast. What will I do when I don't have my great-grandbabies to snuggle?"

"You can snuggle us." Dillan grins. "Just sayin'. We might not be as cute, but we won't smear ketchup on your dress."

Gran laughs and traps Dillan's face between her palms. "Who says yer not as cute? Yer adorable my wee man."

Dillan wrinkles his nose and makes a face. "Guys don't want to be adorable, Gran."

"How about handsome then? Will that work?"

"Handsome works." He kisses her cheek before meeting Granda for a chest-to-chest welcome. The two pat one another's backs as men do and step back.

Dillan undoes his shirt and runs a hand over the purple dragon resting within him. He brushes a finger over her snout and smiles. "We're on the island, sweet girl. Do you want to go play with the dragons?"

Rory bursts free of her resting place and flutters around us a few laps before the little pseudo-dragon soars toward the opening in the wall that leads off to the balcony.

"Did Calum and Kevin not come with ye?" Granda asks.

"Not this time." I watch Rory spin in the air as she goes off to find Dart and the others. "Kevin's boss is out of town for the weekend, so he's running the gallery. Calum's keeping him company and Bizzy is having a play day with Imari at the compound in Africa."

"Lovely. What do ye have there?" Gran points at the autumn centerpiece arrangement we made with the kids this morning. "Is that to brighten the table of yer uncles' home?"

Jackson grins. "Yeah, we got the stuff from the grove. I picked the big leaves. Auntie Fi said we needed lots of color. Meggie picked mostly sticks. They aren't pretty."

"Och, sticks are pretty too in their way. How about I put this on the hutch so everyone who comes in here will see it? Is that a good spot, do ye think?"

Jackson nods. "That's good."

An excited squeal has me turning to see what's going on across the room. Meg is getting eaten up by Emmet, Brenny, and Dionysus.

I knew they were having a video game marathon last night and by the bags under their eyes, it might still be going.

"Where are our hugs from you two?" Granda asks. "It's been donkey's years since we've seen ye."

It hasn't, but I won't complain. I take my turn hugging my grandparents, thankful as I am every minute of every day that they sought us out and reunited our family. "Hey, Gran. Hey Granda. Howeyah?"

After a side hug from each of them, Gran steps in and takes Carragh from me.

Sloan hugs them both, and Granda takes Ireland. Once they have the twins, they pepper them with kisses, take the diaper bag, and head across the hall. "Nap time."

I laugh and wrap my arms around Sloan. "I guess we're officially off duty."

He chuckles. "I guess so."

"Break it up, married people." Tarzan sticks his hands between Sloan and me and pries us apart. "You've had your alone time. It's the Greeks' turn for some Fi lurve."

"Speaking of Greeks in the plural, where is Nikon?"

"He went to say hello to Sarah and invite her to join us."

Interesting. Nikon's interest in Sarah seems to have escalated since the two of them have been working as the magical seals for the Boundary Gate. I've seen her with Emmet, and I've seen her with Nikon, and I honestly can't say who might be a better match.

Not that I get a vote.

Dionysus leans into my line of sight. "Where'd you go just then? Fi, I've been patient. I want my best friend back."

I chuckle and step in to hug him. "Sorry, Tarzan. I didn't mean to neglect you, sweetie."

I meet Sloan's gaze, and he winks at me. "I guess I have been monopolizin' ye a bit."

"Hey, no complaints here."

Dionysus rolls his eyes. "Yeah, yeah, Irish is the hunkiest hunk of a man, and you get warm and tingly in all your lady bits when he flashes those mint green eyes at you. We know. Now, enough eye-fucking. Nicky and I are claiming our turn."

I peg him with a look. "Eye-fucking?"

"Yes, that ocular intercourse the two of you share like we can't read your gazes."

"I don't know what—"

He tilts forward, shaking his head. "Don't even try to deny it. You're so easy to read it's embarrassing. You're also over-sexed right now, so your mind and body are craving. Trust me. I know the signs. The best thing to get back to a balanced life is to go cold turkey."

I laugh as he tugs me toward the buffet and points at a flaky croissant stacked high with yumminess. "Eat that."

I accept the sandwich when he hands it to me and glance at the stacked meat beneath the sliced gouda, lettuce, and tomato. "What's this?"

"Hellooo, Jane." He snaps his fingers in front of my face and hits me with an unblinking stare. "It's cold turkey. We just went over that."

I laugh and catch up with his train of thought. "You realize going cold turkey doesn't mean…"

He's watching me with the face of a god and the innocence of a boy, and my heart lurches inside my chest. "Never mind. This is me going cold turkey."

"Good girl."

I take a bite of the sandwich and groan. "It's delicious. Thank you, Tarzan."

"You're welcome. Now come with me. There's so much I've been waiting to tell you." He steps in tight to side hug me and directs me toward the outer balcony. As we walk, he holds out his hand, and a scroll of parchment unfurls as gravity takes the free end toward the ground. "I made a list."

CHAPTER TWO

As Dionysus goes through his list of things he wants to share with me, I lean on the balcony railing, chew my sandwich, and gaze down over the enchanted city. Since my wedding weekend when the sentient city held us captive, we've been working to repopulate Isilon.

At first, there was a huge surge of beings that sought haven within the city's walls, but over the past weeks, that influx has eased.

"Contessa McSparkles ate two of my Chia pets during one of my parties. Is it possible for a pegasus unicorn to be jealous? I looked it up on the Internet, but there's nothing about that anywhere. I found stuff about misbehaving dogs, cats, horses, and goats, but nothing that helped me."

I chuckle and set my hand on his wrist in support. "Either she was making a point, or she was hungry. Which do you think it was?"

"I don't think she was hungry."

"Then maybe if you're going to have a party and won't have any time to lavish on her, you can take her to the savanna for a visit with Imari. She'll get plenty of attention there and won't murder your Chia pets."

Dionysus sighs and hugs me, his cheek pressing down on the top of my head. "This is why I need you, Jane."

I breathe him in and hug him tighter. "I've missed you too, sweetie."

It takes another five minutes to go through the other talking points on his list, but when we get to the end, he seems content. "Thanks for listening, Jane."

"Always, buddy." The two of us fall silent, and I smile at my blue boy dancing in the afternoon sky with Saxa and his dragon siblings. "I appreciate you giving Sloan and me time to enjoy the beginning of our married life, but I'm back now."

The dragons continue to play when Dart leaves them to fly over to us. He does a front roll before hovering in front of us. Hanging in the pale pink sky, his mighty wings flap in a powerful *whoosh, whoosh, whoosh.*

"Hey, buddy. How're things?"

Good. We're glad you're here. Saxa and I want to come back to the city with you for a few days.

"I'd love that. Absolutely. Is there any reason or do you miss your den?"

Nesting with everyone is wonderful and we enjoy it, but we were accustomed to having our own space. Yes, we miss our den.

"I totally get that. Yeah, tonight, after we get the monkeys home and settled, Sloan and I will ride with you through the stones."

Excellent. I'll tell Saxa. Thank you.

"There's no need to thank me, sweetie. It's your home. I'm thrilled to have you with me. I only ever want you to be happy."

Then you're in luck because I am happy.

My boy flies away, and Dionysus rolls his eyes. "Even your dragons are obsessed."

I laugh and pop the last bite of my sandwich into my mouth.

I finished a cinnamon bun and hot chocolate right before we got here, but I figure it's the same idea as having my dessert before my meal. "So, are we good? Should we rejoin the others?"

"Not yet. There's one more thing I want to tell you." He points down the main street toward the city gates, and I follow his gesture.

I see it then. "You've worked on the Craic House."

He nods. "I have. Emmet, Brendan, Nikky, and I wanted to give it a facelift so I restored the main floor, renovated the second-floor rooms for the inn, and built a lovely cocktail patio oasis on the roof."

"Has Liam seen it yet?"

Emmet joins us. "Nope. We finished it this afternoon." He steps beside me on the opposite side of Dionysus and drapes an arm across my shoulders. "I think you're going to like it. If there's anything you'd do differently, now is the time to tell us because we're having the grand reopening next weekend."

I twist to look at him. "Grand reopening?"

"Yeah, we figured since the tavern was last open a thousand years ago, it was probably due."

"I suppose you have a point." I pick up my plate and brush the crumbs off and into the air. "All right, let me keep my promise to Jackson first, then we'll go see it. The suspense is killing me."

Despite Kinu's fears to the contrary, I'm quite safety conscious when it comes to the monkeys. I love them to death and would never put them in harm's way. From my perspective—and my perspective is the most qualified about dragon-riding—she's worried over something she truly doesn't understand.

There's the height aspect, but I am right there. Sloan's portaling ability is close at hand, Dionysus' god powers are too, and with Dart's grace in the air, there is nothing to be panicked about.

"Widen your feet, buddy, and two hands on the saddle handles. That's right." I take my position directly behind him, standing at the first spike. I moved the second saddle forward and lower so Jackson could hold on and remain in the shelter of my body.

When he's all set, I stretch around him to look at his expression and ensure he isn't having second thoughts. "Are you good?"

"Yep."

"Not afraid? We don't have to do this if any part of you is scared."

"I'm not scared." There's nothing but resolution in his tone, so I wink and straighten. "Don't let go of your handles. Promise me."

"I promise."

To be sure, I cast a rooting spell to keep his feet firmly locked to the scales of Dart's back. When I've done everything I can think of to mitigate danger, I glance at where Sloan is standing on Saxa's back and Dionysus is mounted on Contessa McSparkles. "Everybody ready?"

"Aye, all set here, luv."

Dionysus flashes his pearly whites at me and points at his shirt. The navy T-shirt stretched over his chest starts blinking Born Ready.

I laugh. "Okay, then let's go for a dragon ride."

After a tour through the sky, Sloan and I get Jackson off Dart. The kid is a natural and whether Kinu and Aiden like it or not, I truly don't think anything will deter him from claiming his druid heritage.

Dionysus dismounts Contessa and sends her off to continue flying with the dragons. "You guys take Jackson back, and I'll meet you at the tavern. There are a couple of last-minute things I want in place before you get there for the first impression."

I blow him a kiss and take Jackson's hand. "Okay, Tarzan. We'll see you soon."

While Dionysus snaps off to the tavern, Sloan *poofs* Jackson and me back to the palace. We drop him off with my grandparents and strike off to find Brendan and Emmet to let them know we're off to the tavern next. "Did you know about the tavern remodel?"

"No. They didn't mention anything to me."

Huh, usually the guys chat it up and whisper behind the scenes worse than a blue-haired knitting group.

We take the stone stairs and wind down toward the main floor and don't find them. Pulling out my phone, I send a text.

Em? Brenny? Where'd you guys disappear to?

Top floor. The Light Weavers' suite.

I read Emmet's reply and hold my phone out for Sloan to see. "We're headed in the wrong direction."

"Goin' up." He takes my hand, and the familiar warmth of his power signature washes over me. Sloan *poofs* us to the top floor of the palace tower, to the massive private suite that once belonged to Emmet's predecessors, the Light Weavers.

When we materialize, my gaze narrows, and I scan the changes in our surroundings. "Okay... You boys are all about remodeling these days. What's going on?"

At first blush, it reminds me of Dionysus' loft, but instead of a frat boy bachelor pad vibe, it's more urban chic meets homey. "You've been redecorating."

Emmet and Brendan stand in the center of the room looking a little anxious. "It's our wedding present for the two of you," Brendan says.

"When you and Irish mentioned maybe spending dinners and nights here, it got us thinking," Emmet says. "We decided we wanted a space that felt like home instead of like we're squatting in someone else's palace."

I grin and take the space in. "Well, I like it. And yeah, I'm glad. I want you guys to have a real home here."

Brenny shrugs and comes over to hug me. "It's not just for us. You talked about wanting to spend more time here and we thought if you had a space to call your own, it might seem more appealing."

"Are you serious?"

Emmet nods. "The portal door to get you back and forth from Toronto is great, but I know you, little sista. You need your family close the same way I do. This way, when you stay here—however often that is—you have a real home."

Brendan twists and points around the room. "We had Dionysus change it from three monstrous bedroom suites around the outside to six smaller ones."

I follow his gesture and take in the three extra doors.

"Wow, I admit, when we came up here to find Syma's crystal the space stole my breath, but..."

"You don't need to decide anything right now," Emmet says, holding up his hands. "We just wanted a place to call our home and knew it would never be right unless there was enough space for you two, Calum and Kev, and Dillan and Eva."

"Aiden opted out and picked out a suite downstairs." Brenny chuckles. "Who are we kidding? He almost needs a six-bedroom suite to himself."

True story.

I step farther into the space and take in the furnishings and finishes. There's a huge navy blue leather sectional with an antique pine coffee table and a massive television.

There's a beautiful live edge dining table with turquoise resin snaking up the center like a tropical river. There are ten chairs along each side and two on the ends. More than enough to ensure everyone can sit for a family meal.

Floor-to-ceiling bookshelves filled with ancient tomes cover an entire section of the back wall. "I take it the table is for me, and the books are to entice Sloan?"

Emmet grins. "Is it working? We lugged the books up from a couple of the libraries on the other floors. We thought about bringing up the ones from the Light Weavers' temple but figured they might've locked them away for good reason."

Sloan nods. "That's sound logic. I think it's best not to bring more than a couple at a time up here until I've had a chance to read through them and make sure there's nothing delicate within their pages."

I chuckle and wander over to a section of the wall that's floor-to-ceiling glass. It leads out to a balcony that wraps around the entire tower giving us an incredible view of the city.

"You really want us to live here?"

"Yeah, we do, baby girl," Brenny says.

Emmet nods. "At least maybe part-time? We know you have your own lives and want your space, but with the portal back to Toronto, we're hoping you, Calum, Kev, Dillan, and Eva will be here more."

"We miss the hell out of you guys," Brenny adds. "And since we're kinda stuck here…."

"Not that we're guilting you into anything." Emmet raises his hands. "You have your lives. We get that. We just want to see you more than we do."

I meet Sloan's gaze. I love the idea, but there are two of us to consider now. "Hotness? What do you think? When we talked about this, you were clear you wanted to make sure we had our own space."

"I stand by that, but we can split time between here and our house fer a bit and see how things go." He holds up a finger to halt their premature celebration. "Fi's right, though. We're a newly married couple, and I want to have time with her all to myself. I love yer family, but ye tend to take over situations with yer…Cumhaill-ness."

Emmet chuckles. "That's totally fair. Not all of your time, just more."

"Definitely more," I agree.

That had been our intention with installing the direct portal door into our kitchen pantry. It hasn't happened much yet because we were working as fae liaisons for the human world and are still riding the wave of our honeymoon.

"Are you going to like being on the seventh floor, though? That's a lot of stairs every day," I point out.

Brenny grins, grabs my wrist, and pulls me over to an amazing barn door hung on black iron rails. *"Voila."*

He tugs a long iron handle, and the massive panel of aged wood slides along the rails to reveal two shiny brushed chrome doors.

"An elevator?" I laugh and look between them.

The smile on Brenny's face is infectious. "Having Dionysus in the family is good for more than drunken debauchery. Although, that's a strong selling point too."

Emmet laughs and waves away his comment. "Yes, we have an elevator. Not all of us can teleport."

Agreed, but I'm not ready to move past Brendan's comment. "Has our God of Good Times been hooking you boys up?"

We talked about Brenny being lonely and wanting female companionship on my wedding weekend, but I forgot about that.

Brenny grins. "You have no idea."

Emmet shakes his head. "No, she doesn't, and she doesn't need to. There's a reason she and Sloan leave Dionysus' parties early. They have different interests and don't need to know about the naughty things her brothers do in the wee hours of his parties."

"Yep. What he said." I point at Emmet and tap my finger on

my nose with my other hand. "Speaking of Tarzan. He's waiting for us at the tavern. He's super excited to give us a tour of the renovations, and I don't want to keep him waiting."

Sloan nods. "With the tavern's revival, a bartending schedule will have to be worked out. Ye gave Liam yer word ye'd take that on with him."

"Hells yeah. I'm super excited about that."

When we divvied up the duties for the restoration and repopulation of the city, I agreed to Liam's terms of tending bar with him once a week for event nights. Now that the tavern is ready to roll, I suppose it's time to get—

A wave of energy hits me, and I can see by Emmet's and Sloan's reactions that they felt it too.

"What the hell was that?" I ask Emmet.

He scowls and strides forward. "Irish, if you don't mind, can you give me a lift to the security office? I think someone broke through our wards."

CHAPTER THREE

Sloan *poofs* Emmet, Brendan, and me to the windowless bronze building in the city center. When we arrive, Emmet calls for the AI helper of Isilon. "Astrid, can you come to speak with us, please?"

A four-foot female with purple and turquoise spotted wings appears in front of him almost immediately. "Hello, Emmet. How can I be of aid?"

I breathe a sigh of thanks that she no longer addresses us in rhyme.

Emmet takes charge, and I'm proud to see him settling into his position of authority. Having grown up in the shadow of our four strong and admirable older brothers, he doesn't have as much confidence in his awesomeness as he should.

"We felt a power flux a few minutes ago," he says. "Can you help me figure out what caused it?"

"Of course, if you'll join me at the console..." She leads Emmet to the side as Nikon and Sarah snap in.

Nikon sees the rest of us standing there and his expression washes with a moment of guilt. No one other than me notices.

He clears his throat and reclaims his normal, charming air before hustling over to hug me. "Hey, Red. It's good to see you."

"You too, Greek." I ease back from his hug and smile at Sarah. "I take it you two felt the power fluctuate as well?"

"Aye, we did." Her cheeks flush a rosy pink. "If ye'll excuse me, I should join Emmet and see what's happened." She spins without looking at Nikon, and I almost laugh.

My 'caught in the act' meter is redlining here, Greek. Sorry the universe interrupted.

Nikon rubs the back of his neck. *You're imagining things, Red.*

I laugh. *Both of your lips are swollen, you're both acting guilty as hell, and Sarah's hair has a tousled look that women get when their head has been thoroughly getting to know a mattress.*

Nikon pegs me with a look. *Please don't embarrass her. It's new, and she hasn't talked to Emmet yet.*

Dude! Have you talked to him?

Of course. He's still hung up on Ciara and gave me his blessing. He doesn't want to let her down twice, and they've become really good friends over the months of living here and working in the city. Still, Sarah's super sweet and doesn't want to hurt him.

Well, you know me, Greek. I only ever want the people I love to be happy. So, it's over with Danika?

Yeah. I think it's good we had a chance to revisit our feelings and clear the air, but when it came down to it, we're different people now, and we have different priorities. She's great, but with her everything was always a push and pull. I don't want that. I want to sink into a relationship and be at peace.

I get that, and if you're happy and Emmet's cool, then I'm happy for you. I adore Sarah.

Thanks, Red. I nod and get back to the conversation already in progress. "So, what do we know?"

Sloan glances down at me, and his gaze flicks to Nikon. "Everything all right, luv?"

"Perfectly fine. What do we know?"

"It wasn't the wards." Emmet is frowning as he points at the console screen. "Nothing surged with the Boundary Gate, and I've got nothing coming in from the shifting forest or the skies."

"What do you think it was?"

Emmet checks with Sloan and they both look blank.

Brenny curses. "Damn it. I feel so fucking out of my depths with this empowered world shit. I used to rock the streets like a badass. Now I'm useless."

"You're not useless," I argue, but now was not the time to get into a philosophical discussion with my oldest brother. "You're not alone in feeling out of your depth. More often than not, we don't know what we're dealing with or what to do about it. Don't feel bad."

Sloan frowns. "Astrid, can ye sense any areas of the city or systems that might need our attention?"

Astrid falls silent for a moment before answering. "Nothing is registering as a concern."

"What about an abnormality and not a concern?" I take a shot at it. "Maybe a change in one of the systems that isn't registering as a danger."

She grows still for another moment. "Nothing is registering as a change."

I frown and look at the others. "I got nothing."

Sarah shrugs and looks at Nikon. "If you don't mind portaling me around to the different sectors of the city, I can try a few spells, and maybe we can figure out what happened."

Nikon shrugs. "Sure. I'm game."

Sarah looks back at us and smiles. "It's always an adventure when you guys show up. We'll look around and catch up with you in a bit."

"Do you want us to come help?" I ask.

"No, that's fine. I don't expect to find anything. Enjoy your visit. We'll meet up later."

"We're heading to the tavern," Emmet tells her. "Meet us there when you finish, and we'll have a drink and talk about anything you find."

When Sarah and Nikon snap out, I slide my palm against Sloan's and link our fingers. With my free hand, I connect with Brendan and Emmet. Sloan *poofs* us to the street outside the tavern, and we head inside.

My favorite of the tavern's unofficial names is the Craic House—craic being the Celtic word for fun. It tips a hat to our Irish heritage and the atmosphere we want to instill in the tavern.

The boys aren't sold. Considering it's more their island than mine, their votes carry more weight. It's their background as cops and the crack reference.

Still, I think it's funny.

"Come in. Come in." Dionysus rushes around the bar and greets us inside the entrance. "Let me take you on a tour."

Wrapping my hand around his elbow, he turns us toward the interior. A couple with moss-green skin is sitting in a booth along the far wall, but other than that, the place is empty.

I glance around, but honestly don't see any changes.

"Don't look so puzzled. We already worked on the tavern part for your wedding weekend," he says, reading my expression. "We've spruced things up a little, but yes, I already replaced the counters, added the booths, and updated this area."

"And added the mechanical bull and padded corral."

Dionysus grins. "That too, yes. We've been having more than our fair share of fun on old Ditch here."

"You named him Ditch?"

"Yeah, because that's what he does. He ditches you."

Sloan chuckles. "I like it."

Fine, I'll give them that. "So, if the big reveal isn't here, show me what else you got."

Before we take five steps, HaiLe exits the kitchen door behind the bar. She smiles when she sees Sloan and me. Over the past two months, she and her children have settled in nicely and are adjusting to their new life. "Fiona. Sloan. How are you both?"

When she comes over, she finishes wiping her paws with the bar towel and tosses the cloth onto the bar. "Your brothers didn't mention you were coming."

"It was Jackson's idea. He asked if we could visit, so we invited our grandparents to join us. Dionysus was kind enough to pick them up on short notice so we could have a couple of hours this afternoon."

Dionysus scoffs. "It's no imposition. Gran and Granda are family. I'm sorry Da and Shannon weren't around to join in."

I shrug. "They have Shannon's family in Dublin to visit too. Besides, we aren't here for long today. Just a quick visit because Jackson wanted a dragon ride."

"So, you're not staying for a meal?" HaiLe asks.

I notice the black apron tied around her hips when she gestures at the booths along the side wall. "Are you working here now?"

"Yes. I wanted a way to support my cubs and give back to your brothers and the community. I love to cook and ensure everyone's bellies are full, so it made sense to take on running the tavern."

"Awesomesauce. Can the kids manage without you?"

She grins. "Pi and Binx watched the little ones back home while I worked, so it's nothing new. If they need me, they can come to get Kidok or me."

Dionysus grins. "HaiLe claimed the two-story across the street and Kidok the house next to it."

"It's convenient," HaiLe says. "If the tavern starts getting busy, I might want to find a quieter place, but for now, having my young close is exactly what we need."

"I'm happy for you. That's awesome."

Dionysus nods. "Come. Let me show you the rooms for the inn before you leave to return the small humans to their parents."

I let Dionysus tug me into motion to move on to the next part of our tour.

Since the last time I was here, the rooms of the tavern above were halved in number but doubled in size. The renovations have taken the accommodations from this being a rustic spot to lay your head into luxury weekend away territory.

Dionysus is proud and excited to show me all the upgrades. "To accommodate the loss of rooms, I copied and pasted the same thing for another floor. Then I added a rooftop garden patio with a hot tub on top of the building."

"Wow. You went all out."

"It was so much fun."

"Well, you've got a gift."

"Jane, I have many." His eyebrows dance under his loose brown curls, and I bust out laughing.

"I'm sure that's true." I walk through the rooms, smiling at his thoughtful attention to detail. The little basket of toiletries on all the vanities. Maps of this section of the city and the city square. A binder of houses in the city, their locations, some highlights for those who might need to claim a house, and much more. "You've thought of everything."

"Thank you for noticing," he says as we finish with the first floor and move toward the stairs to climb to the second. "We've got sheets of Egyptian cotton, silk, or the ones that keep hot people cool and cool people warm. The towels feel like you're wrapping your nethers in the softest fur. You can spend the day naked and indecent and love every minute."

"That sounds like you're speaking from experience."

He flashes me a saucy look. "Maybe."

We wander through the third floor, and it's the same as the floor below. "Did you notice each room has a fae theme in the decorating? We have pixie woodland, elven forest, and fairy meadows... Oh! And I forgot to tell you the most exciting part!"

"What?" I laugh, trying to match his energy.

"I put together an assortment of massage and aphrodisiac oils for our guests looking for a next-level tavern experience and I had an epiphany."

"Which was?"

"I'm going into business. I've put together a line of sensual toys and naughty accouterments. I'm stuck on what to call it."

"Your own line of adult amusement accessories? I'm surprised that hasn't come up sooner."

He laughs. "Right? I'm late to sail on that boat, but I think I've got the know-how to dominate the market."

"I have no doubt about that."

"So, my only issue is what to call it."

"What about something Greek? What's the word for sexual desire?"

Dionysus wrinkles his nose. "Eros."

"Uh. Really?"

He nods. "In Greek, *Eros* means physical love or sexual desire but also encompasses passion, lust, and romance."

"Well, you're not naming your products after him. He's a tool, and his ego is already big enough. What other love words do we have to work with?"

"We've got a lot of words that mean love, but they don't apply."

"Such as?"

"Well, *Philia* is affectionate love between friends. *Mania* is an obsessive stalker love. *Storge* is the natural love that family members have for one another. *Agape* is unconditional, sacrificial love. That's what we have."

He smiles at me and brings my knuckles to his lips. "*Agape* is the kind of love where you're willing to do anything for another, including sacrificing yourself with no expectations in return."

My heart melts and I reach up to kiss his cheek. "I *agape* you hard, Tarzan."

"I *agape* you too, Jane."

"You're right, none of those work. I guess we'll have to figure out something that's either not Greek or not love."

"What about Latin?" His eyes spark with excitement as his smile widens. "*Ludus* is a word we use, but it's Latin. It means playful, noncommittal love. *Ludus* covers things like flirting, seduction, and casual sex."

"Okay, now we're talking. Seduction and casual sex sounds promising."

He nods vigorously. "People wanting *ludus* are looking for fun and exploration of physical pleasures."

"Bingo. I think that's a definite possibility. Plus, it sounds like lewd, which gets the point across."

"I like it. Thanks, Jane."

We continue up the last flight of stairs and emerge in the rooftop garden. "Wow. You've really outdone yourself up here too. This place is amazing."

"I wanted it to be special and have a Hanging Gardens of Babylon feel."

"Nailed it."

He warms under the praise. "Shenanigans is a touchstone in your lives and means so much to your family. I wanted to create that same experience for the people moving here. This will be a place where new arrivals can recover from their ordeals, meet other community members, and heal their wounds so they can move forward."

I step into his space and wrap my arms around him. "You're incredible. You know that, right?"

His shoulder bounces against my cheek. "I *do* know that, but it never gets old hearing it. Go ahead. Tell me more."

Brendan, Emmet, and Sloan are gathered in the front corner when we get back downstairs. They've carved out a little business nook by the windows looking out onto the street. "This is new. I didn't notice it when I came in. Are you boys setting up shop here?"

Emmet grabs two more glasses from the credenza behind him and flips them up on his desk. Brendan hands him the bottle of Redbreast Whiskey, and he pours for us. "Brenny and I think it's less imposing for new arrivals to contact us here if they need something rather than having to come up to the palace and try to find us."

"*Annnd* it's also an excuse to hang out at the tavern," I add.

Emmet grins and raises his glass. "There's that too."

We laugh about that, and I slide onto Sloan's lap where he's seated in one of the two padded armchairs facing the desk. "I like it. It makes going to the office much less onerous."

Brenny hitches his thumb over his shoulder and grins. "Good food, lots to drink, and damn good music."

I laugh at Shakira's *Hips Don't Lie* playing on the sound system.

Nikon and Sarah snap in, and Brendan waves them over. "Welcome. Do you two want a drink?"

Nikon nods. "Count me in. I'll never turn down a chance to raise a glass with you guys."

Sarah eyes the bottle of whiskey and passes.

Dionysus snaps his fingers and offers her a glass of Guinness. "Is this more to your liking, milady?"

She giggles and accepts the dark stout. "Yer a true gentleman, sir. Thanks fer includin' my preferences."

"That's what I do." He winks and swipes his hand through the air as if gesturing at an invisible marquee. "Dionysus: inclusion, preferences, and putting smiles on faces for millennia."

Sarah's cheeks flush bright red, but I don't feel bad for her. If she's going to hang around us, she'll have to get used to the ribald comments and innuendo.

Nikon changes the subject. "So, do you want to ask us about our hour away?"

"Hells yeah." Emmet's chair creaks as he leans back and swivels. "Did you figure out what that power blip was all about?"

"Nope. We've got nothing. We scoured the city. Sarah did her witchy best, but still nothing."

"That was anticlimactic after the buildup," I remark.

"Sorry. If we had anything to tell you, we would."

Brenny swivels the tumbler in his hands, watching the amber liquid swirl in gentle waves. "Then I guess we chalk it up to being a one-time unexplained event, or we wait until it happens again, and we can get more info on what's going on."

Emmet upends his drink and nods. "I guess so."

I shrug. "In that case, we should finish our drinks and get back to Gran and Granda at the palace. We've got kids to return and stuff to get done at home."

CHAPTER FOUR

"How do I look?" I'm standing in front of the full-length mirror in our bedroom getting ready for the start of our work week. I've got two meetings back-to-back, and we'll be off to solve a fae fiasco somewhere in the world, no doubt.

"Ye always look lovely, *a ghra*. The question is, why are ye anxious about it when ye wear a cloak fer the meetings anyway?"

I chuckle. He's got a point.

I finish with the mulberry lip gloss I'm spreading across my lips and blot with a tissue before straightening. I went with smoky eyes and dramatic liner. As he said, there's only so much a girl can do to make an impression in a room full of black cloaks.

"I've missed the last three Guild Governor meetings and want to hit this one out of the park. With all the tension between the magical and non-magical citizens in the city, it would be nice if we could at least appear to be a united front."

"Ye think havin' yer makeup on just so will help?"

I hear how ridiculous that sounds and shrug. "It couldn't hurt."

"No. I suppose not." Sloan finishes buttoning his navy shirt and turns the arms up until they sit folded at his elbows.

It doesn't escape my notice that he's exposed the new tattoo he had Merlin ink on his forearm. I know the ancient script is a tribute to me somehow, but he won't tell me what it says.

Every time I ask him, he grins and says I enjoy a good mystery, so he's giving me one.

He's not wrong...still, I'm very curious.

"This is the first time ye'll be in a room with Xavier since our island lockdown. Does it make ye anxious?"

Anyone who doesn't know Sloan the way I do might hear that question and think it was a simple inquiry about a potentially awkward moment between acquaintances.

I hear all the subtext he doesn't want to pile on me. "Benjamin said Karuna wasn't hurt or angry. She was grateful Xavier was able to feed from someone she trusted."

"Ye believe that's the end of it?"

I hear the skepticism in his voice. "You don't?"

He backs up to the footboard of King Henry and crosses his ankles and arms. "I hope fer yer sake it's that simple, luv, but Xavier is a proud and powerful man, and ye saw him when he felt he wasn't in control. I worry his frustration might come out at ye in anger."

I finish futzing with my hair and toss my lip gloss into my pants pocket. "I've been on the receiving end of Xavier's anger more times than I can count. It'll be fine. Besides, Garnet will be there to referee if things don't go well."

He pushes off the end of our bed and closes the distance to kiss me goodbye. Since I just finished putting my lips together, he brushes his lips along my jaw. "Be safe, love, and text me when yer done and headed to the Batcave."

"You'll be downstairs at STOA?"

"Aye, I've been delinquent in getting the McWinn collection cataloged and tested."

I grin. "Who would've thought it? Sloan Mackenzie, a delinquent."

He chuckles. "Yer a bad influence. If ye weren't so damned addictive, I might've been able to get my work done."

"Well, the honeymoon is over, so I guess we're on the slippery slope to becoming mundane married people."

He arches a brow. "Mundane? Do ye really think ye've got it in ye to be mundane?"

I wave my fingers at him. "Go to work. Nikon's meeting me downstairs in two minutes. He might be here already. Off you go."

"Make sure ye take Bruin with ye."

"Yes, dear."

"Don't forget to text me when yer done."

I laugh. "Go."

Nikon portals the two of us to the headquarters of the Lakeshore Guild of Empowered Ones. I grab a couple of the robes left hanging against the corridor wall outside the meeting room. It takes a bit to check the tags until I find mine and his, but in the end, we get ourselves covered and are ready to roll.

"We're not even the last ones here this time." I point at the last robes hanging.

Nikon laughs. "Finally, we're not the bad kids."

"I like us being the bad kids."

He grins and grabs the door handle, opening the way for me to go first. "Yeah, I totally do too. Well-behaved guild governors rarely make history, right?"

"Right."

With a steady swish of black fabric, Nikon and I step into the large conference room where the Guild of Governors holds their monthly meeting. There's a large buffet table set up with all the brunch fixings, and the other governors are still milling around getting their coffee and plates ready.

"Two minutes, people," Garnet says.

Nikon makes a face. "Divide and conquer. I'll get the java. You get the food."

"Got it." The two of us split up, and I grab two plates and start a hasty run down the food line. As I pick up tongs and make my selections, I find it kind of funny I know all his likes and dislikes and he knows mine.

He didn't have to ask how I want my coffee, and I don't have to ask to know he loves bacon but hates sausage. He also will take buttermilk biscuits over croissants and croissants over buns.

I smile as I race through the food selections in a frenzy.

"Hey, girlfriend."

I glance up at the familiar voice and greet Suede standing at the end of the table.

"Ten... nine..." Garnet has his arm up and is counting us down.

Dammit. I wanted to dip some of the fresh pineapple and strawberries into the melted chocolate, but I've run out of time.

With the large spoon, I scoop a small mountain of each into the empty bowls at the end of the table, and then—since I'm the last one—I contaminate the spoon and scoop chocolate into another bowl. "Grab those, will you?"

"Six... five..."

She's known me long enough not to be surprised. "Sure. I've got cutlery too."

Three... two...

The two of us scurry over, and she drops my bowls off and hustles to the opposite end of the table. Nikon has our coffees set up and waits until I've set down our plates to tuck my chair in for me.

We are ass in seat by zero and damn proud of it. I high-five him, and we straighten and sober as the entire table of governors stares at us.

Whatevs.

When I first started coming to these meetings, I detested the idea that the seating was from what they considered the most powerful to the least. It's elitist and stupid.

Suede is the governor for the Toronto elven community on behalf of her father. Because their empowerment is nature-based instead of magic, she's way down at the far end.

She's next to Zxata, Myra's brother. He's here to represent the ash nymphs. Same thing. They don't possess active magic, so they're in the cheap seats.

Xavier ranks as being more powerful, but how he's farther down the table than High Priestess Drippy-Face representing the Toronto witches, I'll never understand.

Garnet told me once that it's because the leader of the witches can call on and amass the power of the women in her coven. Even though she might not be incredibly powerful herself, when she taps into the Wiccan well, she is.

Honestly, I stopped caring. There's only so long you can fight for something on behalf of others before you give up because they don't care. I fought Garnet for months to dismantle the hierarchal system.

He didn't because unlike me, the other governors find comfort in knowing where they stand.

I don't get it.

Nikon and I have been jockeying for the first chair over the past year. Sometimes Garnet has me directly beside him and Nikon to my left. Sometimes Nikon is beside Garnet, and I sit to his left.

Since Nikon leveled up after the veil dropped and started manipulating spatial energy through his connection with the Source, he has solidly won the right to sit in the first chair.

Which is amazeballs.

I'm so thrilled he finally has an active component to his power, and it's more than his family being immortal and having a connection with fae prana.

"Good morning, everyone." Garnet scans the faces of those

gathered. "For those of you who haven't been here for a bit, welcome back. Your absence was noticed. For the rest of you, thank you as always for making these meetings a priority."

I blink. *Was that shot across the bow for me?*

Nikon casts me a sidelong glance and bites his lip to keep from chuckling. *Me thinks you're in the hot seat for poor attendance, Red.*

Rude. I was on liaison business for two of the three and on my honeymoon for the other.

He's gotta call you out, or he'll lose attendance when other people decide they don't want to come.

I suppose. I stab a pineapple square with my fork and dip it in the chocolate. *It's still rude.*

Nah, you know you're his favorite. You got him and Myra back together and found them a daughter to love. He gave you a little love tap because he knows you can take it.

He's right. I can.

Garnet opens the folder in front of him and starts the meeting. "It's been nine months since the fall of the veil, and for the most part, things are starting to quiet down. The protests have all but ended, the outburst of violence is down considerably, and we seem to be returning to a state of business as usual."

"Says you," Malachi grumbles at the far end of the room. "Things always look better from the glass tower."

I fight not to roll my eyes.

Malachi and his swamp nixie community were a huge part of the uprisal to expose the fae world to humans. They incited the protest at Ripley's Museum and caused all kinds of damage—not only physical but to our directives of secrecy as well.

Now that the world knows about the fae, he's *still* complaining.

"Some people are never happy," Ng says, down the table past Xavier. "Do you honestly believe that because the human population knows about you, you should rise in the hierarchy and laud yourself over them?"

A'tym snorts. "You are no more or less than you ever were, nixie. Get over yourself."

Garnet glances out at the group, and though I can practically hear his growl pushing for freedom, the threatening rumble of his lion doesn't come.

He's in his impartial leader mode and is trying to be PC. "All empowered communities have had to make adjustments, that's true, but I think we keep well informed about the species within the city—even from up in the glass tower."

Malachi doesn't say much after that.

Garnet discusses a few issues that came up since the last meeting, but mostly this is a rinse-and-repeat gathering.

The gist of it is simple.

Those who are outed to the world, mind your manners in the public eye. Those who still live behind the veil of secrecy, keep a low profile and your head down.

After he has his say, he opens the floor to anyone with questions or concerns. High Priestess Drippy-Face straightens and takes her turn with the talking stick.

Hey, Red? Is everything okay between you and Xavier?

Why do you ask?

Just a vibe I'm getting from how sternly he's not looking at you. He was fine at the wedding, but then he didn't help us defend the Boundary Gate, and he practically vanished without a word when Isilon lifted the lockdown. Is he on your shit list?

No. Nothing like that.

But something did happen.

Something private, yes.

Gotcha. As long as it's nothing that will blow back on you or bite you in the ass, I can stay out of it.

I appreciate it. It's not. Sloan counseled me to give him time. I think I should talk to him.

Without knowing the details, I can't weigh in. However, your instincts are bang on. You know best how to handle things.

Thanks, Greek.

He reaches into my lap and squeezes my hand under the table. *You're welcome. I got you.*

CHAPTER FIVE

"How was yer meeting, luv?" Sloan asks two hours later when we arrive at the Team Trouble Monday morning case files meeting.

"The food was good, the company great, but the meeting itself was meh."

Garnet grunts. "Are you still pissy about my comment during the morning welcome?"

"Me? Noooo. Why would I be pissy?"

Sloan looks from me to Garnet to Nikon and back again. Garnet doesn't bother to hang around. He strides over to the offices unapologetically. "What comment?"

I flick my hand and roll my eyes. "It's fine. I'm over it. Garnet rapped my knuckles in front of the other kids to make a point. Moving on."

"What about that other matter we spoke about?" Worries cloud his gaze.

Right. Xavier. "Nothing transpired. He didn't meet my gaze and must've exited in a blur afterward because I never saw him once Garnet wrapped things up."

"Maybe that's for the best for now."

I don't see how two months isn't enough time to get over the fact that he fed on me, but hey, I'm not an autocratic, obsessive vampire king, so what do I know? "How did your object assessing stuff go?"

Sloan walks me to the Team Trouble conference table. Amusement lights his eyes. "It went well. A few hours of quiet time. Some interesting pieces to research. A few letters of provenance to track down. I can't complain."

"Well, good. I'm glad you enjoyed it. If you're in the thick of it, you don't have to liaise with us. You can do your thing."

He shakes his head and turns down my suggestion. "I wouldn't be able to concentrate if ye were out on a case. I prefer to keep an eye on ye, lest ye go missin' or are hexed or stabbed or hunted by a demon."

Diesel is already seated on the far side of the table with Brody and Jenna. When we sit, the big guy meets my gaze. "He made that sound random, but all those things have happened to you, haven't they?"

Sloan reaches into the center of the table and pours me, then himself, a glass of water. "Aye, they have, and a great deal more."

I take a sip and set my glass on one of the black leather coasters. "He's being a drama llama and making it sound worse than it is."

"No, I'm not."

I glance at Nikon, Dionysus, Calum, and Dillan taking their seats. "Help me out here. He's making me sound like a train wreck."

Calum chuckles as he sits and moves his chair closer to the table. "Would if I could, baby girl, but Irish is right. You can't be trusted alone in the world of mayhem and monsters. Your Fianna mark draws the chaos of the world toward you like blood chumming shark-infested waters."

"Iron filings to a super magnet," Dillan says.

"Horny moths to a porch light," Dionysus adds.

I roll my eyes. "I think they get the idea."

Aiden comes through the elevator doors wearing his blues, and I get up to meet him and walk him in. It's rare that I get a chance to see him socially these days, and I miss him.

"Hey, big brother. What's the craic?" I lift my arms for a hug, and he doesn't hesitate to collect.

"Och, not much craic these days, I'm afraid," he says in an Irish accent that mimics our father's perfectly.

"You're in uniform?"

"I had a court appearance this morning and didn't have time to go home to change out of my blues."

I glance at the offices. Garnet and Maxwell are still chatting with Andromeda, so I have a few minutes. "Hey, are *we* okay?"

Aiden steps back and kisses the top of my head. "We're always okay. Don't worry about that."

"Well, I *do* worry about that. I don't know what more I can say or do to fix whatever is broken between us and it's starting to really piss me off. You're my brother. The kids are my nieces and nephew. I'd never do anything to put them in harm's way, and I'm sick of being the fall guy for the universe's plans."

Aiden's expression is tight as he sighs. "Don't make me choose, Fi. I couldn't handle it."

I squeeze his arm. "I would never do that to you. I'm just saying that I'm past being apologetic for something I didn't do. I've tried, and it's like the past ten years of her being my sister never happened."

Aiden nods. "I don't know how to fix it either. I've told her you didn't do anything to cause Jackson's mark. I've explained to her that if you hadn't accepted the druid world, Granda would be dead. I've told her that I'm the one who decided to accept that side of my heritage."

I can tell by the defeatist tone his arguments have done no good. "Thanks for trying, bro. I miss you guys. These past two months of my marriage have been incredible, and I want to share that with you."

He nods. "I'm sorry, baby girl."

I draw a deep breath and sigh. "Not your fault. I'm sure you got an earful when Jackson told you about riding on Dart."

Aiden's eyes widened. "What's that now?"

"I'm shocked he didn't tell you. Yesterday he asked to visit Em and Brenny and outsmarted me into taking him up for a ride. I rooted him in place, stood tight to him, and had Dionysus and Sloan in the air with me to ensure nothing could happen, but yeah, he had a trip through the skies of Isilon."

"The wee bugger never said a thing."

I hold up my hands. "I never told him to keep it quiet. I'm fully prepared to fall on my sword and take the blame."

He shakes his head. "He's picked up on Kinu's tension since the island and has been trying hard not to upset her. Last night I even said how a weekend with you guys brightened his spirits."

"Well, we certainly had fun, but yeah, that also involved dragon-riding."

Aiden looks torn about what to do about that.

"Good morning, everyone." Maxwell crosses the room with several files in his hands and Garnet following. "Are we ready to do this?"

I hold up my fist for a knuckle bump, and the two of us break it up and take our seats.

"It's a slow week so far," Maxwell says.

I snort. "Now you've gone and jinxed us."

"Hopefully not." Our silver fox leader grins. "I know how hard you've all been pushing these past months and I'm so proud and grateful. This task force is everything I hoped it would be and we're getting recognition from all over North America and the European Union."

"Yay team." I pump my palms in the air to give the group a little cheer. "So, what's on the agenda, Max?"

"The biggest thing we have is down in Texas. The incumbent governor, Tucker Boseman, has had more than a couple of bumps on his campaign trail. He's asked that our team join him for the week and see if maybe it's something empowered and not a string of odd occurrences."

"I thought we don't touch politics," Dillan remarks.

"We don't, but we protected the mayor of Montréal, and I think the precedent stands. It has nothing to do with the politician and everything to do with the possibility of a fae or empowered event impacting a human citizen."

"Okay, so we're babysitting a governor on his bus trip across Texas. What else?"

"We've got anti-Wicca picketers causing trouble in Lily Dale, New York. Locally, a few empowered groups in the city are planning a full magic Halloween bash and need a reminder of what we are and are not showing the public."

Huh. That does sound tame compared to the usual shitshow we deal with.

Maxwell drums his fingertips on the table and smiles. "It seems the tension of the past nine months is finally dying. I hope we're easing into a new normal...one that doesn't involve riots and chaos."

"Wouldn't that be nice," Dillan agrees.

Garnet takes over the conversation. "Aiden? I take it you'll want the local beat?"

Aiden nods. "That works for me, thanks."

Brody raises his hand. "If it's possible, I'd like to stick around. My mate needs me close to home for the next few days. She's having pack issues."

Garnet nods. "Do what you need to do when you need to do it. Be sure to let us know so your partners don't end up shorthanded. If the pack issues escalate and you need backup, I'm always available to be your alpha and step in."

Brody drops his gaze to the table. "Thank you, Alpha."

Garnet waits for him to raise his gaze. Then he addresses the rest of us sitting around the table. "Does anyone else have preferences?"

I raise my fingers. "If strange things are happening, it might be a good one for Bruin and me. He can suss out issues in his ghost form that the rest of us can't."

Maxwell slides me that file. "Garnet and I thought the same thing. Sloan, Dionysus, and Calum are with you. Dan couldn't get here until later. I'll put him with Aiden and Brody here in the city. Nikon, you'll portal Dillan and Jenna to quell the issues in New York."

"Any questions?" Garnet asks.

I flip the file folder open and scan the political itinerary, meeting places, and public forums Governor Boseman will be attending. "It looks straightforward."

"We're good," Aiden acknowledges, reading through his.

"Yep. We're on it." Dillan slides the info over to Nikon.

Garnet stands. "Excellent, then let's get to work."

We *poof* back to the house to change and prepare for our case. Sloan pulls out our medium-sized suitcase and flops it on the mattress of King Henry, and I follow him into our walk-in closet. "Political rallies and event luncheons are more of a blouse and slacks assignment than I'm used to."

Sloan pushes the hangers of his dress shirts along the rail and sorts them to gather half a dozen to put into a garment bag. "Agreed, but bring some casual clothes. We might want to blend in with the crowd at public events, so we'll need jeans and tees too."

"Oh, grab that sage green Henley tee. It looks amazing against your skin and sets off the color of your eyes."

He chuckles. "It's lovely of ye to notice. I'll add it in if only to know yer oglin' me on the job."

If he only knew how often I do. "I'm not wearing heels. I'll do boots, but there's no way I'm going into battle wearing slingbacks, no matter what the fashion critics might say."

He chuckles. "Are ye really worried about the fashion police?"

"Nope. I'm letting you know that your rep as a clothes whore might suffer by being in my presence."

"Fer better or fer worse, wasn't it? I'll manage the blight on my reputation. Don't worry." He takes my blouse and slacks selections and slides them into his garment bag and pulls the hooks of the hangers through the slot at the top.

Then we search through our dressers for jeans, tees, and underthings. When everything is packed, Sloan snaps his fingers and runs back into the closet. When he returns, he's got a suit jacket on.

Mhmm...I am one lucky lady.

His soft chuckle brings my attention to him watching me watch him. "Like what ye see, do ye, wife?"

"As a matter of fact, I do. You're very pretty."

He adjusts his sleeves along his forearms and the thought of that tattoo taunts me again. I need to take a photo of it while he's sleeping so I can research the hell out of it.

By the time the two of us stroll downstairs, Calum is back from checking in with Kevin, and Dionysus has changed into jeans, cowboy boots, and a black cowboy hat. He grips his belt on both sides of a massive silver belt buckle and flashes me a smile.

"Who are you, Garth Brooks?"

"Jane. Don't be a hater. It takes a certain kind of man to wear a hat like this. I put the dude into dude ranch. I'm the stud from the stud farm. I'm the—"

I hold up my hand to stop him. Dionysus gains momentum as he goes and it's best to end this sooner rather than later. "I get it, sweetie. You rock the casbah. So, are you ready to git along little doggie?"

"Yes, ma'am."

Calum snorts and grabs the raised handle of his wheelie case. "Ready."

I find the address of where the governor should be right now and show Dionysus. "Oh, dear."

"What, luv?"

I wave away his question and get back to telling Dionysus where we need to go. "Okay, so our first stop is at the University of Texas in Austin."

Dionysus' eyes light up much too quickly. "University? Could this day get any better?"

I hold up a finger to slow his roll. "Remember. We're going there as professionals, and we're representing the governor and his team."

"What are you saying?"

"I'm saying that while you might love university students—"

"There is no *'might'* about it. I do love them. I luuurve them. They are my demographic. My peeps. My tribe. All that drinking and sexual abandon—"

"Is not on the menu today. Sorry, Tarzan, but you have to lock it down and at least pretend to be a respectable professional."

His excitement falls considerably. "How respectable are we talking?"

"Think Tommy Lee Jones in *Men in Black*."

"I'm Agent K? He was the ballbuster bore. I don't do boring. Can't I at least be J?"

"Nope. Not this time. I'm sure it won't be as bad as you think. If you want, you can pretend to be one of the personal guards, you know, with the earpiece and the black sunglasses?"

That cheers him up a little. "Fine. I won't initiate any freshmen, but it's September, and they'll be ripe to try new things and prove themselves, so I want it on record that this is officially a missed opportunity."

"Your opinion is noted and valid, but my decision stands. We're strait-laced secret agents."

Dionysus exhales, and black sunglasses appear in his hand. "Fine, I'll be K, but you owe me some good time cheering up later."

"I'll make it up to you, I promise."

"Aye, now that's settled, can we be on our way?" Sloan asks.

"I'm coming too." Manx rushes through the doggy door in the back. His long gray coat has a golden sheen in certain light as he trots to the front of the house.

Bruin materializes behind him and lumbers our way. "I told Manx about our investigation, and he's keen to come."

"The more the merrier," I agree.

Sloan reaches out his hand and scrubs Manx's long, black ear tufts between his fingers. "We're glad to have ye, sham. What sparked the interest?"

"Bruin said you packed for a week away. I don't mind when you're gone for the day or overnight, but if you're gone for a week, I want to come."

"Aye, I'm glad. Hopefully, this one is more in yer wheelhouse than crypts in New Orleans."

"I'm sure most things are. Maybe we'll get a few nature stops on tour. Governors make speeches in city parks too, don't they?"

"I suppose it's possible. I've never really followed a campaign trail before."

Manx glances up at me. His smile lifts his whiskers. "Then I guess it'll be an adventure."

"Excellent, let's make tracks," Sloan says.

With that settled, Dionysus looks at the sheet with our destination, and we're off.

CHAPTER SIX

We arrive in front of the UT tower, and it quickly becomes apparent where we're supposed to be. A long walkway has trees on both sides that have grown a canopy thick enough to meet above and shade the length of the path. A massive gathering of people on that walkway and the grassy area on either side are listening to the man at the podium.

"I think that's our guy." I point at the distinguished guy in his early fifties wearing suit pants and an orange T-shirt with a longhorn on the front.

Flipping the flap of our case file open, I verify against the photo we've got and confirm it. "Yep. That's our governor."

I glance around and see a line of black Escalades with tinted windows and a tour bus against the curb in the distance. "I assume that's our ride. Calum, try to offload our suitcases so we can circulate better."

"Don't start anything fun without me."

"No promises."

Calum rolls off and Sloan, Dionysus, Manx, and I people-watch.

After a few minutes, I release Bruin. *Buddy, why don't you look around and see if you notice anything?*

Sure. Is there anything you want me to look for?

From what I read in the file, it seems like the governor's problems are less about sabotage and more about a series of misfortunate events.

Aye, I'll keep my eyes open fer Count Olaf.

I snort at the Lemony Snicket reference. *Point for you, Bear. Good one. You do that.*

There's a soft *pop* as he bursts free from my chest and swirls around me in the rush of a warm breeze. I lift my face and smile, then he zooms off, and my hair settles back against my blouse.

While Bruin's off doing that, I step away from the others and assess the governor's staff. He has a decent-sized posse with him.

From what I can tell from the outside, a woman is running his visit here at the event. Another woman with a padded folder and an iPad keeps checking her watch.

They appear to be the organizers.

Two human hulks stand four feet behind the governor with their attention on the students and staff who showed up, with another four dotted among the crowd.

Nothing seems out of order.

When the governor finishes his speech, he opens things up for questions. I make my way over to the woman keeping the schedule. "Are you Maggie Fuentes?"

The brunette meets my gaze. Her warm brown eyes hold confidence and intelligence. "I am. Do you need something?"

I extend my hand and smile. "I'm Fiona Cumhaill, Fae Liaison of Toronto. My team leader was contacted and told you might have an empowered-related issue that needs sorting out."

The polite warmth of her greeting dissolves before my eyes. "Ah, the fae woo-woo girl from Canada. Yes, Jonah mentioned he called your office."

She has no intention of shaking my hand, so I withdraw the offer. *Woo-woo girl? Seriously?* "I'm not sure who called for us, but you're listed as our contact person. Should I be speaking to someone else?"

One of the professors asks Boseman a question. She taps on the screen of her iPad and makes a note. "No. I handle everything to do with Governor Boseman's re-election campaign. I will deal with you."

I bristle. "You don't need to deal with us. I assure you we're self-sufficient and excellent at what we do. We can be as visible or invisible as you need us to be."

A quiet *ding* has her glancing at a timer on her phone, and she flashes the governor two fingers.

"One last question," Governor Boseman says in response.

Maggie slides her iPad and phone into the leather bag hanging on her hip and nods at the two men behind the governor. Then she turns to the woman on her opposite side and shakes her hand, thanking her for the opportunity to have Governor Boseman address her group.

When the next *ding* sounds, she nods at the muscle men, and everyone moves in a coordinated and well-practiced choreography.

Governor Boseman waves as he steps back from the microphone. "It's been wonderful talking with you today. Go Longhorns!"

I follow Ms. Fuentes and the governor and glance over my shoulder to make sure Sloan and the others are with me.

As we get close to the bus, a clean-cut blond hops out of the middle Escalade and steps out of the way as Boseman and his guards load him in.

"Jonah, your wizards are here." Maggie throws a careless gesture back at where we're following. "You're on the bus with them. Next stop, the senior center."

Jonah meets my gaze and thrusts a hand toward me. "Thank all y'all so much for coming. I'm grateful."

"Not a problem. It's what we do."

The security staff I pegged for crowd control approach with another five in plain clothes. They pass us, load into the Escalade parade, and the engines rumble awake.

"We best get loaded." Jonah gestures at the bus and hustles off. "There's no slack in Maggie's rope. All y'all know that saying, 'No man gets left behind?' That doesn't apply to Mags. If folks aren't on the ball, they're left in the dust."

Bruin? Are you with me?

A rush of magical energy hits my chest, and my bear flutters around and settles. *All set, Red.*

We climb onto the bus and are bombarded by the overlapping chatter of a dozen people sitting in the front seats with phones to their ears and laptops open. They all wear plastic ID tags around their necks and barely acknowledge our arrival.

Jonah says a few quick hellos as he passes them, and we slip behind a curtained area. The bus transforms from forward-facing seats to a living room setup with slim couches against both sides and a restaurant booth and kitchenette at the back.

"Take a load off. Can I get all y'all something to drink? Water, juice, or a Coke?"

"I'd be grateful fer water." Sloan settles on the couch beside me and Manx sits at his feet. "The heat is a shock if yer not used to it and my friend here has fur."

Jonah glances at Manx. "He's a handsome boy."

"Aye, he is."

He turns to the small drink fridge sitting on the counter. "I've been reading up on druids. All y'all can talk with animals, right?"

"Aye, that's right."

"They understand what's said?"

"As well as you do."

He grabs a handful of bottled water from the fridge and hands them out. "Do all y'all have animals? You don't call them pets, do you?"

"No, they're our companions."

He nods. "So, do all druids have companions?"

"Aye, most, but not all. I have Manx and Calum has a precious wee skunk named Daisy."

"I have a bear named Bruin," I add. "You'll meet him later. This bus isn't big enough for him to ride with us."

Sloan nods. "Dionysus isn't a druid, nor is he bonded with an animal."

Dionysus adds, "I have a pegasus unicorn named Contessa McSparkles, but she's a free agent and comes and goes as she pleases."

"A pegasus unicorn," he repeats, his expression warring between skepticism and wonder. "All y'all are yanking my chain."

I chuckle. "No. Contessa McSparkles is real. A little girl named her."

"If that wasn't apparent," Calum adds.

Jonah grabs a bowl from one of the upper cabinets and hands it to Sloan. "Did you say, Dionysus?"

"The one and only," I confirm.

Tarzan swirls his hands in front of himself and bows forward. "God of Wine, Feasts, and Debauchery, at your service."

The guy looks stunned. "Wow. I didn't expect that."

"Don't let the name scare you. I'm an ordinary demi-guy."

I laugh and recap the introductions. "So, Fiona, Sloan, Dionysus, Manx, and that's my brother, Calum."

Jonah extends his hand and takes an extra moment to hold it. Then his glance falls on Calum's wedding band, and he steps back. "Well, I'm tickled all y'all are here. I know with the way of the world, there's no grass growing under boots these days. I appreciate having the extra eyes on hand."

I crack the seal on my water bottle and twist off the lid. "Excuse me for saying so, but I get the feeling Maggie doesn't share that opinion."

"Aw...Mags is all right. She worked her tail off to get where she is and hasn't adapted to the world changing around us. She pretends nothing has changed and keeps her focus on Tucker and his needs."

"She seemed very efficient."

Jonah nods. "She is at that. Which is why when things started going sideways, she dug her heels in and got even more focused."

I sit on the couch next to Sloan and Jonah perches on the edge of the opposite couch near Calum. "Tell us a bit about what's been happening."

Jonah spends the next ten minutes of our bus ride through Austin telling us about the incidents listed in our file. "While we were on the WWII aircraft carrier, the USS *Lexington*, it fired up and pulled away from the port at Corpus Christi. When we were at the Fort Worth Zoo, a bunch of the pens unlocked, and the animals got free."

"I'm not sure this falls in our wheelhouse," I point out.

"It could be a run of bad luck, I understand that, but I think it's more. Maggie is sharp as a tack. I could see one incident or maybe two...but with four separate and unrelated incidents...it's more."

"I'm a huge supporter of respecting your instincts. We'll see what we can do to help, but it might take some time. From what you've told us, there could be an empowered influence interfering but knowing that isn't enough for us to stop it. It could be a ghost haunting, a brownie or pixie pissed off with one of you, a witch hexing you, or any number of other things."

Jonah's excitement falls. "I was hoping all y'all would know."

"Not yet, but once we experience an incident firsthand, we'll know much more."

"How so?"

"Magic carries a signature. It tells us the source—whether it's wizardry or elven or from which pantheon of gods it comes.

Once we experience that, we can tighten the scope to recognize the caster."

Jonah chuckles. "So instead of praying nothing happens, I should pray something goes cattywampus near one of all y'all?"

I chuckle. "Something like that."

He sits deeper on the couch to consider that. "Well, we've got two more stops today. Then we're off to San Antonio for a few days. Maybe luck will shine on us, and something will happen. Then, all y'all can shut it down, and we'll know what's been going on."

Sloan arches a brow at me and smiles. "Aye, in a perfect world, that could happen."

Jonah reads Sloan's subtext and sighs. "This is far from a perfect world, ain't it?"

"Aye, it is."

The bus eases to a stop, and the brakes squeal our arrival at the Lone Star Active Living Retirement Community. Jonah leads us off the bus and points for us to follow the security team. "Knox, hold up. This here is the team from Toronto."

One of the crowd control hulks stops and waits for us to catch up. He eyes me up and down and doesn't think much about what he sees. That's fine. I love proving tough guys wrong.

"Hey. I'm Fiona Cumhaill." I step a few inches further into his personal space than he'll be comfortable with and smile. "This is my team, Sloan, Dionysus, Calum, and Manx."

He inhales deeply, and I can practically hear the shoulder seams of his jacket protesting. "I vetted you and cleared you to tag along. Don't interfere with us or our duties protecting the governor. If you get in our way, you'll be treated as a hostile."

Noice. Nothing like a warm welcome.

"What about saving his life if we see something before you do?

What about immobilizing a hostile or stopping a bullet you can't get to?"

"That won't happen."

"No? How many vengeful spirits have you dealt with? Tricksters? Bored goddesses? Minor demons? Can you honestly say you know more than we do about what might happen?"

His gaze narrows on me, and I'm beginning to regret our proximity. If he Hulks out, he could have his freakishly giant man hands around my throat in an instant.

Hulk crush puny girl's windpipe.

He tilts his head to Jonah standing beside us. "The kid insisted on calling you in. For some reason, the governor agreed. Whether or not something is going on, you're here to show he is open to accepting the fae community."

"Ah, we're his way to secure the fae vote."

"While you may have some party tricks, the fact is, my men are trained in personal security, and you're..." He waves his fingers between us dismissively. "You're whatever you are."

I want to laugh and show him exactly what I am, but I take the high road and backpedal for the sake of civility.

"How about this? My team will focus on all things empowered and your team will continue to guard the governor and control the crowds. We won't kick up anything in your sandbox unless it's necessary. If we do, our focus will remain on the empowered event. Your toes will be spared."

His brow pinches like he's not following.

"No one will step on your toes."

He rolls his eyes. "Fine. Stay in your lane and know where we stand. Jonah, you're babysitting them."

Before I can respond, he strikes off to join his team and continue with his safety assessment before Governor Boseman makes his appearance.

Jonah's hazel gaze is warm with sympathy. "I'm sorry they're giving you such a hard time."

"Bah, don't worry about it. Trust me. My skin is a lot tougher than anything they can throw at me."

Calum chuckles. "True story."

Sloan leans in and points at four buildings that overlook the courtyard where the governor will speak. "Bruin should do an aerial sweep on the rooftops and upper floors of those buildings."

"On it. Did you get that, buddy?"

Aye, I did. I'll take a look around.

"You better stay in ghost form. You're liable to cause a wave of heart attacks if you materialize in this crowd."

He's highly amused at the thought.

"Dude, that would be a bad thing."

Oh, aye. It tickles me to know ye still find me fearsome.

"Was there ever any doubt?"

Weel, it never hurts to hear.

I laugh. "You're fearsome, buddy. The baddest of the badasses."

Och, thank ye, Red. Yer sweet.

When he leaves, I'm left with Jonah frowning at me. "Do all y'all have a ghost on the team?"

"No. You asked on the bus about my animal companion. Well, Bruin is a little different than Manx and Daisy."

"Because he's not an animal companion," Sloan interjects, stating his opinion in the argument we've had for two years. "He's a bonded battle beast."

I shrug. "Potato-Tomato."

"Yer ridiculous, Mrs. Mackenzie."

"You picked me. No takebacks."

CHAPTER SEVEN

Jonah doesn't seem to consider himself our babysitter. He's more than helpful. He should be...they asked us to come here. If we're here, there are other places we're unable to visit.

Still, we stay out of everyone's way while the governor makes his appearance, and other than Manx drawing the attention and affections of a lot of old people, we fade into the woodwork.

"Is the campaign trail this same sort of thing day in and day out?" I ask Jonah later.

"Maggie schedules days at a time like this but there are also traveling days and days when we sit in a hotel somewhere, and Governor Boseman leaves to perform his duties."

"The people on the bus are press?"

He nods. "When we started, we had half a dozen tagging along from the major publications and networks. Since things started going wonky, we've gathered a few more. Honestly, I think they're less interested in covering the governor's campaign and more interested in being here when the next thing happens."

I glance around at a few of the folks with the press passes. "Have you considered the possibility that there's nothing empowered about the events and it's someone deliberately trying to break a story?"

"We've considered it, but most of the press team has been following the governor for years and know him. When we're on the road like this, everyone gets to know everyone else. We don't think it's them."

The *ding* of Maggie's timer brings this session to a close. Knox and his team move the governor toward the vehicles.

We're a hurried group, exiting the old folks' home and closing the distance between us and the bus. The day's warmth hits the moment we're outside, and I scan the sky looking for any of the usual fae messages and cloud writing we get in Toronto.

"Governor Boseman, a word?"

"Yes, ma'am—"

The strain in his voice grabs my attention, and I catch the speed at which he tilts back his head and examines the blue sky.

What the—as quickly as my alarm bells ring, I dismiss the danger. It's a spectacle, not conflict.

The woman standing in front of him is pushing her eighties and is nakey and swinging her cans—literally.

She's got a tin can in each hand and is swinging them, rattling the contents inside like she's playing the maracas at Cinco de Mayo.

"Spare change, Governor?" She takes a couple of staggering steps closer and extends her hands. As her arms shake, there's a startling ripple effect. Her sagging boobs slide across her navel and the loose skin under her arms swings like the sails of an inverted sailboat.

Knox and his security detail look flummoxed.

Seriously? They're prepared to take down assailants, but they're freaked out by a naked old lady.

"Someone take care of this," Boseman snaps, refusing to drop his focus from the clouds. "Maggie, this woman doesn't have a stitch of clothing on."

"Maggie is still inside finishing up with the coordinator, sir," Knox informs him.

Since I'm the only other woman around, I guess this falls on me. I step around the wall of security muscles and engage. "All right, what's your name, Ms..."

"Clutterbuck. Gerty Clutterbuck."

Of course, it is.

Why does this feel like this situation is about to become a giant Clutterbuck? "Okay, Gerty, we gotta get you covered up. You're naked. Do you realize that?"

"Oh sure, I'm getting ready for my Playboy shoot. I was hoping for July, but Hef gave me November."

"Uh-huh, well, it's September right now, so you're early. We can't very well keep you nakey for two months, so let's work on covering things up."

"Gerty, what the blazes?" A woman in nursing scrubs jogs over from the parking lot. "Lordy, woman, you're burning out everyone's retinas."

Gerty ignores that and rattles her cans in the governor's face again. "Feed the poor is one of your campaign promises, Governor. Pay up."

He lets out a long-suffering sigh, digs into his pockets, and releases a handful of change into her can. "Ma'am, I believe your nurse wants to take you inside."

"Tarzan, the woman needs a robe," I say.

Dionysus raises his hand, and a red silk Japanese robe is in his grasp. "Here we are, Gerty. A beautiful coverup for a beautiful lady."

He holds open the draping fabric, hooks one of her arms through—can and all—and moves in front of her while draping the robe across her back.

While he's focused on getting her other arm through the sleeve, he lets out a high-pitched shout of alarm.

"What's wrong, Tarzan?"

He straightens, startled. "Dirty Gerty's got my junk."

I try not to laugh as I push in to help him. The old girl has a good handful and doesn't seem eager to let go.

"This is not okay, Gerty." Dionysus grips her wrist and works to pull her hold away. "Not cool. Wrangling ancient lady bits and being sexually objectified goes beyond our job description."

Gerty laughs and makes a play to pinch his nipples.

He evades the secondary assault and wags a finger at her. "No means no, Gerty. Although I applaud your conviction, I'm more than eye candy."

I laugh and help the nurse finish double-knotting the tie of the silk robe. "There you are. Ready to head back into the Playboy mansion."

The nurse gives Tarzan and me a nod of thanks and hustles the old girl along the sidewalk toward the main entrance.

When that's taken care of, Knox pats the governor's arm. "All clear, sir. Your honor is safe."

Tucker Boseman surprises me by laughing. "This job. I tell you. It's never the same day twice."

"No, sir."

The governor gathers himself quickly enough, and Knox and his team rush him off to get into the center Escalade.

"You're welcome." Dionysus waves.

I grab his hand as his middle finger leaves the others behind and lace our fingers together. "We're here to do a job, not for recognition."

"I get that, but my man parts deserve recognition for their service."

I giggle. "You can retell the heroic tale tonight in bed with a few admiring strangers and have someone massage them all better."

He grins. "That's a good idea. I'll do that."

After collecting Bruin, we climb onto the bus and flop on the couches. Traveling on a tour bus is kinda fun. I feel like a rockstar.

Dionysus could snap us anywhere we need to be in a blink, but if we are going to be with Team Boseman for the week, it can't hurt to spend time walking in their shoes.

Besides, if this isn't an empowered problem and someone is sabotaging the campaign, we might be able to shed some light on that too.

Jonah is looking expectantly at me. "Did all y'all sense any magic? Do all y'all know what's going on?"

I shake my head. "Nope. That seemed like an eccentric old bird who likes to get naked. I don't think that fell in our wheelhouse."

He looks disappointed by that.

"Don't worry. We'll stick around and see what happens next. You still could be right. One thing doesn't negate the other."

He sighs. "I really don't want to be wrong about this."

I run my fingers through Manx's coat and play with the silk of his fur. "We'll be here either way. What's next on the schedule?"

"Now we leave Austin and head to San Antonio. The governor has a few private commitments to attend to there. Then he'll join us at the hotel. He has a cocktail mixer tonight on the Riverwalk, but that's not until ten."

The Menger Hotel reigns as the oldest continuously operating hotel west of the Mississippi. It's got Old World charm, architectural grandeur, and mango ice cream. What more could anyone need?

"It says in the brochure we're directly on Alamo Plaza and adjacent to the Rivercenter Mall and the Riverwalk." Calum shows me the pictures in the welcome binder on our desk.

I'm kind of excited. Usually, when we're on a case, the world is crashing around us, and we don't get a chance to enjoy the sights and local flavor.

"Apparently there are amazing restaurants on the Riverwalk." He flips back a couple of pages. "Check this out. You can call the restaurants, and some of them will cater your meal on a boat as you cruise along the river."

"Oh, let's do that," Dionysus interjects.

I love that idea. "I don't see why we can't. The governor won't be doing anything until ten. Until then, we've got free time."

Calum sets the binder down on the desk and pulls out his phone. "Should we invite Jonah?"

"Definitely. He's been good to us."

"If Kinu will watch Bizzy, can I invite Kev?"

I shrug. "No objection here."

Dionysus nods. "I can get him. No problem."

"You know what? You better put it in the chat and see who else might like to come. If Nikon and Dillan finished with their assignment in Lily Dale, they might want to join the fun."

"Family boat cruise dinner!" Dionysus shouts.

Sloan comes out of the bathroom, fresh from the shower and wearing only his boxers. He pulls on a fresh dress shirt and smiles at Dionysus doing a happy dance. "What did I miss?"

"Tarzan's excited about our dinner plan."

"Which is?"

I wave him over to show him the picture of the bright blue, orange, and pink boats cruising the lazy river past all the shops and restaurants. "Calum's seeing who all wants to attend. It says here we can have up to twenty on the boat but is most comfortable with sixteen or fewer. We're thinking of our gang and maybe Jonah."

"Sounds wonderful. I'm going to finish getting dressed. Grab my card out of my wallet if ye need to secure the boat."

I lean forward and kiss him. "Thanks, Sugar Daddy."

He rolls his eyes, laughing as he heads back into the washroom.

"Okay, Kev, Dillan, Eva, Nikon, and Andy are in."

"Andromeda's coming? Awesome. This is going to be so much fun." I squee and hustle over to where Sloan hung our garment bag. Picking out a simple floral sundress, I rethink my boycott of shoes. "Calum, can you please beg Nikon to grab my gladiator sandals from our bedroom closet?"

My brother laughs and sends the message. His notification whistles when the response comes back, and he laughs. "He says no gladiator ever wore shoes like that, but for you, he'll pretend not to judge."

"Send him hearts and kisses from me."

When the boat is reserved and everyone is on track for our night out, I run across the hall to knock on Jonah's door.

He opens the door, and I smile. Jonah is a looker, fit, and sweet. He looks good dressed as a professional, but even better in khaki shorts and a black T-shirt stretched across his chest. "Fiona? Do all y'all need something?"

I stop admiring and wave away his concerns. "No. Since the governor won't be going out until ten, we phoned a few friends and booked a catered Riverwalk dinner cruise. Do you want to join us? We have room in the boat."

"I wouldn't want to impose if all y'all want an evening with friends."

"We are impossible to impose upon." I laugh at what a mouthful that was. "No, really. Our friends are our family, and we do this at least once or twice a week. Come. You'll have fun, I promise."

"Then yes. I'd love to. What time are you leaving?"

"Our cruise is seven until nine, so we'll head down around six thirty and get the lay of the land."

"Perfect. I look forward to it."

September in Texas is hot but not scorching. With evening falling and being on the water, I have to ask Sloan to *poof* back to the room to grab me a light sweater. Our group is laughing and chatting, and when Sloan returns, we're ready to start our evening. "Thanks, hotness."

He winks and helps me shrug into my sweater. "My pleasure, luv."

"Mackenzie, party of ten."

Eva squeals and the guys let us lead the way to the peacock blue boat awaiting us. Long and flat, the oval boat is more like a motor-driven floating dock than any other boat I've been on. Still, it has metal railing walls to keep us from falling off and comfy seats around a table elegantly set for dinner so there's nothing to complain about.

I draw a deep breath and groan. "That smells *soooo* good it's making my stomach growl."

"Mine too," Andromeda agrees.

Nikon's younger sister is a stunning blonde with more brains and poise than any other woman I know, but the beauty of her is that when she's out with friends, she's also fun and funny and a pleasure to be around. Much like her brother.

I slide my arm around hers and hug it. "I'm so excited you decided to come. We don't see enough of you outside the Batcave."

Jonah glances over at the mention of the Batcave, and I make a mental note to explain that to him later.

A man wearing a white shirt, red tie, and glasses waves from the end of the boat and we quiet down. "Welcome aboard, everyone. I am Roberto, and this gentleman beside me is our riverboat captain, Javier. Please, take your seats and we'll begin. Is everyone hungry?"

"Hells yeah!" Dillan, Calum, and I exclaim at the same time.

Yeah, you can't take us anywhere.

"Tonight, we've created an Italian experience full of fresh ingredients, bold flavors, and legendary dishes like our famous shrimp paesano."

I waggle my eyebrows at Sloan, and he rolls his eyes at me.

"I promise when our time together ultimately ends—after toasting with world-class wines and stealing bites off each other's plates—you'll truly know the meaning of *buon appetito*."

"Opa!" Dionysus calls.

"This was a fabulous idea." Jonah is leaning back in his chair taking in our crazy group. "All y'all are amazing."

I sip from my wine glass and wink at Dionysus across from me. "Yeah, we're blessed."

The evening begins with a little salad and wine and a lot of laughter and conversation. The boat quietly chugs along the bends of the river while on both sides, we pass quaint shops, restaurant patios, and beautiful cypress trees draping over the water.

"So, tell me. Are they all empowered?" Jonah asks me while Roberto gathers the used salad plates.

I glance around to take stock of who is here and shake my head. "No. Kevin has been Calum's best friend and boyfriend since we were kids. They got married last summer on the beach. He's completely human and has no superpowers other than being an incredible artist and an amazing daddy to their little girl, Bizzy."

Calum catches my comment on the breeze and smiles at us. "Oh, he's got superpowers all right. They're just more of a private nature."

Kevin hears that and leans close, whispering something into Calum's ear. Calum, who's impossible to embarrass, blushes and laughs. "Check, please."

I laugh and get back to Jonah. "Ignore them."

He's taking in a visual account of the rest of the group.

"Everyone else has magic?" By the way his voice pitches at the end of his question, I take it he's surprised by that. "Sorry. Is it rude to ask who has what kind of powers?"

"In some circles, yes. Here with us, no, it's fine."

His cheeks blotch with a flush, and he glares at his wineglass. "Maybe the wine's making me too familiar."

I laugh. "That's an impossibility with us. If someone doesn't end up naked, talking about orgies, or reliving some incredibly inappropriate story by the night's end, it'll be a San Antonio miracle."

He chokes on his wine and pounds his chest. "Really? That's what I should expect?"

"Prepare yourself. We don't filter, so there's no reason for you to worry about it. What's on your mind?"

He sets his glass down on the table, and I do the same. Sloan sees we're both about to be empty, reaches over, and pours us some more.

"That husband of yours is going to get me drunk."

"Don't worry. Someone will get you upstairs and into bed. We're good like that."

He shakes his head and laughs. "All right. I'll trust all y'all with my well-being."

"You're in good hands."

"Let me see what I've learned so far." He takes in our group. "Calum and Kevin are married."

"Yes."

"Calum and Dillan are your brothers, and you're all druids along with Sloan."

"Correct."

"Nikon and Andromeda are siblings."

"Yep."

"Are they twins? They look about the same age."

"No. Nikon is older."

"Really? He looks like he just turned twenty-one."

"That's a long story involving an angry goddess and a lot of heartache. Try not to bring it up."

"Consider it a dead subject."

"Thanks."

"Dillan's wife is the one with the curls." He points at Eva down the table. "I haven't figured out what she is yet."

"Do you want a hint?"

"Sure."

Dionysus, get your camera ready on the sly. I'm going to blow Jonah's mind.

Yes ma'am.

"Hey, Eva, Jonah here is curious about your designation. Can you give him a peek at your feathers?"

Eva grins. "What, here?"

"Sure. Sloan can cast us a privacy spell, can't you, hotness?"

"As you wish, wife."

When Sloan's magical signature tingles over the surface of my skin, I give Eva the go-ahead.

She stands, holds open her palms, and stunning golden wings unfurl behind her shoulders. Her wingspan is close to eight feet, and her feathers shimmer in the evening sun.

"Hot damn. Are those real?"

"If I had a dollar for every time a guy asked me that…" Andromeda laughs.

Calum and Kevin bust up.

Dillan snorts. "Real? As opposed to what, her buying them at a costume store?"

As always, the brilliant warmth of Heaven's light focuses down on her and lights her up from above.

"She's an angel, right?"

I nod. "A guardian angel. She used to be a reaper, but she changed her designation."

"Can she fly?"

Eva grins. "With these wings, not really. I can make a powerful leap and get air, but they're for battle. If I need to fly, I do this."

She launches off the boat's platform in her white dove form, does a few aerial spins, returns to us, and reclaims her form. When she slides into her seat, Dillan leans over and kisses her. "Damn, that never gets old, babe."

She giggles and reclaims her wine glass, lifting it toward Jonah. "Welcome to the inner circle, Jonah."

He's sitting there, jaw dropped. "Wow. An angel. That's incredible. You're incredible, Eva. You're so incredibly beautiful."

"Yes, she is." Dillan turns his attention fully on Jonah. "And she's taken."

Calum chuckles. "I think your claim is safe, brother."

Jonah blushes again. "It's just that she's so..."

I laugh. "Incredible. We know."

Dionysus is chuckling as he scans the pictures he's taken and turns his phone around for me to see.

Hilarious.

Jonah catches sight of it and shakes his head. "That's cruel. Don't show that around or I'll never get laid."

Dionysus' brows pop. "I can't imagine that being a problem for you."

Jonah blinks and shakes his head, glaring at his wine glass. "I'm sorry. I'm supposed to be the contact person for all y'all. I shouldn't be drinking like this."

"Pfft." Dionysus waves that away. "Around us, everyone should be drinking like this. Irish, I think we need to do this lazy river dinner and drink at least once a month. See if you can get us a standing reservation."

I laugh. "Oh, no. San Antonio won't survive if we become regulars."

Sloan checks his watch. "It's coming on nine, *a ghra*. Our time is nearly up."

"*Noooo*," Andy and Eva both moan.

I don't blame them. I don't want this feel-good family party to end either.

Dionysus raises a hand. "Javier, if we pay you a thousand dollars for another two hours of lazy boat cruising, will you pilot us?"

Our boat operator looks stunned. "Are you serious?"

Dionysus looks insulted. "About extending the party and drinking more? I would never joke about something like that."

Javier's gaze darts around as if he's working out the logistics of how to make it happen. "I'll have to dock to let Roberto off with the catering supplies. Do you want to restock anything?"

"Not necessary, my friend." Dionysus sinks back in his seat, grinning. "I am all we'll ever need for a party."

True story.

"So, are we getting an encore?" Dillan asks.

"Hells yeah, we are." Dionysus waves. "Pay the man, Nikki."

Nikon laughs at the imperious order but doesn't hesitate. He pulls out his wallet and fingers through the bills. "Javier, here's a thousand for you plus a thank you tip you were getting anyway, and Roberto, here's yours. Money well spent."

Jonah looks at me, his eyes wild. "Does he walk around with a couple of grand in his pocket?"

I shrug. "Apparently tonight he does."

"Should I offer to pay my share?"

I laugh. "No. It took me years to understand how much he and Sloan love to treat the people they love. Trust me. They wouldn't offer if they didn't genuinely want to cover the tab. They have more money than they know what to do with."

Sloan sets a hand on my shoulder and tops us up again. "Aye, listen to her, sham. All yer meant to do tonight is enjoy yerself."

"As much as I love all of this, I have a feeling we're going to pay for this in the morning."

Dillan waves that away. "Dude…we've got magic on our side. We'll set you up. Don't worry."

CHAPTER EIGHT

By ten o'clock, it's obvious Jonah won't join us on the Governor Boseman overwatch mission, but that's okay. He's having a good time, and after speaking with him, I get the feeling he doesn't rank very high in the pecking order and usually ends up getting pecked.

"Take good care of Jonah, boys and girls." I leave him on our floating family fun fest, and Sloan *poofs* us to solid ground. "All ashore who are going ashore."

In the end, Calum stays with Kev, Jonah, Dionysus, Dillan, Eva, and Andromeda while Nikon, Sloan, Manx, and I move on to guard duty.

Doesn't matter.

We had a damn good night, and if they can keep on having fun, I'm glad.

The moment my sandals touch down, I keel to the side. Sloan has to grab me and stand me upright. "Are ye drunk, luv?"

"I don't think so. Pleasantly buzzed for sure, but I think that was me getting my sea legs."

He laughs. "Ye got it backward. Ye get yer sea legs when yer on the water, not on land. It's in the phrase."

"Fine. I'm losing my sea legs. How's that?"

He rolls his eyes. "Och, much better."

With a gentle hand on the small of my back, Sloan guides us through the bustle of bodies spending social time milling along the Riverwalk.

Over the past three hours, we've circled the area, watching as the colorful shops grew shadowed. Then the white lights of the tourist destination turned on and changed the atmosphere entirely.

"It's magical," I say.

"It's also incredibly busy and will be difficult to keep watch." Sloan frowns.

We make our way to the high-end cocktail bar where the governor is meeting some power players for a drink after a long day.

"This is the right place." I tilt my head at where Maggie perches on a tall stool in an outdoor patio area. She's nibbling on finger foods and drinking a club soda and lime.

Knox and his men are here too. The big guy is standing with his back against the brick wall of the building as Governor Boseman sits with four other gentlemen sharing drinks.

"You put in long days." I shift to stand opposite Maggie but move to press my back to the rail overlooking the boats so we both can still see the governor.

"Oh, are you still here?"

"Yep." The dismissal in her comment makes me chuckle. Whatevs. Haters gotta hate. "How did it go this afternoon? Did you have any trouble?"

"Not a bit."

"Good. That's good."

She picks at the food on her plate, and I let her enjoy her downtime without forcing conversation. It's a beautiful night, and I'm happily riding a wine wave of wonder.

"You look like a tourist."

I glance down at my dress and sandals. "I sorta am a tourist. I've never been here before, and we were off duty for the past five or six hours."

"You're still off duty. You don't work for the governor."

"No, but if something magical is going on, we're here to help."

I'm not sure what bug crawled up her butt, but there's no mistaking her disdain for all things magical.

Not my circus. Not my monkeys.

With the conversational part of our interaction over, I settle in to watch the governor and enjoy the evening.

Ms. Fuentes doesn't have to be my best friend. I have plenty of those. We simply need to coexist for a couple of days until we determine if what's happening around the governor is an empowered something or not.

You doing okay, Red? You look a little sleepy.

I meet Nikon's gaze across the outdoor seating area and smile. *A great night with friends and maybe a little too much wine will do that to me.*

It was a great night.

I entertain myself by reviewing the highlights as we watch the scene. Man, I don't envy Knox. Doing this every day all day must be boring as hell.

A splash catches my attention, and I lean back to glance down the length of the rail. Did someone fall into the water?

Another splash on the other side of me has my full attention. What are the odds of two people falling in within seconds of one another?

Four more people to my right stop chatting with their companions and step off the edge of the walkway, dropping into the dark water.

It's a bizarre, slow-motion oddity where well-dressed people follow the late-night plunge crowd like lemmings.

"What's going on?" Maggie stands, frowning at the people around us.

"Something isn't right." I step away from the rail and yeah, whatever is going on, the governor is affected.

Governor Boseman and all four of his party have abandoned their table and are heading over to the section of the walkway that doesn't have a barrier.

Knox and two of his men are positioning themselves between the governor and the water. Short of tackling the men, there's nothing they can do. "Governor Boseman? I need you to step back. Governor, what's wrong? What's going on?"

The governor isn't registering anything.

"Knox, grab hold of the governor and one of the others. You boys too. Nikon, take them to the Ambassador Suite of the hotel—third floor. My guess is as soon as they're away from here, the compulsion will break."

"Stay back." Knox glares at Nikon and me. "Stay in your lane, Red."

"Greek, do it." Despite the protests of the Hulk brigade, Nikon listens to me. With a rush of his spatial energy, Knox, his men, Boseman, and his drinking buddies are gone.

"What the hell? Where did they go?" Maggie snaps.

"Nikon is securing them at the hotel. Sloan and Manx, you're with me. Let's figure out what's going on."

Sloan pats Manx's side. "See if ye can catch the scent of magic, sham."

When they trot off, I try to do the same thing.

Detect Magic. My powers come online, and my cells burst to life. Opening my senses, I try to pinpoint where the compulsion is coming from.

I've got nothing.

Sloan doesn't look like he's doing any better.

Nikon snaps back, and he's got Dionysus and Dillan with him.

"Help. She can't swim!" The plea for help draws us out of the patio area. A frantic woman points at her friend thrashing and splashing in the water.

"Well, balls." I glance around, looking for a rope or pole we could offer her.

"Got her." Dionysus cannonballs into the water next to the frantic woman. I'll have to explain to him later why jumping or diving might've been better because his drowning victim is now being toppled and rolled by the massive waves he made.

"It's a mocker, fer sure." Sloan frowns and gazes around us, searching. "I can taste the acrid magic on the back of my tongue."

Ew...I'm not sure what to say about that.

"Well, if it's a hex, there's a source or caster here somewhere. We need to find it. Spread out."

Since the Riverwalk lemmings all came from the establishment Governor Boseman was at, I run back there.

Dillan's with me, and he's got his cloak on.

"Where'd you get that?"

"Don't leave home without it."

"You've had it all night?"

"Eva did. I'll explain spatial pockets to you later. Right now, aren't we supposed to be finding a hex bag or something?"

Good point.

I follow Dillan's lead, hoping that with his Cloak of Knowledge on he'll be able to pick up on something. "Irish is right, there's hex energy here, but I think it's a caster and not hex bags."

"What makes you say that?"

"Because on all the occasions when we've had to track down the hex where hex bags created a perimeter, the magical source has felt dispersed—like a cloud permeating the air. This doesn't. This feels like a point of magic radiating."

I'm thankful Sloan and Dillan have the ability to focus on magical sources and signatures as much as they do.

They say it takes a village.

In our case, it takes a talented clan.

Dillan steps back to see around the fabric of the open umbrellas above the tables.

I lift my gaze too. "What are we looking for?"

"Our caster is up there, somewhere."

I follow his pointed finger toward an upper patio packed with diners. Normally, I'd search for the one with their attention focused on the chaos, but people randomly plopping off the walkway into the river has everyone's attention.

"Any idea which one?"

"Nope, but I think we're about to find out."

I open my mouth to question him on that when my focus is drawn to a stunning black man looking sexy as ever mingling through the people above. "Manx must've caught the scent. Sloan will be able to root out the source."

"So, we watch and wait," Dillan says, grinning.

Sloan slips unnoticed through the crowd of probably forty people. He brushes a casual hand over one man's shoulder, then the hand of a woman as he passes, then he guides the waitress to the side as someone moves toward them.

His subtle gestures seem to be nothing more than a courteous man navigating a crowd, but we know what he's doing.

He's gauging their power.

"There! The waiter with the blue tie. Does he look distressed?"

"Why yes, he does," Dillan agrees.

"I'm on it." Nikon snaps up to the balcony patio in a flash and grips the waiter by the shoulder. The moment he touches him, he snaps back down to us.

The guy realizes he's caught and struggles, lashing out with fists and fury. "Get the fuck off me."

All eyes turn, and now we are the spectacle.

"Immobilize." I end the struggle.

The waiter falls still as Sloan and Manx *poof* down to join us.

Dillan grins. "Got him."

A huge burst of energy knocks us staggering back. I hit the ground, and my butt screams in protest. That's going to leave a bruise.

The waiter crumples to the ground as a white wolf appears and bolts away.

"On your horses, boys. Our caster is a shapeshifter." I race after him, weaving through the startled tourists throwing themselves out of the way.

Up ahead, one of the cocktail cruises is letting off, and there's total congestion in our path. "Got you, asshole."

On the fly, the wolf shrinks down to a ferret, and I curse. He ducks between the legs of the people, and there's no way I can follow.

"Water Walk." As the spell takes hold, I launch off the walkway's edge and race across the river's surface. My spell keeps my feet from sinking, and other than the splashing of water with each step, it's no different than running on solid ground.

On your toes, Red. I'm forcing him your way. Nikon's words have me searching the edge of the people. I'm watching...waiting.

Ready when you are, Greek.

Coming to you in three, two, one....

I lock onto the flash of fur and change course to intercept. The moment the ferret is about to hit the water, it shifts again. Now it's a Jesus Lizard racing away from me on its back legs.

"Those little legs won't outrun me, asshole." Pumping my arms, I pick up speed. "I'm gaining on you."

He runs straight at one of the boats and leaps into the air. Clearing the colorful metal wall, he launches aboard.

I'm right behind him.

Throwing my feet to the side, I'm up and over in one quick move. Dropping to a crouch, I search the floor, moving my head to see around the people. Thankfully, this isn't a dinner cruise, so he has no tables and chairs to hide behind.

It's only people.

Too many people.

I don't think they read the part on the brochure about keeping the party under sixteen.

A woman screeches at the far end of the boat, and I rush forward. Throwing my hands out, I try a containment spell, but he's too quick, and too many people block me.

With a grunt of frustration, I try again.

Bumping shoulders and squeezing through the crowd, I search for a clean line of sight.

Before I can release the spell a second time, the lizard throws itself off the side of the boat and transforms again. The cardinal spreads his wings, flaps hard, and launches into the sky in a scarlet streak.

Breathless, I edge over to solid ground.

"Dammit."

The shapeshifter swings around and flips its wing at us before soaring into the darkness.

"Did that prick flip us off?" Dillan asks.

"Yep. Without a doubt."

CHAPTER NINE

I take a couple of extra minutes in the shower letting the hot water ease the knots in my back. Somewhere between the drinking and the chasing, I tweaked something. Normally, I'd ask Sloan to give me one of his magical massages and all would be right in the world, but he's not here.

New city. New sights. I'm not surprised he's taken the opportunity to wander around. He's an early riser. I'm a worshiper of Hypnos—the god of slumber.

The mirror is foggy when I step out of the shower, so I wrap a towel around my hair, another under my armpits, and go out to pick my clothes for the day.

Calum is sitting at the table by the window, sipping from a large Tim's mug. When he notices me coming out, he pushes a medium cup my way. "Morning."

"*Noice*. Where did you get Tim Horton's here?"

"Nowhere. Nikon dropped Kev and me home last night and picked me up this morning."

"Which explains why I didn't hear you come in." I glance at the second queen-sized bed in the room, and yeah, it's untouched. "I wonder where Dionysus ended up last night."

Calum chuckles. "That's a dangerous game to play."

"True story." Sifting through my clothes, I choose pants I can run and battle in for the day. If last night taught us anything, something is going on, and we'll need to be ready for it.

I take my outfit into the bathroom and leave the door open enough to let the humid air out and still hear my brother while I get dressed. "What do we know about shapeshifters?"

"Not a hell of a lot. I'm sure Dionysus will know more. Assuming that's what we're dealing with."

I pull on my underwear and step into the legs of my pants, straightening to do up the fastener. "What else can shift like that?"

"Gods, druids, demons, fairies, witches, wizards."

Right. "I suppose narrowing it down after one encounter would be too easy."

"Wouldn't it be nice?"

"It would." I pull the towel off my hair and slip into my top. With my hairbrush in hand, I walk out of the room. "Any idea where my hubby is?"

He shakes his head. "None. Nikon dropped me here, and he was already gone."

I stand in front of the mirror and battle the tangles before tossing my brush into my suitcase and giving my ends another scrunch with the towel. "I sent Garnet and Maxwell our progress report last night."

"Did they have anything to say?"

"No. Just to keep them posted." After hanging the towel over the rod, I settle into the chair opposite my brother and open the plastic lid. "Mmm, thanks."

The *beep* of the pass key scanner has us both turning to welcome Sloan and Manx back to the room. "Did you enjoy your walkabout, boys?"

Sloan grins and lifts a carrier of drinks with a paper bag resting on top. "It seems Calum beat me to the punch."

Calum shrugs and sets his coffee back on the table. "Only on the drinks. What did you bring us to eat?"

"A selection of chocolate croissants, sweet tarts, empanadas, cookies, conchas... Really, I pointed at all the things I thought Fi would enjoy."

I curl my fingers into a heart and press them against my chest. "This is why I married you."

He chuckles and hands me the bag of treasures. "For the baked goods?"

"Don't underestimate a woman's need for sweet treats." I set a couple of napkins on the table and pull out some of the selection. The fact that sugar and cinnamon dusts my fingers before I start eating is a good sign.

I take a bite and groan. "I *agape* you, hotness."

"I'm sorry?" Sloan's brow arches and I remember he wasn't around for that conversation.

"According to Tarzan, there are a bunch of words for love in the Greek language, and they all have different degrees and meanings. *Agape* is unconditional, sacrificial love. The kind of love where you're willing to do anything for another."

The smile that earns me warms all my girlie parts. "That's lovely. In that case, I *agape* ye right back."

Calum clears his throat. "Before the two of you devolve into your usual lovey-dovey, might I remind you that we're expected in the lobby in fifteen minutes? If you need me to leave, I will vacate, but Fi needs to eat. We all know what happens when you're in the world on an empty stomach."

It's true. Hangry Fi is...difficult.

I sigh and side with responsibility. "You're right. No time for fun and games now. Since we have extra drinks, I'll pop a coffee and a treat across the hall for Jonah and let him know we're almost ready."

I move one of the breakfast empanadas onto a napkin and grab a coffee and some cream and sugar.

After flipping the metal arm of the deadlock to keep the door from closing all the way, I saunter across the hall, gifts in hand.

I knock and step back. "Jonah, it's Fi. I come bearing baked goods."

"Baked goods?" Dionysus swings the door open, and I avert my gaze by looking past his nakedness, and *shit*, now I'm getting an eyeful of Jonah's nakedness inside the suite.

"Tarzan. What are the rules about being naked?"

His smile falls. "Friends don't want to see other friends naked."

"Right. Now, take this coffee and empanada, get dressed, and when you are both decent, come over to our room. We've got more coffee and more treats."

"Okay. We'll be there in a few." He looks so crestfallen I can't stand it. I exhale my annoyance and smile. "Get dressed, sweetie. I *agape* you. Forever and always."

Back in our room, Sloan and Calum are fighting back laughter.

"By the sounds of it, you got an eyeful," Calum says.

"Yep. Nothing like interrupting men with morning wood. Good times."

Sloan points at the empty chair I vacated. "Sit and eat, luv. Time is running out, and by the sounds of it, this promises to be an interesting day."

I sink into my chair and huff. "Aren't they all?"

Dionysus comes to our room almost immediately. He's dressed and showered and completely presentable once more. "Are there any treats left?"

I gesture for him to help himself. "What's with sexing up Jonah? I thought you were Agent K and playing professional."

Dionysus shrugs. "When you left us in the boat, you told us to take good care of him. You also said I should find someone to massage my balls and ease the indignation of being palmed by one of the *Golden Girls*."

Calum chuckles. "He has you on both accounts."

"Yeah, I know he does. At least tell me the two of you aren't going to make things weird today."

"Nothing weird." Jonah pushes the door open and steps tentatively inside. "Sorry about the flash and dash in my room."

I wave that away. "As I told you yesterday. If someone doesn't end up naked, it would be a miracle."

He laughs. "I thought that was all y'all exaggerating for comedic effect."

Calum busts up laughing. "Not even a little. Come in. How are you feeling this morning?"

"Right as rain. I can't believe it. I was steeped last night but feel normal this morning. Truth be told, I feel better than normal."

"You're welcome." Dionysus grins and bows.

Calum laughs. "You're taking credit for that, are you, Greek?"

"Yes, I am. Not to be graphic, but Jonah has been thoroughly infused with my godly awesomesauce."

I groan. "Okay, that was way too graphic. I'm out. Time to go to work."

By the time we get downstairs, Maggie is in full dictator mode, and Knox is escorting Governor Boseman over to the line of Escalades in the pickup lane outside.

Jonah wasn't kidding when he said Maggie's got no slack in her rope. I wouldn't be surprised if she grew up an Army brat and had a drill sergeant for a parent.

We hurry out of the lobby and are headed toward the bus when Knox calls, "Red. Come here for a moment."

I change course and head over to where he's standing beside the center vehicle's open door to the back seat. When I arrive, he tilts his head toward the door, and Governor Boseman gets out to stand.

After he straightens, he extends his hand. "We were never formally introduced. I'm Tucker Boseman."

"Fiona Cumhaill. It's a pleasure, sir."

He passes an assessing gaze over me and nods. "Jonah sent me the press kit for your group. I admit I didn't take the time to look at it until this morning. You've done some good work."

"Thank you, sir."

"Everyone, move out." Maggie waves a finger over her head and marches for us, the angry *click, click, click* of her heels beating out a frantic rhythm.

I glance back at the bus as the engine starts. I don't want to miss my ride, but if the big boss wants to say something, I'm not going to disrespect him by leaving.

"You're going to miss your bus, witch."

I force a smile. "I'm a druid."

"I don't care. We're leaving."

Governor Boseman sends his assistant an indulgent smile. "Maggie keeps the schedule tight. We can't mess with that. Join me in my car for the ride, will you, Ms. Cumhaill?"

"Of course, sir. Whatever you like."

He slides back into his seat, and when Maggie opens the door to join him, he holds out his hand. "Allow Ms. Cumhaill to sit with me for the ride, Mags. I'd like to speak with her."

Maggie looks like she's about to choke, but Boseman doesn't see it. She makes very sure that I do, though. "Of course, sir. I'll catch a ride in the lead car."

Before I climb in, Knox steps into my path and looks me up and down. "Are you carrying?"

"A gun? No. I don't use them."

"May I ask what you do use?"

I hold my hand up and flex my palm, calling Birga forward.

The shock on his face and the small step he takes back is a big win, and I'm petty enough to giggle. "This is Birga. She's an enchanted necromancy spear."

"I don't suppose you'll let me take possession of that thing while you're in the convoy?"

"Nope. She and I are bonded." I pull back my sleeve and show him my bare forearm. Then, I send Birga back to her resting place. When the spear tattoo appears, I drop my sleeve and meet his gaze. "I'll give you my word that I have no violent intentions toward the governor."

He swallows, his frame still taut with tension. "That's the only weapon you carry?"

I shake my head. "Not even close."

He eyes me up and down, and while my clothes are tasteful and professional, they cling to my curves well enough that he knows my weapons can't be physically on me.

"It's fine, Knox," the governor interjects. "We need to leave, or Maggie will lose her mind."

Knox stares at me and his gaze narrows. "I'm trusting you. Last night you didn't stay in your lane, but it worked out. Don't go off script again."

I chuckle. "Don't bench your best players, big guy. Give them room and see what they can do on the field."

He grunts and steps back. "I can tell you're going to be a major pain in my ass."

I chuckle again. "I've been called much worse."

When I'm seated in the Escalade next to the governor, I close my eyes and reach out to Dionysus. *The governor asked me to ride with him. I'm in the center car. Can you let everyone know?*

Will do. Enjoy the upgrade.

I smile and return my attention to Boseman. He's staring at me with a curious look. "What were you doing just now? It looked like you were meditating."

"No. I was talking to one of my team members in the bus to let them know I'm en route with them, but I'm up here. My husband is a worrier, and my brother's not much better."

"You can talk telepathically with your team?"

"Only among certain members. It's their ability, not mine."

Knox's gaze shifts to the rearview mirror, and he studies me silently from the front seat.

Boseman reaches into the console between us and offers me a drink. He chooses water, so I do the same. "And teleporting? That's how you evacuated my party from the event last night, isn't it?"

"That's right. Several of my team have the ability to portal."

"Is that a common ability?"

I consider how much to tell him. The boons of speaking telepathically and having access to teleportation aren't lost on me. A man in his position might solely want to strengthen his team, but often people in power want more power.

Giving them ideas is a dangerous thing.

Still, in his position, he has access to the answers to these questions anyway. "Portaling can be common, depending on the race of the empowered person. It's also a trait that happens by chance with others."

"So, who has what powers?" He turns in his seat and opens his water. In a casual setting like this, he's much more charismatic than when he has his politician façade in place.

"That's a loaded question, sir, and not one I'm prepared to answer."

"All right, I'll ask it a different way. If I were interested in adding empowered people to my staff—so we had some of the abilities available to us that you do—how would you advise me to start the process?"

I see the warning brewing in Knox's gaze and feel for the guy. It's obvious he loves his job and doesn't want to be rendered obsolete, but to the governor's point, there are bigger, stronger, and faster options out there.

"Moon Called can pretty much all portal short distances. Those are what you'd know as shifters."

"Like werewolves?"

"Not exactly. The power of a were-creature comes from being infected with lycanthropy. They can't teleport. They are usually super strong but can't choose when or when not to shift. The Moon Called is a magical species that shift to one animal form at will and can teleport."

He nods. "Would you recommend Moon Called shifters in a security setting?"

"Sure, if you find ones who are qualified and form loyalty to you. But with Moon Called, their loyalty will always be to their alpha and pack first."

"That's good to know. Is your man that teleports a Moon Called shifter?"

"No. The guy who teleported all of you back to the hotel last night is a Greek immortal. Spatial energy is simply his affinity. It's not a thing among immortals. We also have Dionysus—he's a demi-god, and most gods and goddesses can teleport—and my husband Sloan. A druid who can teleport is called a wayfarer."

He sits back and sighs. "You have three people on your team who can teleport?"

"Three of the ones here today, yes."

"It's a great deal more complicated than I realized."

"We're trying not to release too much information too quickly. We don't want to overwhelm society or spike a panic."

"Or start a black-market frenzy," Knox adds. "There are a lot of powerful humans in the world who won't like not being at the top of the food chain. I could easily see individuals with these abilities being rounded up and sold, like the gun and sex trades."

"Yeah, that's a fear of ours as well."

We drive along in silence for a while, and I watch the busy streets of San Antonio grow quieter as the landscape changes. With all the excitement in the hotel this morning, I didn't take note of where we are heading.

Definitely outside the city.

"Tell me what you know about what is happening around me." Boseman takes a long drink from his water bottle. "Maggie said you got a look at the thing that's stirring up trouble."

"Sort of, not really. We were able to determine the magic used was a hex. Knowing that, we searched for the source. With hexes, the source is either a person or an object placed in the vicinity."

"And it was a person."

"It was. At first, we thought it was a waiter, but the waiter was innocent and being inhabited—" My mind spins out on that.

"Is something wrong, Ms. Cumhaill?"

"Fiona, please, or Fi." I mull over that tidbit of realization and shake my head. "No. Nothing's wrong. This morning my brother and I were throwing around the types of beings who can change forms. There were too many to narrow down. Being able to change form and also possess a human...that's a much smaller group. I hadn't thought of that until now."

"So, do you think you can solve it?"

"Oh, we can solve it. I hope it's sooner rather than later."

CHAPTER TEN

When we pull off the road and the Escalade slows, I look out my window and read the sign for Big Bend National Park. Right. I remember seeing that on the list of stops for San Antonio.

The area's landscape is stunning.

As a druid, a surge of power comes from being in a truly natural setting.

Big Bend doesn't disappoint.

"Oh, it's lovely." I take in the desert landscape, the limestone cliffs, and the canyon in the distance.

When the driver pulls into a parking space to stop, he and Knox get out. I wait until the governor is set and given the go-ahead to open the back door before I get out.

I'm already on Knox's shit list.

There's no need to give him a chance to say I endangered the governor.

I brush a hand down my pants and flick my hair behind my shoulders before taking inventory of my surroundings.

The Chisos Basin Visitor Center at Big Bend National Park is a modest beige and brown bungalow with access to washrooms from the outside.

It's the first building in a long U-shaped parking lot that stretches off three hundred feet into the distance before looping back around.

Half a dozen more bungalow buildings sit around the loop, all with the same long, one-story floor plan.

Behind them, all the way around the loop, low mountains form the backdrop.

There's no bus parking, so the tour bus drives perpendicularly across the lines for the vehicle parking spots and takes up seven spaces in front of the convenience store next door.

Maggie hustles over to check on the governor and zips over to where a female ranger is waiting to greet her.

I wander down the sidewalk to meet my guys. Jonah steps off the bus first and sends me an amused smile. Calum's next. He's laughing too. Knowing them as well as I do, there's no telling what kind of craziness they've gotten into.

I'm not sure I want to know.

It couldn't be too bad, though. Sloan was back there, and my hubs is the prince of responsibility and maturity. When he steps off the bus, he's red-faced and wiping tears from his eyes.

Or maybe not.

"What did I miss?"

Sloan shakes his head and sobers. "Och, luv. As a gentleman, I couldn't even begin to repeat it."

After Manx, Dionysus steps off next. Hilarious. He's snapped himself into a ranger uniform complete with a wildlife whistle and a ball cap that says, Park Rangers do it in the woods.

When he sees me reading his hat, he waggles his brows at me.

"Hey, Jane. You like the look?"

"You make beige and brown look good."

He grins. "Thank you for noticing. So, is there a crowd at this stop? I'm curious to see what the constituents think of my outfit."

Jonah shakes his head. "Not this time. This stop is to go over the wildlife and conservation directives Governor Boseman put into place and to take some photos to use in media spots. The press probably won't even get off the bus."

Dionysus frowns. "And I got all dolled up too."

I link my arm through his and laugh. "You'll have to make do with us as your adoring fans."

The six of us set off along the sidewalk, heading back to the visitor's center. Together we take in the gray-green mountains and rising peaks. Toronto is amazing in many ways, but other than the view of Lake Ontario or the cityscape, there isn't much horizon scenery.

Here, there's nothing *but* beautiful backdrops. I'm half-turned to chat with my brother when Dionysus jolts to a stop and a shrill whistle sounds.

My heart hammers. "What the hell, dude? You scared the bejeebers out of me."

Dionysus is paying no attention. He's standing transfixed with his whistle still pursed between his lips.

When I open my mouth to question him, he points at the sand, dirt, and grass combo beyond the sidewalk's edge. Slithering into the shade of a huge prickly pear cactus two feet away is a large, heavy-bodied, flat-headed snake.

"Is that a rattler?" A chill races down my spine.

"It's a bullsnake, Jane, but the pattern is similar. The bullsnake also hisses and shakes its tail when threatened. When it does this in dry brush, the effect is similar to a buzzing rattlesnake. Isn't she a beauty?"

Calum busts up laughing. "Are you channeling Steve Irwin now, Greek?"

I wait until our new friend slithers under the cactus and give her a wide berth.

Dionysus is watching me, amusement plain on his face. "You're a druid, Jane. She's a creature of nature."

"I realize that, and while I have no ill will toward her, I prefer my wildlife to have fur or feathers."

"What about Dart?"

I frown. "I don't consider him to be wildlife. He's more of a mythical marvel."

"Bruin qualifies for that too," Calum adds.

I often forget that Bear is *the* Bear of the Native American mythos until moments like this. I rub my chest and send him a rush of love. "Yeah. Definitely, him too."

"I can't believe you have a wildlife prejudice, Jane. I'll have to rethink my opinion of you."

I roll my eyes. "Can't a girl like kittens more than spiders?"

"Jonah and I like snakes more than beavers," Calum says.

Jonah snorts. "That is true."

I smack my brother's arm. "Be professional. Jonah's got a job to do, and we don't want to make him look bad in front of his peers."

"Speakin' of somethin' lookin' bad..." Sloan points at where Maggie, Knox, the governor, and a female ranger are having an intense conversation.

I release my hold on Dionysus' arm and put on my game face. "I'll go see what's going on."

As brusque as Maggie Fuentes can be, she's efficient at her job. From what I saw yesterday and the stories Jonah told us last night, I have no doubt that ordinarily, everything runs like clockwork around her.

When it doesn't...she looks like that.

Under the calm exterior, Maggie Fuentes is raging.

"It's not safe," the ranger is saying. "I'm sorry, but I can't in good conscience allow all y'all to go out as planned. Not with the bears like that."

"The bears like what?" I ask.

Maggie spins and glares at me. "This is none of your concern, witch."

I roll my eyes. "I'm a druid, not a witch. Huge difference. One of the most notable differences being that my powers are rooted in nature magic. The key word there being *nature*. If you've got bear problems, it's more our concern than anyone else here."

The park ranger looks me over. "All y'all have experience with bears?"

"More than you can imagine. In fact, my best friend is a bear."

Yeah no, she doesn't buy that.

Governor Boseman rubs a hand over his face. "Jonah said druids communicate with animals. Is that right?"

"It is. If you've got trouble with your wildlife, we're happy to step in and help."

The ranger seems undecided.

Governor Boseman nods. "I say we trust Fiona and her team. From what I've seen and heard, I believe in her abilities."

The ranger doesn't look sure but how do you say no to your governor? "Come inside, and I'll call my boss."

I wave for the guys to join me and let the others enter. Once I fill them in on what's going on, we join them.

"Oh, that's nice." Calum stops under the air vent in the ceiling of the breezeway and raises his face to the flow of cool air.

"Yeah, so stop hogging it." I push him from behind.

He closes his eyes for a moment, draws a deep breath, and moves on to give the rest of us a chance to get inside.

The welcome center is a long public area centered around an artistic display of a stuffed cougar and other desert animals mounted on a platform of smooth, tan rocks. I hope these animals died of natural causes and are displayed as teaching points.

They would have to be, right?

As we join the discussion already in progress, the ranger hangs up the phone. "All right. He says if all y'all are confident and the governor is standing behind it, I'm to let all y'all take a crack at it."

Knox crosses his arms, showing off his manly guns. He looks all kinds of skeptical. "I don't like it. Wildlife is unpredictable. What if you can't get through to them? This could put the governor in a dangerous situation."

"It won't. We'll fix the bear situation while the governor waits here in the air conditioning safe and sound."

That appeases the Hulk. "You're sure you can do this?"

"Easy-peasy. Any one of us could talk a bear down. If not, we can use magic to stop it from whatever it's doing, and if for some crazy reason we can't, then Bruin can."

Jonah has his hands in his pockets and looks up at the mention of my bear. "Bruin? That's your animal companion, right?"

"Yes. Bruin will have no problem finding out what's going on with the bears. We'll go, sort out the issue, and be back in a flash."

Knox huffs. "Where do you need to go to get your animal friend? Are you going to teleport?"

"No need. Bruin is always close by, aren't you, buddy?" I release my bear, and he gains his freedom and manifests at my side.

"Oh, my Lanta!" Maggie stops dead in her tracks as the hands of Knox and the ranger go straight for the weapons holstered on their hips.

I throw up a fast and dirty shield and step forward. "Don't do that. Bruin is no threat to you unless you intend to threaten him."

Dionysus, Sloan, and Calum react fast and step in beside me to form a united front.

"He's the one who can help with the bears?" the ranger asks. Then she notices Manx beside Sloan. "Are they your pets?"

I glance from Bruin to Manx. "No. They're part of our family. We're druids."

The ranger gathers her wits before Knox and Maggie, Jonah is wide-eyed and grinning, and Governor Boseman seems to be in shock and taking it all in.

The ranger holds up her palms. "My apologies. I'm Mia Martinez."

"It's good to meet you." I take a couple of steps toward the glass wall and the cougar display to get their eyes off Bruin. "Tell us what's going on. So far all you've said is that you're having trouble with the bears. Could you elaborate on that?"

Dionysus has caught Mia's eye and I'm not sure if she's attracted to the man or amused by his ranger impersonation. "We noticed the bears displaying non-typical behavior a couple of days ago. We're at a loss."

"How many bears are we talking?" Dionysus asks.

"At last count, we had between thirty and forty black bears in the park. There's no way to know for sure if they're all affected or only the ones that have drawn our attention."

"What are the bears doing?" I ask.

"Two were found jumping on the trampoline of a park neighbor."

Calum laughs. "I've seen YouTube videos of bears doing that."

"And high-fiving campers."

"Okay, that's a little less common."

"And breaking into the rented cottages to sit at the tables and eat our guests' breakfasts right out of their bowls."

Dionysus nods. "Ah, yes. The old reverse Goldilocks maneuver."

I blink at him and look at Bruin. "Is that a thing?"

Bruin snorts. "Of course not, Red. The man's a loon."

Well, yeah, but he got me on that one.

Mia pulls up pictures on her phone and turns them around to show us. Yep. There they are. Three black bears sitting at the table eating out of bowls.

"Okay, that *is* odd." Although I wouldn't admit this out loud, it does remind me of a reverse Goldilocks maneuver.

Mia's gaze narrows on us. "How exactly does your team

work? You can't harm the bears. This is a natural area, and we have directives to enforce."

"Och, no. We'd never harm an animal, Ms. Martinez." Sloan joins the conversation, and now Mia is eyeing him up and down. "We're guardians of nature. Our priority is to safeguard the earth and all her creatures."

"What will all y'all need from me to get that done?"

"If ye could take us to the area where you last saw the bears, that would be helpful. From there, Bruin and Manx can track them, and we can find out what's happened."

Mia's head tilts as she studies each of our boys. "They're trained well enough to do that for you?"

Bruin grunts and growls.

Maggie retreats a few steps and glares at me.

What did *I* do?

"They aren't our pets and aren't trained. They are intelligent, self-aware team members and are as skilled as you and me. If you have questions, you can ask them directly. If it's a complicated answer, any of us can understand them to translate."

"Are you all druids?" she asks.

"No. Only the three of us." I gesture between Sloan, Calum, and me.

"I'm in a category all my own," Dionysus says before I can explain. "And hard to explain."

Sloan meets my gaze, and I shrug.

"I'm Dionysus, by the way." He offers her a million-dollar smile.

The girl shakes his hand with flushed cheeks.

"All righty then." I clap and gesture at the door. "Let's go meet up with your bears."

Mia grabs a set of keys off a hook behind the reception desk and marches toward the door. "Let's see if we can find them."

Mia and Knox ride in the front seat of the GMC Sierra King Cab while Calum and I take the back seat. I thought Bruin would ghost out and leave Sloan and Dionysus to sit in the truck bed with Manx, but he shook off that idea and remained on the physical plane. There isn't much room left in the truck bed once he's in there.

Until we know what's going on, I'd rather not draw attention to me not being a typical bear when out here. If there's a wizard or a god behind the things happening around the governor, I'd rather be an unknown entity.

It's your call, Bear. This mission has your name written all over it.

He meets my gaze through the glass window in the back seat and grins. *That's new fer me. I gotta say, I like bein' the lead on a case. Watch out, or I might go after yer job.*

I laugh. *Most days I'd give it to you without a fight.*

Mia drives us from the visitor center, past the convenience store, and around the loop. We wind up a slope to the Chisos Mountains Lodge. "We have guests in here year-round. People bring in their RVs, and we've got camping, the lodge, and several cottages to rent. The last thing we need is bad publicity about bear problems."

Calum grins. "If you think about it though, bouncing on trampolines and eating someone's Cheerios are more hilarious than dangerous. The way the world is these days, if it got out you might go viral and end up having more business, not less."

Agreed. "It could be much worse."

Mia meets our gaze in the rearview mirror. "That still doesn't negate our need to resolve the problem and figure out why it's happening in the first place."

"Do you have any ideas yet?" Knox asks.

"Dude, we haven't even gotten started. Give us a chance. This is what we do, and we're damn good at it. You'll see."

Mia appreciates that.

Knox...not so much.

When the truck stops, the tires slide and *crunch* on the sandy gravel mixture. Once Mia shuts off the engine and pulls the keys, we all pile out.

Dionysus, Sloan, and Manx jump down from the truck bed right away. Bruin follows. The truck springs creak as the vehicle jostles and it's almost as if the Sierra breathes a sigh of relief.

On the ground, my boy scans the landscape, his nose raised to the warm breeze.

"This one is made for you, buddy." Calum raps his hands on the truck bed. "Community bear relations is all you."

"Yeah, it is." Dionysus approaches Bruin with his palm raised. When Bruin meets his high-five, he grins. "To celebrate your promotion, I got you a hat too."

Dionysus magically produces a second hat. It's huge and has a wide brim and a chin string. He holds it out for us to read the slogan. "Bears do it in the woods, too."

Dionysus grins. "We're going to rock this one, bear."

Bruin lifts his ebony nose into the air and chuckles. *When do we not rock it?*

"Fair point, my ursine friend."

I run my fingers through the coarse brown guard hairs of his coat into the silky fur beneath.

Bruin and Manx lift their noses to the warm breeze and fill their lungs.

Manx glances at Bruin with a quizzical look clouding his warm golden eyes. *Do ye smell that?*

Aye, I do. Bruin shakes his head. *It smells familiar, but it's too faint fer me to place it.*

"You smell something odd?" I ask.

Aye...but I'm not certain what it is.

It's magic of some sort, Manx adds.

Bruin wriggles his nose in the breeze and sneezes. *What kind of magic? That's the question.*

Dionysus places Bruin's hat on his massive, boxy head and

leans under his chin to cinch the clasp. "Excellent. Now you're dressed for success."

"And looking good." I give him two thumbs-up.

Bruin stands on all fours and lifts his face to the breeze. His glossy black nose twitches this way and that as he breathes in. When he's finished, he sneezes again.

"Bless you, buddy. What's on the wind that's making you sneeze?"

He looks at me with his eyes narrowed. *Too soon to tell, Red. Stick close to me though, will ye? I've got a bad feelin' yer magnet is workin' its usual magic.*

Sloan, Calum, and Dionysus all turn their heads when he says that. The only two who don't understand the implications of that are Knox and Mia.

Okay, yeah. Consider me forewarned and let us in on the secret as soon as you figure it out.

Will do.

"Do you smell the bears?"

Manx looks at me and nods. *And magic.*

Manx looks at Bruin, and the two trot off toward the treeline behind the cottages on the hill. The six of us follow, my mind still milling over Bruin's warning. What does it mean that he's got a bad feeling?

CHAPTER ELEVEN

All right, Red. Wait here while we do our thing. Bruin's rounded haunches waddle off into the forest's shadows with Manx's stubby tail twitching happily at his side. Sloan's lynx companion is all lithe reflexes and springy steps while Bruin is rooted power and solid strength. They are opposites and yet as close as two brothers could be.

I should know. I have five.

Sloan strides closer to the edge of the trees and holds his hand open behind him. I take the gesture as he means, and he helps me up a sandy slope.

I'm thankful I wore my hiking boots because this terrain would be hell in tennis shoes.

After seeing the snake back at the welcome center, I'm hyper-vigilant about watching where I put my feet. I'm also listening for any hisses or rattles.

Opening myself up to the nature around us. I reach out with my druid powers to get an idea of who and what is nearby. I sense a couple of armadillos, and a kit fox in a den off to my left. I get a strong coyote vibe…and jackrabbits, some bats…and thankfully no snakes closing in on us.

Red? Can ye bring the others and join us?

Sure, buddy. On our way. I relay the request to the others, and despite the skeptical looks we receive from Knox and Mia, they follow.

The moment we're under the trees' canopy, the Texas sun's heat cuts drastically, and I shiver. The shade isn't cold, but the contrast between the two temperatures is jarring.

"Did your bear tell you why he wanted us to come?" Knox asks.

I scan the forest floor and step over a downed tree. "No. Only that he wanted us to join them."

The throaty vocalizations of bears ahead draw us to where we need to be.

"What are they saying?" Mia asks me.

"They aren't speaking to us. They're speaking to one another, so it's not for us to understand."

"Uh-huh," Knox says.

Whatevs. The nice thing here is that we don't have anything to prove to anyone so they can be as judgy and skeptical as they want.

"It's magic, all right," Bruin says when he finishes speaking to the Big Bend black bears. "The big male with the scar on his shoulder says they've felt light-headed and odd ever since they found a patch of blueberries growing deeper into the forest."

"Blueberries?" I repeat, my mind trying to grasp that one. "I didn't realize blueberries grow here."

Sloan nods. "There are suitable hardy varieties that do well in Texas's desert biome, rabbiteye and Southern highbush varieties in particular."

That's my guy. He's a walking encyclopedia.

"Okay, cool. Well, the bears are saying they began feeling strange around the time they noticed a patch of blueberries growing deeper in the forest."

"Then that's where we need to be," Dionysus states. "Sounds like someone doped the berries."

As much as it sounds like that, I can't help but wonder why? Why would someone go out of their way to drug bears to reduce their inhibitions or even more strangely, to get them to act like fools?

Is this still about the governor's campaign trail?

Having the bears being weird was only going to get the governor's photo op canceled not cause him any embarrassment.

I guide our group in the direction Bruin indicated before the bears and Manx went ahead, and soon we reconvene with them at a robust grouping of fruit-laden blueberry bushes.

I hold my hands out as magic crawls over the surface of my skin. It's hitting me in the belly too. It's like eels are wriggling around in my stomach playing tag. "Wow. That's powerful."

Mia frowns. "What is it? What do you feel?"

"Magic." Sloan reaches out and makes a face. "It's nauseating."

I step back and let him have the access he needs to help figure out what's going on.

When Knox and Mia send us a sidelong glance, I explain. "One of Sloan's affinities is to gauge the strength and designation of magic. Between him and Bruin, we have a good chance of solving this mystery right here and now."

Mia looks relieved.

Knox...not so much.

I'm beginning to wonder if there's more going on beyond him not liking us infringing on his security gig.

"There's something here beyond magic left behind to stir trouble," Sloan says.

"What do you mean, hotness?"

"The blueberry bushes are tainted with a mocker, no argument, but the source of that magic is too strong to simply be the result. The source is here too."

"The source? You mean the one who cast the hex?"

Sloan's gaze narrows as he takes in the bears. "We know our troublemaker can assume other forms."

He takes a slow walk around the group of bears, brushing his hands over them as he passes.

"Believe it or not, this is how we met," I say to Knox. "He came to test the strengths of my family and me. We ended up in a bloody brawl in the alley."

He doesn't care. Fine. I was trying to strike up a bond of familiarity. Never mind.

Sloan finishes walking through the bears and strides over to us. I feel the surge of his power still engaged as he approaches.

Right. Our bad guy can shapeshift, but he can also possess people. He could be standing right here.

Sloan stops directly in front of Knox and Mia.

"If ye don't mind…"

My shield fires to life at the same moment a thundering roar of bears fills the air. Sloan pulls back, and I spin, my gaze piercing the heart of the forest all around us.

Shit. We're surrounded.

Dozens of angry bears gallop toward us with maws open and teeth bared. This is a diversion.

I return my attention to Mia and Knox, reaching out with my instincts. It's an easy choice when my shield is firing up and burning. Grabbing the woman's arm, I pull her away and push her toward Dionysus. "Tarzan, get Mia to the safety of the trees. No one hurt the bears. Knox is controlling them."

A throaty laugh tears from the hulking bodyguard as he raises his hands, and the bears heed his call. "You have no idea what you're playing with, little girl."

Dionysus grabs Mia and snaps out. Calum, Sloan, and I have our hands up and call various shields. I'm running through the plan to handle this when he returns. "Bruin and Manx, call your armor and push the bears back. Calum, you're on animal-influence spells. *Beast Bond. Confusion.* Sloan, try to heal the influence of the hex and cure them of whatever magical poisoning they ingested with the berries."

"What about us, Jane?" Dionysus asks. "If they get to be the bear whisperers, what are we doing?"

I tilt my head toward Knox. Now that he's outed as the source, the glamor he was using to mask his true form is dropping. Our baddie has taken over our hulking security agent. "We're going after the source."

Dionysus holds out his fist for a bump. "I can get behind that."

I call forward my body armor and Fionn's magical bracers ink the entire surface of my skin: bark, roots, leaves...

The power and impenetrability of the Tree of Life protect me within seconds.

I call Birga to my hand, and as my spear responds, Knox's gaze locks on me. "You are a fierce female."

"Well, you know. I try my best."

Bruin roars. Standing on his back paws, he flexes his claws at the attacking bears.

Manx has his armor on, his head dropped, and his ears pinned back. Growling long and low, he darts between the seething bodies of black fur.

Without waiting for an invitation, I move in on the offensive. Dionysus lets me measure the man's skill. A few preliminary strikes. A few assessing looks. A few moments of testing reflexes and vulnerabilities.

"What are you?" Knox's demeanor shifts from annoyance to curiosity as we bat away each other's advances. "You're more than a druid."

"You could say that."

He looks from me to Bruin and frowns. "How did you capture the affections of one such as he?"

The question catches me off-guard.

I'm not sure if it's a ploy or a genuine question, but before I can figure that out, he charges.

His movements are quick and practiced, but I'm ready for him. I kick forward, aiming for his chest. He smacks my foot away without effort and swings for me. Ducking the blow, I dip to the side and crack him with Birga's staff. The strike is solid, and he grunts as he shifts to steady his footing.

Dionysus is circling, letting me take the lead on the confrontation. I wouldn't think anything of it except for his look of puzzlement.

What is it, Tarzan?

I can't spare much of my attention for him with everything happening around us. Knox makes an aggressive play, and I barely miss getting his fist to my temple. I don't escape entirely, though. He grabs my hair and yanks me back.

When I scream, Dionysus throws his hands forward, and the governor's security guard is thrown thirty feet into the trunk of a wide tree.

I blink and recover quickly. "Tarzan, no! You can't use your god powers like that. You only just got them back. Don't do anything to draw the censure of the Fates."

Dionysus has one hand over his head with his fingers extended wide. He isn't giving up whatever magical hold he used to pin Knox in place. "Don't worry, Jane. The Fates only care when I use my powers to alter the lives of humans within the realm. He doesn't qualify."

Knox's eyes flip gold and glitter with wild excitement. "I thought you'd pick up on that."

Shit. I don't know what's happening. Is he saying he's not human, not from this realm, or both?

Snapping brush behind me is the only notice I get before a pack of incensed bears race at me. I spin, my heart pumping blood through my veins at a dizzying rate. "I don't want to hurt you. Please, don't make me."

The lead bear is male, followed by half a dozen smaller, but in no way small, females. They aren't as large as Bruin—few forest bears could be—but gripped by the thrall of the dickwad Dionysus is taking on, they are still dangerous.

Matted with clumps of shaggy black fur, they *galumph* forward, swiping six-inch claws and swinging their heads with canines exposed.

I take on the male, confident my armor will keep me from getting shredded. It won't keep me from getting knocked around and roughed up by a bunch of possessed bears.

"Confusion. Bestial Strength." I push out my intention, hoping to distract and derail this attack. "How are you doing, hotness?"

"Not well. Whomever he is..." Sloan grunts. Outnumbered and overpowered by bears, he's taken to the ground. Before they have him pinned, he *poofs* out and reappears at my side. "He's powerful, luv. It might be best to regroup and come back at it."

Bruin roars, sending several females skittering back. "I remember that scent now. Feckin' hell. Of all the bastards in all the realms..."

I get knocked back and bear-hug the male standing on his hind legs to take me down.

Crappers. Leaning into the struggle, I dig the balls of my feet into the forest floor and strain to remain upright. The dirt beneath me is soft, and the soles of my boots gain traction.

A wild base growl vibrates through the trees as Bruin abandons his position and barrels toward Dionysus and Knox. "Ye no good, lyin', trouble-makin' piece of shite. I'm goin' to sink my teeth into yer mangy coat and tear yer bollocks from—"

Knox's eyes roll back in his head, and his body falls limp to the ground.

A rush of magical breeze whips past me and circles me once, lifting my hair. *Until we meet again, fierce female.*

Bruin ghosts out and a second rush of air blasts past.

The chaos ends without warning. The forest goes quiet in an instant, and the only sound I hear is the thumping of my pulse racing in my veins.

One by one, the bears break the spell and shake their heads, knocking the cobwebs loose.

"Is it over?" I take in the scene.

Calum lowers his *Impenetrable Sphere* and takes in the carnage. "Shit, Irish. Are you okay?"

Sloan is down on one knee, probing a bloody gash on his thigh. As he trails his finger along the damage, the flesh knits back together. "Aye, I'll live. What the hell was that about?"

Dionysus leaves the unconscious Knox lying in the scrub of the forest floor and brushes his hands together. He wraps an arm across his chest. Fresh blood stains his lips. "Not a what, my friend. A who."

I take in the damage to our demi-god, and I'm more concerned than ever. "All right, who then? I've never seen Bruin go after someone like that and you're bleeding. Who the hell did we come up against?"

Calum huffs. "Whoever it was, Bruin wasn't happy about the reunion."

"Yeah, he really doesn't like that guy."

Dionysus frowns, glancing in the direction they exited the forest. "I'm sure his opinion is justified."

"How so?"

"Because that, my dear friends, was Coyote, and by the mess he left here, I'd say he's back to his old tricks."

"Coyote? As in Coyote of the same Indigenous mythos as Bruin?"

Dionysus nods. "Bruin's right to be alarmed, Jane. In my experience, nothing good ever comes from Coyote being around… especially if he's looking for trouble."

CHAPTER TWELVE

After Dionysus is healed, he snaps out to retrieve Mia from wherever he stashed her. At the same time, Sloan works on healing and reviving Knox. Once that's taken care of, we start piecing together the events of the past couple of days.

"He's the one who did it?" Mia asks, her voice thin and pitchy as she points at Knox.

I shake my head. "No, he was possessed by the one who did it. Knox is an ordinary guy who got overtaken by a trickster god."

"Possessed? As in *Exorcist*?"

Dionysus tilts his head from side to side. "Yes and no. Some beings with god powers or those with god-like powers can commandeer people's bodies at will. They aren't demons consuming their souls or anything. They're hopping into a car and taking it for a joy ride."

"But why?" Mia looks at Knox lying there. "What does possessing him and inciting strange bear antics accomplish?"

Bruin materializes back with us and a steady, rumbling growl rolls through the forest.

I start us moving back to the truck.

As Bruin paces off his hostility, he releases his armor and

smacks a few trees as he storms past. Even with the protection of his God-given shielding, he's bloody and mauled as I've never seen him. "The asshole doesn't need a reason beyond bein' an asshole. If he's bored, he gets off causin' a fuss. It's been close to four centuries since I last had a run-in with him, and it's still too soon."

"Is Coyote a bad guy? I thought his mythos says he created animals and can control the rain."

Dionysus sets his hand on the hump of Bruin's back as we walk. The welts and cuts start to mend when his fingers sink into Bruin's thick brown coat. "There are many versions of Coyote's story. Some paint him as neither good nor evil but simply indifferent. Others say he's a mischievous trickster. Still, to see him is an omen of a negative event coming your way."

"Just what we need, another troublesome trickster bringing us unfortunate events."

Mia arches a brow. "Another? These things have happened to you before?"

I don't want to comment. If I could go back to not knowing all the bad and crazy things the world was barfing up around me...

No, maybe I wouldn't want to.

If I didn't know about all the crazy bad, I also wouldn't know all the crazy good. And those heavily outweigh the negatives.

"Yes, we've dealt with tricksters before." I count Discord as the truest example, but Loki was a pain in the ass and qualifies.

"Why the bears?" Knox slumps to sit on the truck's tailgate and lets his boots dangle while he catches his second wind. "And why me?"

Dionysus waves that away. "I'd bet there was nothing about you specifically. You were here, and he was having fun. That's it. That's all it takes when immortals find themselves unchallenged and needing stimulation."

"As for the bears...I'm assuming that relates to disrupting the governor somehow. As far as I know, there haven't been any trickster hexes in Texas other than what's coming at you guys and this campaign."

"But why?" he asks.

"That's the million-dollar question."

Knox is quiet on the ride back to the welcome center, and I feel bad. He's a take charge and control the situation kinda guy, so having his choices stripped from him, even for a short time, would shake his foundation.

When we get there, Jonah, Maggie, and the governor are still waiting in the welcome center. I'm reaching for the door to head inside when a hand gently grabs my elbow. "Hey, Red? I know I probably haven't earned it, but can I ask a favor?"

I meet Knox's gaze and nod. "What do you need?"

"Could one of your teleport people take me back to the hotel for an hour? I need to do some laps in the pool or run my ass off on the treadmill or something. I've got all this pent-up fury inside me, and I'm afraid I'll kill someone who even looks at the governor."

"You don't have to explain. Sure. Give me your phone, and I'll put in my details. Sloan can take you to the hotel, and you can text me when you're ready for a pickup."

"That works. Can I get two minutes to notify my guys...and if you don't mind, can we say I have a lead to run down or something?"

"Not a problem."

He meets my gaze, and the annoyance and anger have subsided for the first time. "Thank you."

"I'll send Sloan over to the Escalades. Do your thing, and he'll be there when you're ready."

When the big guy strides off, I fill Sloan in.

"Aye, well, it's better that he remove himself than to lose his temper and regret his actions."

"Exactly. We'll wait here until you get back."

With that taken care of, Calum, Dionysus, and I head inside to give our report. They're sitting in a small education center with the hard plastic chairs all turned inward into a circle.

Mia filled them in on what happened, so when the questions fly, it's more about why we think it happened than the actual events.

Boseman looks baffled. "What I don't understand is why a mythical trickster god would target me. I've never had any run-ins or dealings with empowered people that I know of and certainly not any gods. Present company excluded, of course."

Dionysus sits forward in his chair. "Maybe something happened that pissed him off. Coyote is known to like desert towns. Maybe you did something in your politics that upset him. Think Nevada, New Mexico, Utah, Arizona...he's said to have a daughter in the Columbia Basin...does any of this ring a bell?"

"No. Nothing. I don't have anything but good relationships with other states, and I'm tough on legislation that impacts the environment."

Maggie shoves her iPad back into her bag and stands. "We've wasted enough time with your investigation and interrogation. I've got photographers here who are getting paid by the hour. We need to take some promotional shots and get back to the city if we hope to salvage the day's schedule."

I chuckle. "Don't let me keep you. We can talk more later. You're welcome, by the way, for cleaning up the mess with the bears so you can go out there."

That earns me a look.

Dionysus and Calum chuckle.

When the room clears out, Jonah looks at them and shrugs. "What's so funny?"

"It's a running joke that Fi can't work with strong women without claws coming out."

I hold up my hands. "Don't even think about putting that on

me. She has hated me since I introduced myself. I did nothing to provoke it and have been nothing but a ray of sunshine."

Calum and Dionysus bust up laughing. Jonah wisely doesn't weigh in.

Sloan returns before their laughter dies down. He holds the door open for Manx, and Bruin ghosts through and takes form in the welcome center. "I'm feckin' starvin'."

I rub the emptiness in my belly. "I know, right? It's amazing how much of an appetite you can work up wrestling bears."

Sloan snorts. "And to think ye say things like that as if it's simply a fact of life."

"Well, it's a fact of *our* life, at least."

"Aye, yer not wrong."

Bruin grunts. "Is there any chance we could eat while we're waitin' on them to finish their photo shoot?"

Dionysus nods. "Ask and ye shall receive, my friend. What are you in the mood for?"

I grin at Jonah and fill him in. "Dionysus loves putting together massive buffets whenever there's a family gathering. Tell him what your favorite foods are and voila, we'll be eating them."

He shakes his head. "Having a god as a friend is amazing."

"It absolutely is." I wink at Dionysus and point at the open area on the floor. "I think if we had a round table here, we could all sit together."

The table appears the moment I've voiced my thought. "To eat, I'd like lasagna and garlic bread with cheese, please and thank you."

"Wings and Guinness," Calum adds.

Sloan nods. "I'm good with those."

"Can you make meatball subs?" Jonah asks.

Dionysus laughs and waves the question away. "Spicy or savory?"

"Spicy."

"Done." He turns to look at Bruin. "And you, Bear? Since you're the man of the hour, what would you like?"

"Smoked salmon and a trough of whiskey."

"That's the spirit." Dionysus points at the table, and it's now filled with all our choices.

My stomach lets out a long growl of approval, and we get up, grab our chairs, and head over to our feast.

When our plates are empty and our bellies are full, I sit back in my chair and study my bear. He emptied the massive pan of whiskey Dionysus manifested for him in record time. "Tell us about the bad blood between you and Coyote, buddy. What's that about?"

"Coyote and I have a colorful and volatile past. Needless to say, there was a female involved."

Calum shakes his head. "Women. It's best to stay away from them at all costs."

Jonah chuckles.

I give them both the finger.

"Then, when you see him after all these centuries, he's torturing your cousins. Rude."

Bruin grunts. "He always was a petty dick."

Calum relays that to Jonah so he can keep up with the conversation.

"Well, at least that explains his interest in me and how we formed our bond," I say.

Bruin stiffens and turns his head as if it's on a pike. "What do ye mean, Red? What did he say?"

I think back to grasp his exact words. "He asked me, how did you capture the affections of one such as he?"

"What was your response? Think carefully. This is important."

I think hard but come up empty. "I never answered him. I was taken aback by the question. Then the forest broke out in chaos, and he charged me."

"Why, Bear?" Tension laces Sloan's voice. "What's got ye so worried?"

Bruin flops back on his haunches and lifts his snout into the air. "As I said, there's bad blood and a female between us. If Coyote figures out Fi and I are bonded or that I love her as much as I do, he'll target her to make me pay."

"I take it you won out with the female," I say.

"Yeah, he did," Dionysus says. "Bruin's a stud."

I laugh. "I'm well aware of his track record."

Bruin lifts his snout and chuckles. "I got the girl, aye, and fer a time I thought that was a win. In the end, she had her own path to take, and we parted."

"Who was this worthy woman who had two mythical beings fighting over her?" I ask.

Bruin casts me a glance and chuckles. "Really? That's what ye got out of that? I tell ye that my mythical nemesis might target ye and come after ye and yer mind gets stuck on who my old girlfriend was?"

Calum chuckles. "Is anyone here surprised?"

By the looks on their faces, that's a no all around.

Whatevs. "Is it wrong that I'm interested in the life and love of my beloved animal companion?"

Sloan chuckles. "Only if ye insist on callin' him that."

I grin at my hubby. From the beginning, when I annoyed him more often than not, he took great offense to me considering Bruin my druid animal companion. Apparently, it still irks him. "He is both my companion and an animal. Thus..."

He chuckles. "Aye, by the rules of a Socratic debate, ye might win, but that doesn't make it so."

Dionysus waves and points outside at the Escalades and the governor returning. "What do we do about them and the fact that it's Coyote meddling in the governor's campaign? We can't kill him, and it'll be tough to convince him to fuck off."

Calum brushes off Dionysus's ranger hat and hands it back. "If Coyote is as much of a pain in the ass as you and Bruin say he is, then I'd bet we're just getting started. We better let Garnet know this is going to take a while."

Bruin grunts again. "Now that he realizes I'm here in Texas and has taken an interest in Fi, I'd wager his game just leveled up."

I fight back the urge to groan. "Oh, goody."

The next stop of the day goes off without any drama, and after the amount of food we ate for lunch, I'm glad. Just because you can, doesn't mean you should. I'll have to do some major training hours to work that off.

Knox joins us when we arrive at the San Antonio Museum of Art and resumes his place as leader of the Hulk squad without missing a beat.

That's a good thing.

I've had my world rocked by empowered incidents enough to know how disruptive they can be to your sense of self. It's nice that he could grab the reins so quickly and pull things back together.

Sloan, Calum, and I work the background at the museum. They won't allow Manx inside, so Dionysus and Jonah stay with him on the bus.

Nothing happens, so we consider it a success.

Governor Boseman walks through the museum with a group of local students who won art prizes. This visit is another photo op, capturing him and the kids as he admires the exhibit of their work.

The nice thing is I think he genuinely enjoys spending time looking at their creations.

When that's over, he says goodbye to the kids and we're off to a women's shelter.

According to the woman at the podium, Governor Boseman is the first politician to listen to their needs and to ensure the shelter's women have what they need physically, legally, emotionally, and spiritually.

By the time we get back to the hotel to change for the evening event, I'm starting to like this guy.

"Fiona." The governor is standing in the hotel's lobby when he waves me over. "I realize Maggie cut off our conversation earlier to salvage the schedule. There's more I'd like to know about what happened today. Can I ask your group to join me in my suite for an update before we get ready for tonight?"

"Of course, sir. If possible, can we have Maggie, Knox, Jonah, and whoever else heads up responsibilities on the campaign trail join us?"

"Do you have new information that affects them?"

"Yes and no. Moreso, I'd like to have a brainstorming discussion now that we know who's against us."

Boseman nods. "Give me ten minutes to change and make the arrangements with the others."

The Ambassador Suite at the Menger Hotel is elegant and damn impressive. The door to the governor's bedroom is closed, so I don't get to peek into that, but the living area with the couches and antique sconces and the table by the window are all very impressive.

When we arrive, Knox raps his knuckles on the closed door to the bedroom, and the governor comes out to join us.

His outfit catches me off-guard. He's wearing nice-fitting

black jeans and a plaid shirt and looks every bit the part of a cowboy.

"Why are you looking at me like that?" he asks.

I blink and wave in front of my face. Heat warms my cheeks, and I know there's no hiding my embarrassment. "Sorry. I've only seen you in governor mode, and the country boy in jeans threw me for a minute. Ignore me. S'all good."

He chuckles. "Well, I'll take that as a compliment. For the sake of your curiosity, I was born and raised on a horse ranch outside of Giddings. I'm more than the governor, Fi. I'm a Texas cowboy through and through."

I run a hand over my cheek, not knowing what to say about that.

After a moment, Sloan chuckles. "It's a rare occasion when my wife is at a loss fer words, sir. So, perhaps I'll start us off."

Yeah, that's good, hotness.

The governor raises a finger to stop the conversation. "When we're out in the world, I'll accept sir, but behind closed doors, please call me Tucker."

"Aye, all right. Is yer assistant Ms. Fuentes joinin' us, Tucker?"

"Yes, she'll be here momentarily. She needed to confirm the details for tonight's appearance at Cowboys." He takes in our group and gestures at the couches. "Please, sit. Can I get anyone a drink? Fi, what's your poison?"

"I'm a whiskey girl if you've got it."

"I'm sure that's not a problem. What about the rest of you?"

"Same," Calum answers.

"Aye, that'll do," Sloan agrees.

"There's no wrong answer as long as it's quality," Dionysus adds.

Boseman nods. "Agreed. Whiskey all around then. Knox, do you mind playing the part of our bartender?"

"Not at all." The big guy moves across the room to the wooden stand-up bar, flips tumblers, and opens a bottle.

The governor is sitting in a club chair to my right. "If you're comfortable with it, I'd like to invite my bear companion to join us. He's the one who has dealt with Coyote before, and I think it would be beneficial for him to be part of the conversation."

Tucker grins. "By all means. I think I was in shock at the welcome center. I'd very much like to meet your companion."

Thankfully, the suite is large enough for Bruin to sit comfortably in the seating area without rearranging the furniture. When I invite him to join us, he stirs inside me a moment before he takes form at my side.

The governor studies him, absorbing the size and awesomeness of my boy, then leans closer. "You're a majestic beast, sir."

I like this guy.

I chuckle. *Me too.*

Knox comes over with a tray in his hand, and seven tumblers with two-finger pours.

True to his word, the whiskey is of good quality and slides down my throat with a warm, smooth burn. With a drink in hand, I relax deeper into my seat on the couch and get this meeting started. "So, there's good and bad in the fact that Coyote is our trickster."

"All right. How so?"

"For one, we can't kill him, we can't really hurt him, and there's probably very little we can do to keep him away."

Boseman frowns. "I hope that's your bad news."

"It is. The good news is he's fickle and likely acting out because of something specific that was said or done. If we can figure out what set him off and address it, he'll likely lose interest and flit off to screw with someone else."

"From your lips to God's ears," Boseman says.

"Right. Another thing that might work in your favor is that Coyote hates Bruin and now, after four centuries of them avoiding one another, the universe saw fit to have the two of them collide."

His gaze narrows on me as he sips from his glass. "How does that work in our favor?"

I shake my head. "No. Not our favor. It works in *your* favor. Bruin believes their animosity is strong enough to pull his focus from his petty hexes to come after us."

Tucker sits forward in his seat and rests his elbows on his knees. "How is that any better? That means you've inherited our problem."

"True, but it's better for you, and that's why we're here. We've had more than our share of angry gods come after us. We're prepared for things like that. You're not. If Coyote's focus shifts to us, we're pretty sure you and your campaign tour will be left alone."

"Why has he targeted us in the first place?"

"I think it's my fault." Maggie's voice pulls our attention to where she's standing inside the entrance. "I think all of this is my fault."

CHAPTER THIRTEEN

In all the time we've seen the governor's assistant, Maggie Fuentes has been put together and professional. Da used to tell me there were two types of people. There are hammers, and there are nails. Over the past two days, Maggie has only ever been a hammer.

Not so now.

Her eyes are red-rimmed, and she looks like she's about to fall apart. "I'm sorry, Tuck. I think all of this is my fault."

Boseman sets his drink on the coffee table and rushes over to greet her. He wraps his arm around her back and brings her to sit in his chair. Kneeling next to her, he rests a hand and squeezes her arm. "What are you going on about, Mags?"

She meets our curious looks, and more tears fall. Dionysus is quick to produce a box of tissues and hand them over.

"Good Lord, this is humiliating," she says in a rush of exhaled breath.

"What's humiliating, Mags? Just tell me what happened, and we'll work it out."

She meets his gaze and draws a deep breath. "I think Coyote might have possessed Chance while we were dating."

"What? Why would you think that?"

"Who's Chance?" Knox asks.

Governor Boseman waits for her to answer, but when she doesn't, he answers for her. "He was a rodeo cowboy Maggie was dating the last couple of months."

"Why do you think Coyote was involved?" I ask.

Maggie looks at me, and all the anger she's been piercing me with is gone. "Chance was a wild fling—totally not my type. He was spontaneous and passionate, and for a few weeks I was lost in everything he represented."

"And then?"

"Then I needed to get my head back into the reality of my life. I had planning to do, and Tucker's tour took priority, so I ended it."

"Ye chose Governor Boseman's campaign and yer job over him," Sloan says.

"That's right."

"How did that go over?" I ask.

"Not well. At first, he played it off like I was giving him a challenge and teasing. When he realized I was serious, he was furious—indignant, really. He told me I should reconsider because people like me are lucky to spend time with him. He said I was choosing the career of an ordinary man over time with a god."

"That selfish asshole always did think too much of himself," Bruin rumbles.

"I thought he was being arrogant and self-important. I never imagined he could be a literal god." She clasps the governor's hand. "I'm so sorry this is blowing back onto you."

The two share a private look, and my affection for Tucker grows even more. No part of him holds her responsible for this.

Nor should he.

"So, he told you he was a god and that you should be honored to have him. Is that the only reason you think this ex-lover of yours was Coyote?" I ask.

She shakes her head. "I ran into Chance while making the arrangements at Cowboys last week. I went over to speak to him, and he looked at me like he'd never seen me. I thought he was being hurtful, but now I think he honestly didn't remember me."

"Oh, Mags, I'm so sorry." The governor pats her hand and signals Knox to go to the bar. "None of this is your fault. From what we've learned, this Coyote fellow is a real horse's ass. There was no way for you to know."

"That's why the bears," Sloan interjects.

I sit back to read his expression. "What's the why about the bears?"

"This afternoon we were wonderin' why he'd affect the bears and cause trouble when it wasn't a public appearance and wouldn't embarrass or reflect poorly on the governor. It's because his objective never was to target the governor. He simply wanted to disrupt Maggie's finely laid plans."

"And possessing the bears almost canceled the photo opportunity and ruined her plans for the promotional materials."

"It could be worse," Tucker points out. "He could've been violent or jealous of your commitment to me. Instead, his pride is stung and he's lashing out like a child."

Maggie wipes her face and accepts the splash of liquid courage Knox brings her. "So, what do we do now?"

"That's easy." I grin. "The next chance we get, you need to grovel and tell Coyote you were a fool."

"What? Why?" Tucker asks.

"Because if his ego is as big as Maggie and Bruin say it is, he'll feel vindicated that he's taught her a lesson. He'll never take her back, but it'll make him feel good to know he's leaving her heartbroken."

"Do you really think that will work?" Maggie asks.

I check with Dionysus and Bruin. "What do you boys think? You're gods. Is my logic sound?"

Dionysus nods. "I think it's the best plan we've got. Yeah, Coyote is so full of himself, it might work."

With the whisper of a plan forming, we adjourn the meeting in Tucker's suite and get ready to go back out. "Man, this political campaigning is exhausting," Calum grouses. "I'd be happy to stay home, have a bath, and put my feet up."

I snort. "Marriage has made you into an old woman."

"No, it hasn't. That's rude and sexist."

"And true. Let me know when you start picking out knitting patterns."

He gives me the finger, and I bust up laughing.

The knock on our door brings Jonah into the mix. "Ride 'em, cowboy. That's a hot look for you, my man."

Jonah blushes and looks from me to Sloan.

"Och, don't give it a second thought. Fi calls it as she sees it. She's not wrong. Ye look good."

When his blush burns brighter, I laugh and knock on the bathroom door. "Tarzan, let's roll. Jonah's here, and we want to get there before the governor to get the lay of the land."

"Coming, coming." Dionysus comes out of the washroom dressed like a cowboy from the pointed tips of his boots to the crease in his hat.

I give him a thumbs-up and step closer to brush my hand over his thigh. "I love the suede chaps. Thank you for wearing jeans underneath."

He shrugs. "I looked even better without the jeans but opted to be professional while we represent the governor and his interests."

"I appreciate that."

He sees Jonah and waggles his brows. "I'm saving the ass

chaps look for later behind closed doors. Have you ever played dude ranch? It's a good time, I promise."

Jonah's cheeks couldn't get any redder. "I appreciate your fine taste in Western wear."

"Or Western not-wear," I add.

Dionysus waggles his brows. "I love that you get me, Jane."

"I do."

Dionysus looks from me to Sloan to Calum and frowns. "This won't do. You don't look country enough. Here, I'll help you."

A rush of Dionysus' power tingles over me, and I glance down at the pink plaid shirt and low-rise jeans I'm now wearing. "Do you think the rhinestone belt buckle is a bit dazzling?"

He shrugs unrepentant. "You can't go to a place called Cowboys wearing battle fatigues and Under Armour."

"When in Texas, I guess."

"Says the girl *not* wearing chaps and spurs." Calum grunts.

I glance down at my brother's heels and chuckle. "Well, thankfully, we're going to a dance hall. You shouldn't need to put those bad boys to use."

Calum rolls his eyes. "Why do I get the feeling you jinxed me?"

Waving that away, I call up the map and show Dionysus where we need to go. We're standing outside a hugely impressive country dance hall a moment later.

Jonah takes the lead and talks to the bouncer for a second. He shows him his Governor Boseman staff credentials and explains that we're the advance team here to ensure everything is going according to Maggie's arrangements.

He sends us inside, and it takes a moment for my eyes to adjust. The ticket area is dark and winds back and forth with chrome rails to keep the packed crowd of customers single file.

We push ahead of the line to talk to the guy working the ticket booth. Jonah does his thing with his pass again, but the guy insists we still need to buy tickets.

"That's fair." Sloan pulls out his wallet.

The people behind us aren't impressed, but hey, if we save their asses from a trickster god, I bet they'll change their tune.

"You look familiar." The ticket guy points at me as he holds the terminal up for Sloan to tap. "Have you been here before?"

I shake my head. "Nope. I'm a first-timer."

Sloan chuckles. "Do ye maybe know of the redhead lass from the Great White North? Fiona Cumhaill, the Fae Liaison of Toronto?"

That sparks a smile, and he leans forward to look closer. "You're the one who put San Francisco back in place, aren't you?"

"That was a group effort, not only me. We do things in teams."

"My sister lives in the Bay Area. That whole disappearing city thing scared the dickens out of our mama."

"I'm glad you have her back."

"Yeah, me too. Dang, now I wish I hadn't charged you to get in."

I wave that away. "Not a problem. We need to get inside and check things out before Governor Boseman gets here."

He looks over our group. "Yeah, of course. Good luck. Nice to meet you."

We take our tickets and work toward the black double doors. They open often enough for us to see the other side. It's too congested to get through in a hurry so I point at the doors and squeeze Sloan's hand. "Can you speed this up and get us in?"

The tingle of Sloan's signature washes over my skin and we're standing in a wide-open area with hundreds of patrons.

The sudden bombardment of stimuli is jarring. We went from the dark ticket area to the light show spilling out onto a massive dance floor to our left and the live band on the raised stage. A bunch of shops line the front wall, people surround the bars, and large wooden barrels have been cut to make beer stations. And...

"This place is amazeballs!" Dionysus shouts above the music. "I love it here!"

"Yeah, it's cool, Tarzan, but let's get our bearings and see what's going on."

"Ooo, a gift shop." Dionysus' eyes widen as he peels off and is gone.

"Squirrel!" Calum laughs.

I lean closer to Jonah so he can hear me. "What is the governor doing here tonight?"

"He's making a public appearance. He's going to spin around the dance floor a couple of times and wave to the crowd on the other side of the building when the rodeo event starts."

Rodeo event?

I am officially intrigued.

Jonah pulls his phone out and tilts his head toward the main bar. "They're pulling up now. I'm supposed to get the bar manager to open the side door for them."

"Sounds good. We'll follow you."

Jonah leads the way, and I'm happy to say that when Maggie's not around and he gets a chance to shine, he's good at what he does. According to him, he handles all the social media and email questions, and is Maggie's backup when needed.

"Over here," the guy says. He escorts us across the massive building to a door by the dance floor. He presses a security pass against the screen, and the alarm turns off long enough to allow Maggie, Tucker, Knox, and two other members of the Hulk squad entry.

Once everyone is in, he steps to the side to talk to Maggie.

"Busy night," Tucker says, smiling at the dance floor. "What do you say, Fi? Do you want to take a twirl across the hardwood with me?"

I snort. "I'm trying to minimize your embarrassment on this tour. Taking me out there would be counterproductive."

Sloan rolls his eyes. "Don't listen to her. She's a wonderful dancer. She just needs a strong lead."

"Well, I can do that." He holds his hand up and bows. "Shall we?"

This is out of my comfort zone on all levels. "Sloan says I can dance, but that's only because I melt into him, and he moves me through the space."

Tucker grins. "Well, we could take that approach, but we'll be headlining in the San Antonio Express by morning if we do. How about you trust me, and we have some fun?"

This is going to be bad.

Feline Finesse.

With my spell awakening in my cells, I at least eliminate the probability of falling on my face.

At the edge of the dance floor, he faces me, places one hand on my back, and clasps my hand with the other. "Now, we're going to do a standard social two-step. It's not as difficult as it looks and for a girl who isn't afraid to take on gods and wrestle possessed bears, it's nothing."

"I'd rather wrestle a bear."

He laughs. "I'm sure that's true. Stand straight. You're going backward, I'm going forward, and we're simply going to walk in a quick, quick, slow, slow, rhythm."

"Are you going to twirl me like that?" I point at the couples zipping past us.

He winks at me. "I just might."

Oh, hell.

The band is playing, and nerves are getting the better of me, but what the hell. The Governor of Texas wants to two-step with me. I'm game.

The song changes, and he steps into the flow of the dancers on the floor. "Remember the rhythm. We're just walking. And go."

At first, I'm concentrating so hard on keeping the rhythm of my walking consistent that I forget to have fun. After a minute or two, I get the hang of it, and we really start doing it.

Tucker twirls me into his arms and back out again, and I realize he was right. As long as I keep my feet walking in that same rhythm, we can get away with all kinds of spins.

"You're a natural, Fi."

I laugh. "Hardly, but it is fun."

The guy of the couple beside us bends, grabs his partner around the hips, and flips her over his shoulder.

I peg the governor with a stern look. "We're not doing that."

Tucker laughs. "I'm flattered you think I've still got that move in me. No. We're not doing that."

CHAPTER FOURTEEN

After me, Tucker takes a few other ladies out onto the dance floor, and Sloan and I give it a try. He, of course, is suave and sure-footed from the moment we step onto the hardwood, and I wonder if there's anything he totally sucks at.

Maybe I've still got blinders on from young love, but I honestly doubt there's a thing he couldn't do if he put his mind to it.

When the music changes from two-step to line dancing, we make our way to the high-top table Jonah and Calum grabbed against the dance floor.

Tucker calls it quits as well. "That was fun." He accepts the beer Jonah has ready for him and wipes his wrist across his damp brow.

"I agree. It definitely was."

Maggie moves into our line of sight and touches her watch. Tucker takes another quick sip before abandoning his beer. "Looks like I'm needed. Excuse me."

I take a long drink from Calum's beer and point at the entrance. "I'm going to run to the ladies' room and see if I can find Dionysus."

"I'll walk with ye, luv."

The two of us pass the shops, and I see our missing demi-god trying on large-rimmed sunglasses with turquoise gemstones.

He sees me watching him and points at the glasses.

I shake my head. No way.

He puts them back and turns the rack to continue the search.

"Who knew a god of the Greek Pantheon would be such a shopping whore?"

Sloan laughs and stops outside the ladies' room.

The line is long and it takes ages before I make my way back out. Calum and Sloan are talking about something and by the looks on their faces, it's not good.

"What is it? What's gone wrong?"

Calum tilts his head back toward the dance floor. "We've got a problem. Maggie needs Tucker to move to the other side of the building for a crowd moment, but he can't stop line dancing."

I blink. "What's that now?"

"Yeah, funny, not funny, I know."

"You're shitting me, right?"

"Nope. It's a boot-scootin' catastrophe and Maggie's back to looking like she's going to cry."

The three of us rush back to the dance floor, but we've lost our spot since we left.

"I can't see anything," Sloan snaps, craning his neck to see what's happening. "There are too many gawkers."

"There, hotness." I point at the mezzanine overlooking the dance floor. "Take us up there, and we'll have a bird's eye view."

Sloan takes my hand, and I grab Calum. The three of us *poof* up to the railing overlooking the dance floor. "How long have they been stuck?"

Calum checks his watch. "Jonah and I didn't realize the problem at first. We weren't paying attention. Maybe fifteen or twenty minutes?"

That could explain why they don't look like they're having fun. Line dancing is tiring.

"Is the hex on the dancers or the floor?" I ask.

The song changes and Luke Bryan's *Country Girl* comes on next. No one moves on or off the dance floor except for the few brave souls delivering beer and water to those stuck in the hex.

Sloan's got his hands out and is testing the atmosphere. Calum's searching the rafters overhead, looking for hex bags or anything out of the ordinary that could be compelling these people to shuffle their feet raw.

"Shit. What's he doing?" Calum points down at Dionysus going out onto the floor.

"Is he looking for us?" I wave my arms, but nope, he's not looking for us as much as taking it all in. When he sees the governor, he joins him. Smiling at a group of girls, he claps and shuffles along to the music.

Calum shrugs, laughing. "Maybe he's taking one for the team. Now we can ask him if he's dancing because he stepped onto that floor and now he can't stop himself or because he's Dionysus."

"It's hard to tell."

"Because he's Dionysus," Sloan states.

We watch for a few more minutes and Calum points. "The ones with the water bottles aren't getting drawn in. My guess is he saw the governor and wanted to dance with pretty girls."

"It has been a long day for him to be focused and serious," I agree.

Sloan nods. "That's true. Ye can't fault a monkey fer swingin' on branches and actin' the fool."

"Are you saying Dionysus is a fool or a monkey?"

"Neither. I'm sayin' ye can't fault someone fer bein' true to their nature. We all know who Dionysus is and we accept him despite it."

I shake my head. "No. We love him *because* of it."

"Aye, sure, that's what I meant."

I'm still chuckling about that when my back grows hot and the stakes are raised. "Crappers. My shield is weighing in, folks. Keep your eyes wide. Something is about to happen."

The next song comes on, and the tempo speeds up.

The dancers below—including Dionysus and the governor—are stepping, kicking, twirling, and clapping wilder than ever. I'm bombarded with flashbacks from *Superstar* and Mary Katherine Gallagher's parents being stomped to death in a terrible line-dancing accident.

Funny but *so* not funny right now.

The only one who still looks like they're having fun is Dionysus.

Sloan and Calum snap to full seriousness and the three of us knuckle down.

"Do either of you see anything here that explains the compulsion to line dance?" I ask.

They don't. Neither do I.

"Then Coyote is here somewhere. Let's get into that crowd and find the fucker."

Sloan takes our hands and *poofs* us down to the dance floor to walk around the edge of the action. "To control this many people at once, he'll have serious eye contact and focus."

The three of us fan out to survey the crowd. Most people are watching, drinking, and chatting with their neighbors about what's happening.

Plenty of people are focusing but not necessarily zoned in with a purpose.

I go over to reassure the governor. "We're on this, sir. There's a hot bath and a soft bed in your future."

He doesn't answer. He's too busy shaking his tail feathers.

"Jane! Look, I'm a cowboy."

I follow the ecstatic whoop and give Dionysus a thumbs-up. "You're rocking it, Tarzan."

"Yeah, I am."

To test a theory, I step closer to my dancing demi-god. "Hey, Greek. I know you're having fun, but everyone else is hexed right now and can't stop dancing. Try to stop and see what happens."

All the glee he'd been gushing a moment before is lost, and he frowns. "Well, that's not good. I'm hooked. The bastard got me."

As upset turns to panic and fury, I hold up my hand. "It's fine, sweetie. We're going to figure this out and get everyone stopped."

"Jane, I don't like this. Dionysus is no one's marionette. I honestly didn't think I'd be sucked in."

I'm still trying to find someone in the crowd, but there are too many people with eyes on us.

Bruin, I need you to burst from me and cause a bit of a stir. I'm thinking the humans in the crowd will be distracted or step back, but if Coyote is here and casting the hex, he'll either abandon the dancers to come for you or he'll be the one still focused when everyone else reacts around him.

Aye, that's a sound plan, Red. Tell me when yer ready and it's a go.

I speak to Dionysus mind-to-mind and relay my plan. *Tell Sloan and Calum. They need to be ready to watch closely for the reactions. Oh, and tell the governor too. I don't want him having a heart attack on the dance floor.*

After a moment, Dionysus nods. *Okay, Jane. They're ready. Good luck.*

I wink at him. *I don't need luck, silly man. I'm Fiona-freakin'-Cumhaill.*

He laughs, and I'm glad I could snap him out of his momentary panic. *Okay, watch the crowd, Tarzan. We're doing this.*

I press my fingers together and push them under my tongue. When I let out a shrill whistle, I release Bruin and give him the go-ahead.

Bruin bursts out of me, materializing on an open section of the dance floor. Standing on his back legs, he waves his head with a ferocious roar. He's convincing and terrifying, and my plan works perfectly…

Maybe a little too perfectly.

Dancers pee their pants.

Onlookers scream and faint.

Not only does Bruin's presence get everyone's attention and make them fall back, it also creates a rioting stampede.

Oops.

The good news is that the crowd is thinning fast, and we've got a real shot at finding this dickwad.

"Hey, you!" I follow Calum's cop voice and see the guy he's pointing at. The moment we've got him in our sights, the four of us move in hard and fast.

The look on his face says we've got the right man. The moment he turns and runs, the dancers fall to the wooden floor sobbing.

"Hex is broken." Dionysus races to catch up with me. "It might have been one of those broken egg scenarios, though."

I push against the mass of bodies rushing for the door, but I'm getting nowhere fast. Bruin *whooshes* past me, blowing over the heads of the people between him and our target.

"What do you mean a broken egg scenario, Tarzan?"

"You know the one. To make a quiche you have to break eggs."

"Right. I suppose that's true, although I think it's making an omelet, not a quiche."

"I like quiche better."

"Then quiche it is." I'm only half paying attention. Then I realize how dumb I'm being. "Tarzan, portal us over there."

In a blink, we're on the opposite side of the mass exodus and are racing to the other end of the building.

"What the what?" Dionysus squeals. "You've got to be kidding me. This place gets more awesome by the minute! Bull riding!"

Yep. On the end of the building opposite the dancehall is a full indoor rodeo area with bull riding, stands, and a live event in progress.

I might never get Dionysus out of here.

"Focus, Tarzan. First, we catch Coyote. Then we can watch the bull riding."

"Who wants to watch? I want to ride a bull."

Right. What was I thinking?

I scan the stands, the walkways, and the beer stations, searching for Sloan and Calum. "Where are they?"

"There." Dionysus points at a spot in front of the stands, and I groan. Calum has the collapsed cowboy Coyote possessed by his arms and is dragging him to safety. Bruin and Sloan are in the event ring facing off with a bull. If I'm not mistaken, it's likely Coyote possessing a beast big and mean enough that he thinks he can take Bruin down.

Like hell.

Racing forward, I call my armor and flex my palm. Birga responds immediately and I'm running full-bore at the safety rails. *"Feline Finesse. Bestial Strength."*

Up and over I sail, arching in the air to land on the sandy floor.

"Ooooweee, did all y'all see that? Looks like we got ourselves a firecracker joining the fun. Will the little lady be able to tame ole Whiskey Run or will fifteen hundred pounds of bucking bull be more than she can handle?"

I blink at the screaming crowd. *Seriously?*

Calum chuckles, jogging back from dropping off his downed cowboy. "Looks like you're part of the show, baby girl."

I don't have time to worry about that.

"Look at that red hair waving, folks. She might as well be wavin' a red flag in front of old Whiskey Run's nose."

Yeah, well, there's not much I can do about that.

Digging into the dirt, I cut the distance between myself and my guys. "Hey, sorry I'm late."

Makin' a grand entrance, Bruin says, grunting as the bull charges at us.

"Savin' the best 'til last." Sloan grabs my wrist and *poofs* us out of the raging bull's path.

The crowd goes wild.

The fanfare is new and odd, but I don't hate it.

"Where's Maggie? Did she already plead her case?"

"Haven't seen her," Sloan says.

I glance around looking for the woman who sparked this whole shit show. "Did she forget what we discussed? What happened to her falling on her sword to save the day?"

"I can't say, luv. Either she changed her mind, or she's occupied with something pressing."

I snort. "More pressing than the Clutterbuck of our current situation."

He chuckles. "Focus, *a ghra*. We can't injure the bull, but we can't let Coyote go unchecked. It's a bit of a conundrum."

"Is there any way to force Coyote out of the bull?"

Sloan shrugs. "That's more of a Bruin question than a me question. There are a dozen ways beings can possess others, and we don't have time to run them all down with possible shoehorn spells."

"No. We don't. So, what's our play?" Bruin is standing on his back legs, intimidating the beast into staying put.

Right. Staying put gives me an idea.

Since we don't want to harm the bull, I release Birga and call on my powers. "I'll hold him in place. You put him to sleep."

Sloan frowns. "The bull or Coyote?"

"The bull. I'm assuming we don't have the juice to affect Coyote."

"I'm glad ye realize that, luv. Be careful, will ye?"

"Always." With my hands up, I focus all my energy on those

four hooves and cast the same spell on the bull that I used on Jackson while he was dragon-riding. Rooting him in place does a lot to strengthen our position against old Whiskey Run.

"Calum, you and Sloan are casting sleep spells on the bull. My guess is Coyote will abandon the beast before he allows his vessel to take him down for a nap."

"Good thinkin', Red." Bruin drops onto all fours as our efforts take hold.

Once we have our objective locked in, putting Whiskey Run to sleep and forcing Coyote to vacate his vessel takes only minutes.

I feel it the moment he ghosts out and zooms past me. Bruin growls and is gone in the same second.

Calum and Sloan drop their hands, and I release my hold on the bull's feet. Then I glance over my shoulder at the rodeo hands standing on the fence rails watching.

I wave them in. "S'all good, boys. You can wake him up again, and he'll be fine. The asshole that possessed him has left the building."

"Ladies and gentlemen, let's welcome the Fae Liaison of Toronto, Fiona Cumhaill, and Team Trouble."

I glance at the announcer's booth wondering how... Oh, the guy from the ticket booth who recognized me is whistling and waving.

I wave at the crowd as we leave the ring and roll my eyes at Sloan and Calum. "Where the hell is Dionysus? He's the only one who gets off on this kind of fanfare, and he's missing it."

"Next up in the ring is a newcomer riding Black Magic. Known as the God of Good Times, the Son of Sparta, give it up for Dionysuuuuus!"

The crowd goes wild, and the three of us spin in time to see the gate open. Dionysus comes flying out, arm in the air, riding a massive black bull.

"There he is." Calum laughs. "Found him."

CHAPTER FIFTEEN

The sun is shining brightly through the crack in the blackout curtains when I open my eyes. Bruin is sleeping on the floor under the window. At some point during the night, he pulled the two curtains open at the split. I blink and look around.

"Good morning, Mrs. Mackenzie."

I smile at Sloan sitting at the little table. He's dressed and ready for his day, sipping coffee and reading something on his phone. I'm not sure if it was the inflated expectations of his parents or his natural drive to be prepared for all situations that made him like this, but I find it admirable.

I could never do it myself, but it's admirable.

Water is running in the bathroom, and the other bed is empty. I stretch and sit up, reluctantly abandoning the comfort of our bed. "Did you bring us more yumminess this morning?"

"What kind of husband would I be if I failed to fulfill yer every want?"

I chuckle and move to the table opposite him. "Well, you wouldn't be you, that's for sure."

I open the spiced tea he brought me and peruse the selection. "You bought extra breakfast empanadas today. Good man."

"I did. They were popular yesterday."

I take a bite of one and moan. "And today too."

Sloan pulls the curtains wide to let in the splendor of the square below, and the two of us chat about nothing in particular. We nibble on pastries and discuss the case, wonder what's happening on the island, and enjoy the calm before the inevitable storm that will be our day.

Calum exits the bathroom wearing cargo pants and toweling off his hair. "Oh, excellent, breakfast."

I give up my chair when he comes over, and we switch spots. "Am I good to take the bathroom?"

"Yeah, just toss my brush onto the bed, and I'm good."

I set my tea on the table and close the tab on the lid. I'm reaching into the closet to grab my outfit for the day when Dionysus opens the door and hobbles inside. He's walking with his feet wide and his gait way off. "Tarzan? What's wrong? Are you all right?"

"No. I'm not. How do I say this delicately..."

"Your balls are swollen?" Calum offers.

Dionysus nods and points at my brother. "What he said. Fun fact, riding a bucking bull for eight seconds in the ring isn't the same as riding a mechanical bull in the tavern."

I try not to laugh but fail miserably. "I'm so sorry, sweetie, but shouldn't your god powers heal what ails you?"

He limps up to the table and eyes the offerings of the morning. "You'd think so, but the Fates are still annoyed about me getting them into trouble with their mother. Lachesis sent me a little message that said if I want to play human, I can share your experiences."

"Rude," Calum objects.

"They're annoyed with *you?*" I repeat, my voice cracking.

"Themis was mad at them because they screwed the pooch and you nearly died. How is that your fault in any way?"

"It's not," Sloan says.

"Yeah, that's bullshit, Tarzan."

He waves away our ire. "Needless to say, I'll be sitting out today."

"But will you be sitting?" Calum ripostes.

"I had an idea about that." Dionysus looks at Sloan with a pleading puppy dog stare. "You don't feel like giving me a little touch healing, do you?"

Sloan's eyebrows arch so high it's hilarious. "No offense, Greek, but I'd rather not massage yer balls if I don't have to. How about an anti-inflammatory potion? Can I get away with that?"

"What happened to your Hippocratic Oath?"

Sloan chuckles. "I'm not a doctor, and even if I was, I don't think it applies."

I meet Sloan's gaze, and he stiffens and shakes his head. "No."

I laugh. "What?"

"Ye've got a soft spot a mile wide fer him, but he's not dyin', and I'm not fondlin' his nuts—"

I hold up my hands. "I didn't say a thing. I was going to suggest that you could pop home and get a jump on that anti-inflammatory potion. I'll text Nikon and ask him to bring you back."

"Oh, aye. Well, sure, I can do that."

Sloan *poofs* out, and I look at Dionysus and laugh. "And on that note."

Dionysus adjusts his pants and pouts. "I'm not sure whether I'm amused or hurt by how quickly and emphatically Sloan rejected the idea of tending to my needs."

Calum and I both laugh. "Aw, sweetie. You know if it were dire, he'd do anything to ease your suffering."

"This *is* dire." He eases into Sloan's chair, wincing and hissing as he settles. With one hand, he produces an icepack and sets it in his lap. With the other hand, he picks up an empanada and starts soothing himself with baked yummies.

"I'm going to get ready. Calum will take good care of you until Sloan gets back." I kiss his cheek and grab my clothes, heading into the bathroom.

By the time I'm showered, dressed, and go out to check on the boys, Sloan and Nikon are back, and Dionysus is swigging back Sloan's potion. The vial drains of its bright purple contents and Dionysus closes his eyes. "How soon will this work?"

"Ye'll feel better within ten or twenty minutes. Ye'll be back to full steam ahead within the hour."

"You're an angel, Irish. I heart you hard."

Sloan chuckles and squeezes his shoulder. "I appreciate that, Greek. I heart ye right back."

Dionysus grins and smiles at me. "He *does* love me."

Sloan rolls his eyes, and I can't help but bust up. "The important thing is that he's taken care of your bits."

Calum shakes his head. "No, the important thing is that you rocked those eight seconds like a boss."

"Yeah, you did." Nikon watches the video on Calum's phone. The boys replay it a couple of times, grimacing at a few spots where Dionysus got especially thrown around. "Good for you, *adelphos*. Some bucket list moments demand sacrifice."

"Consider my testicles thoroughly sacrificed. Dionysus out." Dionysus stuffs another empanada in his mouth and sighs as he closes his eyes.

Tucker, Knox, Maggie, and Jonah are gathered in the lobby when we get there. I don't see the Escalades or the bus outside the front doors, and it makes me wonder what the plan is for today.

Before we get to that, I gesture at Nikon. "This is Nikon Tsambikos of Rhodes. We've swapped out our ancient Greeks this morning. Nikon, this is Governor Tucker Boseman, Maggie Fuentes, you know Jonah, and this is Knox…I'm sorry, I don't know your last name."

"Jordan," the big guy supplies.

"Knox Jordan," I repeat.

Nikon exchanges a handshake with the men, and when Maggie doesn't offer her hand, he gives her a polite smile. "Nice to meet you all."

"Are you a god too?" Tucker asks him.

"No, sir. Just an immortal."

Knox snorts. "Just."

Nikon shrugs and tilts his head toward us. "My apologies. Once you spend a couple of years around Fiona and her team, you realize that simply being unable to die isn't all that impressive."

I scowl. "That's totally not true. Nikon is magnificent. He's being self-deprecating. He wouldn't be one of my very best friends in this world if he wasn't awesomeness personified."

Tucker chuckles. "Awesomeness personified. I'd say that's high praise from a woman like Fi."

Nikon winks at me. "She's a bit of a softy for misfit toys. But it's nice of her to say."

"As heartwarming as all this is, we're on a schedule here. Plans to keep. Events to attend. Appearances to make." Maggie taps her watch in that angry schoolmarm way.

Here I thought we were past the attitude after yesterday's breakthrough. I guess her being a taskmaster wasn't all about the stress of what was going wrong on the tour.

"Speaking of plans to keep, what happened to you last night at

Cowboys? We had Coyote immobilized, and you were nowhere in sight. I thought we agreed you would play the regretful lover and soothe his wounded pride."

"I thought about it and decided that idea was more about you getting back at me for my lack of enthusiasm for you and less about a viable solution."

Hubba—wha? "No. I don't work like that. Sure, it was my idea, but it was only about taking the thorn out of Coyote's paw so he'd lose interest in your tour."

"We'll have to agree to disagree on that."

"Okay, so what is your plan?"

"I'll confront him and tell him to go to hell."

"No, you can't. That will only incite his anger and ramp up his antics. So far, no one has gotten hurt. Beyond property damage and some scrapes and cuts from public panic, there haven't been any casualties. If you outright provoke him, you're endangering innocents."

She rolls her eyes. "That's very dramatic, but I've dealt with arrogant people all my life, and I've learned a thing or two along the way."

I grip my fingers into fists at my side and fight not to call Birga to my hand. "Megalomaniac gods aren't the same as arrogant humans. Like me or don't like me, I don't give a fuck, but don't discount my knowledge of things you can't possibly understand."

Another eye roll and she turns to the glass turnstile door.

Sloan's hand grips my shoulder, and the soothing warmth of his healing energy washes through me. "Take a breath, luv. She's locked her position in and won't listen. There's no sense causin' a scene."

"She's going to get people killed."

"Aye, I don't disagree with ye, but she doesn't see it. We're here to help, not cause more problems."

I let out a long sigh and shake my hands out. When I meet

Tucker's concerned gaze, he's torn. "I'm not wrong about this. Me wanting her to play nice with Coyote is the right call."

He nods. "I'll talk to her."

When he strides off after Maggie, Knox follows. Two more of his men step out from beside the reception desk and behind the pillar by the window. Two more are outside waiting.

I roll my neck and try to feel relieved as the soft cracks signify things readjusting. Jonah walks out with us and gestures along the sidewalk. We follow his lead and walk behind the others. "No carpooling today?"

"No need. Today we're going to the Alamo."

Oh, wonderful. What could possibly go wrong?

The walk to the Alamo takes only a couple of minutes from the hotel. Even so, I've now got sweat sliding in crevices and under my boobs. "Is the Alamo air-conditioned?" I ask Jonah.

"The church is, but we'll be outside on the grounds."

I fight my urge to stomp and growl and wonder if hot Fi might be as temperamental as hangry Fi.

Standing in front of the iconic limestone façade, I study one of the most important historic sites in Texas. It's famous, I get that, but other than knowing there was a standoff here, I realize I don't know why. "Jonah? May I ask a dumb question?"

"Sure."

"Can you give this Canadian girl the Cliffs Notes version of Alamo history, please?"

Jonah doesn't seem to think it's a dumb question. "Basically, the Alamo is a shrine to Texas freedom. In 1836 during the Texas Revolution, a small force including Davy Crockett and James Bowie hunkered down here. They held the fort for thirteen days before falling to the force of three thousand soldiers of the Mexican army. It was a ninety-minute massacre, but the bravery of the stand rallied Texas, and we eventually won our freedom."

I can totally get behind the bravery it would take to make a stand like that. "This is all that's left?"

"Yeah, the church and the long barrack."

While Maggie gets things set up on the grounds and the governor and his bodyguards get into position, I take a few minutes to absorb the importance of the site.

If I were going to take my stand, knowing I would die against insurmountable odds, where would I be? What would I fight for?

My family...for sure.

My house...not so much.

The island...to keep it from falling into the wrong hands, yes.

"*A ghra?* Is everything all right?"

I nod. "Just thinking. Do you remember when Dionysus and I made you watch the rom-com *Leap Year?*"

"The one where the American girl named her suitcase and fell in love with the Irishman?"

"Yeah. Do you remember the part where, before she picked the Irishman, she went home with her fiancé and pulled the fire alarm?"

"Aye, she was testin' herself about what she'd save if it came down to a choice in an emergency."

"Right. I was thinking about the Alamo and what I would die for."

Nikon brushes a hand down my arm. "The sad truth of that question is you've faced it too often already, Red."

He's not wrong. "The answer is always the same. There's not one thing I would die for. It's always about people. My family. My friends. The innocents on the island. The people we protect."

Sloan offers me a soft smile. "It's one of the things I love about ye. It's also the reason yer family and friends tend to rally and get protective around ye."

"Why is that?"

"Because when push comes to shove, ye'll never put yerself first. If yer out there sacrificin' yerself to protect everyone else, someone must be at yer side to safeguard yer well-being."

"Well said, Irish," Nikon praises.

"That pretty much sums it up," Calum agrees.

I press my hand against my chest. "Can a heart burst from being too full of love?"

Sloan shakes his head. "No, it can't. Otherwise, I'd have been dead and gone a thousand times over the past two years."

"Same," Calum says.

"Same," Nikon says.

I take a moment to truly appreciate the love and devotion the guys in my life have for not only me but each other as well.

We are truly blessed.

Jonah is taking all this in, and I laugh. "Sorry. We're not always this sappy, I promise."

He shrugs. "No. Don't apologize. It's amazing. I wish I had this kind of a relationship with anyone in my life."

"Well, you do." I slide an arm around his back to side hug him. "You're our friend now, Jonah. Just because we live in another country doesn't mean we can't stay close. Hell, if you ever get tired of living in Texas, come to Toronto. We've got social media and email to organize and events to attend."

Jonah arches a brow. "Don't say that if all y'all don't want me to end up on the doorstep."

I laugh. "One thing you'll learn about me soon enough. I say what's on my mind and don't make empty promises. I'm serious."

"I'll give it some serious thought. Until then, I better focus on the job I have now."

A loud *crack* rends the air, and we all turn toward where Tucker is addressing a couple of hundred people seated under the shade of some massive old oak trees.

"What was that?" I ask.

"It sounded like musket fire." Nikon looks baffled. "Or I could be crazy because it's been over a century since I heard it."

Another *crack* brings us to full alert, and we jog toward the podium. "Jonah, was there supposed to be a reenactment of any kind?"

"No. Not that I'm aware of."

I search for Maggie. She'll know if the Alamo people had something creative planned. I find her pacing behind one of the trees and I jog over.

The minute I get close enough to read her expression, my insides tighten. "What happened?"

Another musket *crack* sounds, and the crowd searches for the source.

"Did you approve a reenactment?" I ask.

"What? What are you talking about?"

Like popcorn cooking in the microwave, the solitary pops of musket fire gain momentum and we've got our heads on a swivel.

It hits me then. Her mood. "Coyote approached you, didn't he? Now that we know it's him, he spoke to you."

"That's none of your business."

A woman screams and the crowd launches to their feet. The musket fire picks up, and we see them. An endless army of men firing pistols and peppering the air with gunfire is storming across the grass.

I peg Maggie with a glare. "You did this, didn't you? Instead of listening, you pissed him off." I see the truth in the shadows of her eyes. "Fuckety-fuck."

CHAPTER SIXTEEN

The annoying antics of disgruntled Coyote are over. Whatever Maggie said to set the guy has sent him straight into taking off the violence filters.

Just like I knew it would.

In a mad scramble, people run screaming while others are tackled and grabbed by dirty soldiers in period uniforms. Calum runs out from behind the screen of the trees where we're standing and grabs a young girl who's been separated from her mother.

He scoops her off the grass and runs her over to us. "Maybe the hotel? Can Dionysus watch her while we deal with this?"

"Aye, it's a good thought." Sloan takes the girl and *poofs* out. A moment later he's back. "He's got her."

Good. We need to get more people out of here.

My mind is spinning, but I'm formulating a plan. "Hotness, you and Nikon evacuate whomever you can. Calum and I will figure out what's going on."

Regular gunshots sound and I spot Knox and his men facing off against a horde of soldiers going after him and the governor. "Get Tucker and Jonah back to the hotel. They can coordinate the victims as you bring them. If Dionysus is up to it, give them the girl and get him here."

Sloan takes Jonah's hand and *poofs* out.

Nikon appears behind Knox to grab the governor, and he's gone too.

I look for Maggie. Yes, this is her fault, but she's good at organizing, and I won't leave her here to rot no matter how appealing the idea.

Sloan *poofs* back and rushes to help a couple being dragged into the fort.

Watching the chaos is mind-boggling, but we need to figure out how to end it. "Bruin, Coyote is here somewhere. Try not to terrify the locals, but if you get a chance to take Coyote down, do it."

I release my bear and get right back to Calum. "Is this a hex, a mass haunting, or something else?"

"I don't think it's a haunting." Calum points at a guy in jeans and a San Antonio Spurs shirt lying bloody in the grass. "That looks like real dead, not fake dead."

We race across the lawn to check the downed tourist. Blood darkens his chest and neck, and yep, there are holes where there shouldn't be.

Calum drops to one knee and presses his fingers to his neck. "Yeah, that's real dead."

I groan, staring at the carnage. Grabbing my Team Trouble pendant, I press it. I've never invoked an all-call from across the country before, but if I have anything to say about it, there won't be a reboot of the Alamo.

Calum sees me pressing the pendant. "Will that even work from here?"

"No idea." I call forward my body armor and engage with the resurrected army. Birga is singing in my hand as I spin her in the air.

The sheer number of soldiers is what's truly overwhelming.

Jonah said three thousand soldiers attacked the Alamo two centuries ago. I wouldn't be surprised if there are that many here now.

Sloan, Nikon, and Dionysus are evacuating panicked and injured people as fast as their portaling power can take them.

All I can do is keep fighting, hoping Garnet and the others come. Hope Bruin finds Coyote, and we can stop this. And hope this isn't going to be a case of history repeating itself.

At first glance, I didn't realize the period players weren't in full color like the tourists and home crowd.

They're muted with a weird sepia color.

Like an old-fashioned photograph, they've been plucked out of history for a mulligan.

More importantly, not all of them are the enemy. When Coyote resurrected the soldiers of this battle, he reanimated both sides. While thousands of ancient soldiers are trying to take the fort, a couple of hundred Texan soldiers are dying to defend it.

I've cut my way through half a dozen when the air snaps with a familiar magical signature and Garnet arrives with Diesel, Brody, Dillan, Anyx, and Dan the djinn.

"Thank you, baby Yoda. Okay, boys, here's the sitch. This is the Indigenous god Coyote's reboot of the Alamo. Three thousand soldiers opposing the handful of friendlies and innocent people taking refuge in the church. Bruin's trying to find Coyote, and we're portaling people out as fast as we can. No idea if this is a hex, a spell, a haunting, or what. The only thing we know for sure is that they're causing real bodily damage. Dead is dead for reals."

Garnet lets out a long growl. "Fuck."

"Agreed. Now, we've been drafted as defenders of the Alamo, so let's rewrite history."

Dillan flexes his palms and calls his twin daggers.

Brody is going with his vampire speed and strength over his wolf side.

Dan raises his hands and steps into the fray.

Garnet and Anyx launch into the chaos as lions.

Diesel looks me over, frowning at the blood on me as he checks my status. "Are you whole?"

"Perfectly. Not my blood."

He studies me a moment longer, and with that and a nod, the goliath jumps into the fight.

The odds against us are no less insurmountable after our reinforcements arrive but having them here with us is an emotional boon that gets my blood pumping. The spirit of the soldiers fighting to hold the fort is still alive today.

Then I see him. "Is that Davy Crockett?"

I point at the man with a hawkish slope to his nose and a coonskin cap.

Dillan lifts his boot and kicks his opponent off his blades, and his green eyes light up. "Fuck yeah. Calum! It's Davy Crockett."

Calum's head spins, and the two take off to battle next to their childhood hero. Even as Canadian kids in Toronto, my brothers had fur hats with tails and sang the ballad of Davy Crockett over and over again.

This might not be the real him, but it's the closest they'll ever get.

On yer back, Red. Bruin's warning comes a moment before the warmth of my shield cranks up to a burn.

I spin and raise Birga between my arms and brace for the downward strike of a soldier's rifle. The barrel *cracking* against my staff rattles my bones, but my enchanted spear has much more strength than an 1800s gun.

When it splinters, I use the moment of surprise to get my boot up and kick my attacker back into his compatriots.

Bruin materializes beside me and roars. The ghostly soldiers seem confused but continue to press. Bruin has his battle armor on and is in a mood. He's thrashing through our sepia specters growling the entire time.

"Usually battle slaughter puts you in a better mood, Bear."

He grunts. "I've got good news and bad news."

I cartwheel Birga in my hands and smile at her happy whistle as she cuts through the air. "Awesomesauce. Give me the good news first."

"I found Coyote on the rooftop pulling the strings behind this fiasco. When I confronted him, we had it out, and he's no longer going to waste his time on getting back at the governor's assistant."

"Excellent. And the bad news?"

Bruin is only half paying attention as he smacks down conjured soldiers and cuts through the battleground. "I'm pretty sure he's comin' after me instead. The years apart have not warmed him to our past and I'd bet my balls I've given him a new purpose in life."

"How do you think that looks?"

"I don't know, Red. I'm sorry."

Sweat is running down my face and my cracks and crevices front and back. It's damn hot here...and that's before we started to battle.

"Whatever he does, it's not on you, buddy. We can't take on the responsibility for other people's actions."

There's a magical *pop* in the air, and I shake my head as my ears adjust to the new pressure. The sepia crowd dissolves into the ether and leaves us with only the carnage of the modern world.

Sloan *poofs* over to us. "Is it over?"

"Yeah, Bruin got him to stand down."

"Well done, Bear."

Garnet's lion roars, and he flashes back to his tailored suit and tugs on the sleeves of his shirt. "Well done, everyone. Nikon,

Brody, and Sloan, head inside and portal those who need medical assistance to the nearest hospital. The rest of you, clean up this mess."

I glance around at the devastation and sigh. "That might take some doing."

In the end, there are nine fatalities, sixteen people hospitalized, and dozens of people left with cuts and bruises. It's hard to say if that's a win or a loss.

Calum and Dillan are chuffed because to thank us for saving them the gift shop manager gave everyone a souvenir pick of anything we wanted. They chose coonskin hats. Sloan, Bruin, and I did the same.

If Calum and Dillan wear theirs to the island, there's no doubt in my mind that Emmet, Brenny, and possibly Aiden will be wailing for their own.

Since Sloan, Bruin, and I don't care, they can have ours. I'm not a hundred percent sure about Aiden needing one. He might take the mature route and give his to Jackson. Which is also good.

Until then, I'm wearing mine.

Brody, Dan, and Diesel each choose a replica Bowie knife, and Garnet picks an Alamo Christmas ornament for Imari.

Knowing Dionysus will be bummed if all my brothers have a hat and he doesn't, I buy him one too.

Sloan rolls his eyes. "Ye realize he's a god and can magic himself one with a mere thought, right?"

"I know, but he'll like that I thought of him. Besides, he's not used to being in pain and had a rough day. Even though he's at the hotel and missed the cleanup, he was here for part of the battle."

"Aye, yer right about that."

Garnet and Calum finish wrapping things up inside, and

when they come back, our lion leader looks at the tired warriors assembled and nods at Nikon. "Back to the office, if you don't mind."

"You got it, boss man. Home we go."

When the Toronto backup crew goes home, Sloan, Calum, and I walk back to the hotel.

The three of us walk through the lobby of the Menger Hotel, and I don't even recognize the place. It's like in the movies when they commandeer a large public space to use as a disaster triage center.

"Christ, Fi, are you all right?" Tucker rushes over to hug me, and after a quick squeeze, he pulls Sloan in for a back-slap embrace. Calum gets the same treatment. "I don't know where to begin."

I wave that away. "It is what it is. I'm sorry there were so many deaths. That's unacceptable in our book. Those people should never have been lost."

He sobers. "I hear what you're saying, and my heart goes out to the families, but from what I saw, I'm surprised there weren't more losses."

"Still. Every person lost is a sibling, spouse, or parent. Today's events destroyed families."

"I know it won't fix it, but I will personally follow up with and provide aid to all those affected. I swear."

It's bugging the hell out of me that Maggie's hustling around playing the part of the San Antonio angel when a huge part of this fiasco falls at her feet.

There's nothing to be done about that.

If nothing else, Tucker's hands-on response should win him votes in the coming election. The fact that he's also genuine and acting out of concern makes me proud we were able to help him.

"You're a good man, Tucker Boseman."

He nods, and his mouth curls up in a warm smile. "You're a good woman, Fiona Cumhaill."

I'm still heart-heavy and tired, but it's nice of him to say. "I'm glad you're going to take care of things. The good news is we angered Coyote enough that he's no longer interested in stalking Maggie and making her life difficult. As we expected, he's turned his negative energy toward Bruin."

He shakes his head. "I don't consider that an improvement in the situation."

"I know you don't, but we're better prepared to weather the fallout of situations like this. So, in a way, it's a good thing."

He steps back and looks over our group. "What can I do for you? Name it. We owe you so much."

I wave that away. "Be good to the people you serve, and we'll call it even. Good luck. And if you ever need us, call and we'll come."

He hugs me again and smiles. "Be safe, Fi. I don't know how you all do what you do, but I can only hope you'll be safe, so you can keep doing it."

When we get upstairs, Dionysus and Jonah are chatting in the room across the hall. They have the door propped open and come out when we arrive.

Jonah takes a page out of Tucker's book and hugs all three of us. "I'm so flipping impressed by all y'all I can't even tell you. What you did...the way you jumped in to save people against a force like that...it was incredible."

I kiss his cheek and tilt my head toward our room. "I'm going to shower and get this blood washed off before we pack. It was so nice to get to know you, Jonah."

He shakes his head. "Oh, no. All y'all aren't getting away that easy. I'm taking everyone out for Texas barbeque before all y'all leave. My treat."

"You don't have to do that."

"I know I don't have to, but I want to. I'm not letting all y'all leave with the last images of Texas being blood and chaos. We're going to sit, have a fantastic meal, and share a few more laughs before we part ways."

I glance at Sloan and Calum. "Well, I suppose we've gotta eat, right?"

Calum nods. "True story."

Sloan smiles. "All right, we'll go, but there's no way yer payin'. We buy food fer us and Bruin and Manx, so that's too much."

"I don't care."

"I do. I'll get the tab. Ye'll pick the place."

Jonah looks like he wants to argue, but I shake my head. "There's no sense wasting your breath. When he gets like this, it's decided."

"Fine, but I buy the next time."

"If it's a round at the pub, that'll work."

Dionysus grins. "Oh, the tavern! You have to come to the opening of our tavern this weekend. Fi? Can I take Jonah to the island?"

"The island?" Jonah asks.

He presses a finger against his lips. "It's a super secret island for magical refugees. It's like fae WITSEC."

I laugh, and he lifts his finger and points at my head. "Hello? Where's my furry hat?"

I hand him the bag with his hat, and he takes it out and puts it on right away. "Thanks, Jane."

"Anytime, sweetie. Okay, boys, give me fifteen."

I leave them to make the arrangements and get cleaned up. Less than twenty minutes later we're standing outside San Antonio's Smoke Shack.

"TripAdvisor says the best barbecue in San Antonio is Smoke Shack." Calum calls up the restaurant's address and sends it to Nikon in case he wants to join us.

Jonah grins. "Sites like that often miss the true gems the locals know of, but in this case, they're right. All y'all will love this. I'm sure all y'all worked up an appetite."

"We always have an appetite for good food," Dionysus points out.

True story.

Dionysus grins. "Let's get our barbecue on."

While Sloan, Jonah, and Dionysus go inside to order for the group, Calum and I settle at a picnic table under the shade of the trees outside.

Ever since his scuffle with Coyote, Bruin has been foul-tempered and miserable. We decided to eat outside to spare the other patrons and to allow him to dig into a huge helping of brisket and mac and cheese to soothe the beast.

While we wait for them to get back with the food, I check on the worst of Bruin's gashes. Fingering through his blood-matted fur, I'm pleased to see it looks worse than it is. "Your healing is already taking hold, buddy. You should be good as new in another hour."

He grunts at me, and I leave him to his hostilities.

Usually, a brutal fight puts him in more of a chipper mood. Not today. It's obvious his mood is more about the bad blood between him and Coyote than anything that happened today.

Hopefully, a feast to fill his belly will help.

When the boys return, Jonah's carrying two drink trays stacked, Sloan's got large, aluminum catering trays, and Dionysus has one tray and a large brown bag folded on top.

"Wow, that's a lot of food." Nikon snaps in to join us. "What's on the menu?"

Jonah grins. "In the trays we've got brisket, ribs, pulled pork, and mac and cheese. Dionysus has the box of fresh buns, the jalapeño sausages, a tub of coleslaw, and a container of brown beans."

"It certainly smells good." I inhale the savory scent, and my stomach growls in approval.

Sloan is chuckling to himself and smirking as he sets things down.

"Care to share, hotness?"

"When we ordered, they asked if we were havin' a party. Dionysus informed them that every moment with him is a party. Then he clarified by tellin' them that no, there was no party, we are just hungry warriors, a lynx, and a Kodiak battle bear."

I snort. "How did that go over?"

"With a fair bit of wide-eyed skepticism, but I think that's settled now."

I follow his amused gaze across the boulevard to a guy in a white apron and a girl with her camera up taking our picture. They return my wave and go back into the restaurant.

For the next half-hour, we focus our energy on filling our faces. Once we slow down on the food intake, the topic of what to do next circles around.

After unbuttoning my pants, I use the last few bites of my bun to mop up the brisket and sauce on my plate. "We're a long way from home. Even if Coyote's gunning for you, it might take him weeks or months to track you down."

Bruin lifts his saucy maw from one of the aluminum pans we made for him and licks his lips. "We won't have the luxury of time, Red. The guy on the microphone last night introduced ye by name and by yer title as the Fae Liaison of Toronto."

Well, crappers.

"Does he really hate you that much, Bear?" I ask.

"Aye, and then some."

When he doesn't offer any explanation, I leave it alone. If

Bruin wanted to share anything beyond them fighting over a female, he would.

Since he hasn't and he's been gruff and growly since the moment we discovered Coyote was involved, I assume he has stuff to sort out in his mind.

"Well, whenever he comes, we'll be ready."

CHAPTER SEVENTEEN

Our time at the Menger Hotel was lovely, but there's no place like home and no bed like King Henry. When Dionysus portals us into our living room in Toronto, it feels like it's been three weeks away, not three days.

"We did well this week, guys. I'll type up our report tonight and send it to Maxwell. Barring something wildly unexpected, we should be able to sleep late and regroup in the morning."

"Maybe I'll turn off my phone," Calum jokes.

"Maybe we all should," Dionysus agrees.

"Laters, boys."

Dionysus snaps out, and I follow Calum to let him out the front door. When he steps off the porch to jog next door, I lock the deadbolt and sit on the bench to untie my hiking boots.

"Are ye in fer the night then, Red?" Bruin asks.

"That's my plan, buddy. Why? What do you need?"

"Just time to clear my head. If ye don't plan on gettin' yerself kidnapped or attacked anytime soon, I thought I'd stretch my legs fer a few hours in the Don."

The Don Valley River System is a large wild space in the heart of downtown Toronto and can be accessed through the trees at the dead end of our street. Bruin has built himself quite a following of ursine ladies and enjoys his free time away.

I finish with one boot and pull it off before starting on the second. "I never *plan* to get kidnapped, but yeah, enjoy your night. I'm looking forward to a hot bath with aromatherapy, some Internet searching, then to bed."

"Best laid plans." Sloan chuckles and bends to set his boots next to mine on the little rug. "What about you, sham?"

Manx's jaw cracks in a long yawn. "I plan to curl up on my platform and have a cat nap. Then, when I wake, I'll get up and go to bed."

I chuckle. "Sounds restful. Thanks for joining in on this one, buddy. I'm glad you came with us."

Manx yawns wide again and his whiskers quiver in the air beside his furry cheeks. "It was nice to be in the action, but now I need to get my beauty sleep."

When our boys leave, I wrap my hands around the back of Sloan's neck and melt against his chest. "Then there were two."

He slows the world down by pressing a gentle kiss on my lips and breathing in deeply. "How about ye run yer bath while I make us some chamomile tea and grab the laptop? I assume when ye mentioned an Internet search, ye want to know more about Coyote and what we'll face in the next round?"

"Yep. Got it in one, Mackenzie. If he's gunning for Bruin, I want to know what we're up against."

"All right. Up ye go. I'll join ye in a moment."

I grab the suitcase and trudge up the stairs, thinking about how disoriented those people had been at the Alamo. What is Coyote capable of? If he killed people because Maggie gave him the brushoff, what will he do to the guy who won the girl?

I don't like where this is going.

Too many variables. Too many unknowns.

At least with bad guys being driven by greed, revenge, or

power, you can predict their next moves because you can read their intentions.

Tricksters don't work like that.

It's annoying.

Maybe, in this case, Coyote will be a more vengeful god and less trickster asshole. Bruin certainly made it sound like it was serious.

At the top of the stairs, I round the century-old carved newel post and head toward our master suite. When I get to the door to our bedroom, my shield fires to life, and I stop dead in my tracks.

My eyes lock, and the hairs on my body stand on end. "What the fuck are you doing in our bedroom?"

The woman standing at our bedside is holding a family picture from our wedding. She is breathtaking, with a warm East Indian skin tone, long chestnut hair, and stunning turquoise blue eyes that glow like they're backlit.

She's wearing a long-sleeve, ruby cocktail dress that comes up to her neck at the front but plummets and has no back. The hem of the skirt hugs the smooth skin of her upper thighs, and there's no doubt that if she bends more than a few inches, I'll get an intimate knowledge of what kind of underwear she prefers.

Assuming she's wearing any.

"I asked you a question, Kaija. What are you doing here?"

Her eyes light with mirth as a sultry smile spreads across her face. "Och, ye remembered."

It's hard to forget the stunning Bohemian succubus your husband used to sex up during his wild university days. "Yes. I remember. What are you doing here and why the fuck are you in our bedroom?"

"I'm in Toronto because I came to claim the male of my heart.

I'm in yer bedroom because I sense him here and was drawn to his power signature."

At least she doesn't shy away from the truth.

I fight the urge to launch across the room, call Birga, and let my bitch out. "Regardless of what you want, if you had bothered to contact Sloan before you traveled all this way, he could've told you that he's married."

As if on cue, Sloan *poofs* into the room holding the laptop in one hand and two mugs in the other.

His gaze shifts from me to his ex-lover, and he straightens looking furious. "What are ye doin' here, Kaija? Whatever it is, I'll tell ye right now that ye have no business bein' in our private space."

He sets the laptop and the drinks down and extends his hand for me to take it and stand at his side.

The woman grins. "Mac, it's good to see ye. Canadian hospitality must be treatin' ye well. Ye look as delicious as always."

Sloan lifts his chin and raises his left hand to silence her. Her gaze settles on the platinum Claddagh band he wears on his ring finger and shifts to my hand to find its mate. "I'll ask ye not to make comments like that. Especially not in front of my wife."

She grins. "I remember ye bein' a great deal more fun, Mac. It's a shame ye've been domesticated."

Sloan's hand grips my upper arm and keeps me from advancing. I didn't realize I called Birga to my palm, but yeah, I've got deliciously violent visions of spearing her dancing in my mind. "She says she's here to claim the male of her heart."

The horror in his gaze is exactly the reaction I was hoping for. "If ye truly came fer me, ye miscalculated somewhere down the line. If ye merely said that to get a rise out of Fi and ye came fer another reason, we can speak downstairs."

"Or you can leave. That's an option too," I add.

Sloan nods. "Aye, it is. The choice is yers."

Kaija laughs, and the melodious sound is like the chiming of crystals. "So protective of yer female. What is it about her, do ye think? Why is it that great and powerful males rally around her and fight for her favor?"

Sloan stiffens. "What the hell are ye goin' on about? What males? Yer off yer nut."

"No, luv, I'm not. I see things a bit clearer than most, and although I'm sure yer wife has many fine qualities, I fail to see the allure."

Sloan yanks me back when I jolt forward. This time, my advance wasn't an unconscious decision. Now I really do want to skewer her with the jagged green tip of Birga's spearhead.

"Kaija, yer diggin' fer trouble. Why?"

She waves that away. "Not trouble, luv. Just takin' the piss. Besides, yer not the ones I'm here for."

That brings me up short. If she's here and she doesn't want me or Sloan, who is she after? I think back to the only time we crossed paths with her in Dublin a few years ago.

Sloan was hexed with festerbugs, and I'd had a bad reaction to a witch's ward. There was a group of us there, but the only other one she interacted with was...

"Dillan's married now too, so you can forget about him being your payment for anything you think is owed to you. Actually, why don't you make your play? His wife is deadly with a scythe, and I'd love to see what she does to you."

Kaija's amusement bubbles to the surface, and she tips her head back and laughs harder. "I'm beginning to see it. Ye've got a bite to yer tongue and the stones of a well-hung warrior."

Um...ew. That doesn't paint a very nice picture in my head. "Can we cut out the bullshit and get down to who or what you're here for so we can tell you to go to hell?"

She chuckles and bites her bottom lip. I'm sure, to any straight male on the planet, that subtle gesture of demure seduction would turn the tables of any conversation in her favor, but Sloan is immune.

He doesn't flinch. His gaze doesn't flicker.

"Fi asked ye, Kaija, and I'm tellin' ye. Yer options are to go downstairs and tell us what the hell ye want or get the fuck out of our home."

The mask of the seductress drops, and the female left standing before us is something else…something "other." Those turquoise blue eyes glow brighter, and her cool expression grows downright cold. "I'll leave when I'm ready and not before I have what I came for."

I grunt, my shield now weighing in on this. "Oh, really? What exactly did you come for?"

"My bear. I've come to collect my mate."

Exsqueeze me? Her bear? Her mate? "What the actual fuck are you talking about?" I release Birga to her resting place because if my spear is in my hand, I am going to make this succubus into a succu-bob. "Now you're saying you came for Bear? My Bear?"

Her lips curl at the corners. "Oh, I assure you, princess, he's not yours. He's mine, has been for millennia, and always will be."

As if to prove her point, she holds out her palm. Before our eyes, the warm brown of her skin shifts, revealing a tribal symbol with a raven sitting on the hunched shoulder of a bear.

Sloan frowns down at it and his brow pinches. "Wait. Are ye sayin' yer true identity is Raven—*the* Raven?"

She meets his gaze and grins. "There ye go. Now yer catchin' on. Now, where is he?"

I shake my head and take Sloan's hand. "No. Not here. If we're talking about this, we're going downstairs where I can pour myself a drink."

Sloan laces his fingers with mine and reaches out to touch Kaija…or Raven…or whoever the fuck she is.

Without waiting for him to make contact with her, she flicks her fingers and disappears.

I frown at Sloan. "Right. I suppose if she's Raven, she doesn't need a ride downstairs."

There have been very few times over the past two years when Sloan has looked truly mind-fucked and thrown. This is one of those times.

I squeeze his hand. "It's fine, hotness. There's nothing she can do or say that affects our family at its core. We'll let her speak her piece, and we'll deal with it together as always."

Sloan leans sideways and kisses my forehead. "As much as I knew that, it's good to hear. Thanks, *a ghra*. I love ye more than ye know."

I shrug. "How could you not? I'm fabulous."

He chuckles. "Aye, ye are. Now, let's go see what all this is about, shall we?"

The three of us stare at one another across the table. I try to wrap my gray matter around Sloan's sex-tracurricular plaything being *not* a succubus Bohemian from Dublin but the immortal mythical Raven. Then there's the part about her being mated to Bruin.

Seriously? If that's true, wouldn't I know? He's been bound to me and living within me for two years.

The "talking" doesn't go any better in the kitchen than it did upstairs. She's giving us nothing and keeps insisting we stop bear-blocking her and tell her what she wants to know. "I know he's close. I can feel him. Do us all a favor and tell me where he is."

"Nuh-uh. I still don't know why you're here, and even if I did, there's no way I'm setting you loose on someone I care about until I'm sure you're not full of shit."

Her chin lowers, and she raises her gaze to peg me with an icy glare. "Don't play games with me, princess. I sensed him on you when I healed you years ago. I've kept apprised of you and your family ever since."

"You've been watching us? Stalker much?"

Sloan squeezes my thigh under the table. "I think what Fi means is that if ye had a keen interest in Bruin and he's yer mate—"

"*If* he's her mate—and that's a big if," I add for emphasis.

Sloan nods. "*If* he's your mate, why would ye spend two years watchin' and waitin' instead of comin' to visit to address yer interests?"

She sits back and arches a brow. "The short answer is that it's none of yer business."

I roll my eyes. "Okay, what's the long answer?"

"That's also none of yer business."

I laugh. "Oh, good talk. Don't let the door hit your ass on the way out."

Except she doesn't get up or make any attempt to leave. Damn. Why couldn't the Fates toss me an easy lob for once?

The answer is obvious.

Because that's not how my life works.

Not seeing any other way to handle this, I reach out and see if Bruin's within range.

Communication over our bond link doesn't have a huge distance of coverage, but if he's in the treed area close to home, he'll be able to hear me. *Hey, buddy? Are you around?*

Yeah, Red? What's wrong?

Uh...I'm not sure yet. We have a visitor, and she's insisting she's Raven and she's your mate.

Feckin' hell. I'm on my way.

Bruin? Is it true?

There's a long silence. Then a growl rumbles between us. *Aye. Technically it's true, but it's a great deal more complicated than that.*

Well, just so you know, she says she's come for you.

Weel, she's a few centuries too late fer that. I'll be home in a shake.

I finish speaking and get up to start the kettle. "I'm having a hot toddy. Any takers?"

Sloan gets up to join me in the kitchen. He's been quiet through this whole thing, and I'm sure he's chastising himself for this coming back to bite us, but really, what are the odds of this happening?

She couldn't have seduced Sloan because of Bruin being with me because she was with Sloan five or more years before that. So, how did she manage this?

Coincidence? I call bullshit on that one.

Before I come up with a plausible answer, Bruin materializes in the kitchen and rears up on his back paws.

Kaija rakes her gaze over his mighty presence and moves around the table to stand before him. The female didn't strike me as being particularly small, but next to Bruin standing like this, she seems tiny.

She raises her palm, stroking the side of his cheek, her smile softening for the first time since she's been here. When she speaks, I don't understand the words. It's an Indigenous language and Bruin responds in kind.

Turning off the kettle, I hold out my hand to Sloan. "On second thought, how about we *poof* upstairs and mind our own?"

"Sounds good to me, luv."

I turn back to the estranged couple and wonder how it all worked.

Bruin turns toward me and snorts. "Don't hurt yerself, Red. We'll talk later."

I nod. "We're upstairs if you need us."

Twenty minutes later, my bath is drawn, I'm soaking in the bubbles, breathing in the invigoration of a citrus bath bomb, and trying not to think about my husband and my brother both having carnal knowledge of my best friend's immortal mate.

It hurts my brain.

"This obviously comes back to Coyote." I open my eyes and sip the chamomile tea Sloan had brought up with the laptop earlier. "Bruin said the bad blood between them began with a woman."

"And in comes Raven."

I swallow and set the mug on my bath caddy. "Right. So, they both have a thing for her. She makes the best decision and chooses Bruin. They mate and get their mating brands. Then what?"

"That's something only Bruin can tell us."

A sharp pang goes off in my chest. "It hurts that he never mentioned any of this."

Sloan sets his tea on the bathroom counter and moves the little makeup stool from the vanity to sit behind our freestanding tub. With strong hands, he grips the tension in my shoulders.

As he kneads away the knots, I try to let the hurt go. "I mean...we're closer than most besties, right? He lives inside me. I feel his emotions and moods, and he feels mine. Never once has he let on that he's mated to anyone, let alone an immortal of his pantheon."

"Perhaps relationships within the community of his people work differently than ours."

"Maybe, but it still hurts."

Sloan pinches a particularly sore knot and bends down to kiss the round of my shoulder when I groan. "If there's one thing I know fer certain, it's that Bruin would never knowingly hurt ye. He loves ye with the same protective vigor ye hold fer him."

"I know, but that doesn't answer any of the dozens of questions I have milling around in my head."

"No. I don't suppose it would, but I'm sure ye'll get yer

answers. Just give him a chance to sort things out in his mind first."

I grin and take another sip of my tea. "Are you implying I'm impatient?"

"Never." He winks and kisses my cheek. "I'm not implyin' it. I'm sayin' it outright."

"Rude." My laugh turns into a yawn, and I'm suddenly being pulled under by the weight of the day. "Do we stay up or can we go to bed?"

Sloan moves my bath caddy over to the counter and comes back to hold a towel up for me. "We go to bed. Bruin has never been shy about wakin' us up if he needs us. If he doesn't need us, there's no sense sacrificin' a night's sleep when Coyote could pull us into his games at any moment."

I accept the heated towel and groan at the decadence of its warmth. I love Sloan for not only the broad strokes of what he's brought to my life but the small details as well.

Heated towels are one of them.

"All right, you convinced me. Let's get ready for bed. I'm done with today."

CHAPTER EIGHTEEN

The person who coined the phrase "everything looks better in the morning" didn't know shit. When I roll out of bed and find Bruin sitting in the middle of our bedroom floor with Sloan reading by the window waiting for me to wake up, I know this isn't going to be good.

Swinging my legs free from the blankets, I rest my heels on the wooden frame of King Henry. "Morning, boys."

Sloan walks over and brings me a hazelnut coffee. It smells divine, and the mug is warm against my palms. I take a tentative sip and fight the urge to groan. "All right, Bruin. Tell me what the hell is going on."

He does.

He tells me of his life, long before I knew of him when I went back to Arthur's court and met Merlin for the first time. That was centuries before he moved to Ireland to await my arrival in his life. He tells me of a time when a much younger version of himself, filled with hubris and glory, won the heart and hand of Raven.

"I was too young and blinded by her beauty and power to

realize the kind of female she was deep down. I didn't figure that out until much later."

"But you stayed mated to her." There's no judgment in my words. It's a statement of the facts as I understand them.

"There's no untyin' that particular knot. The two of us were bound and bound we shall remain evermore even if we've lived separate lives for millennia."

"That's a long time."

"Aye, it is, at that." Sadness coats the deep timbre of his words.

I shake off my hurt to address his. "Do you still love her?"

"Not in the same way ye love Sloan, no. I love her for what we were way back when, and fer the man I was when we were together, and a great many things."

"But?"

"But the relationship we had—the affection of two hearts and bodies—became her thinkin' she owned me. She can be wickedly possessive and cruel. I learned that lesson too late, and by the time I walked away it had torn our love to shreds."

"Did she come after you? If she's claiming you now, what does she want?"

"That's the question, isn't it? She isn't sayin' yet, but you can bet yer britches it has somethin' to do with our run-in with Coyote."

I take a long sip of my coffee and let the java bliss warm the core of my chest. "Raven was the woman who caused the bad blood between you two."

"Aye. Where Raven and I were a match fer power, passions, and thinkin' ourselves above the others, she and Coyote were more well-suited in their disdain and disregard fer humanity. They got up to some nasty tricks when we used to socialize."

"That didn't raise any red flags?"

He grunts. "At the time, I was too lovestruck to see it. I thought Coyote was leadin' her down a dark path and that if I loved her enough and got her away from him, it would all work out."

"But it didn't."

"It did not."

I drink more of my coffee and let that all sink in. "Can I ask an inappropriate question?"

He chuckles and lifts his jaw. "Go ahead. I've been waitin' fer it."

I straighten. "Am I that predictable?"

Sloan laughs but doesn't comment. He simply turns the page of his book and keeps reading.

"It's one of the reasons I love ye so, Red," Bruin says. "Ye say what ye mean and ye mean what ye say, and I can always tell what yer thinkin' because it's written all over yer face."

My cheeks warm under that scrutiny. "All right, so answer the question I'm thinking and prove it."

"Ye want to know how a bear and a raven can share their passions and if Raven can take an anthropomorphic form, do I."

Huh... "Okay, two points for you. What are the answers?"

"Yes, I share the ability to take over a human form and yes, that's how we were able to be together as a mated pair."

I narrow my gaze on him. "Take over a human form?"

"That's right. I don't have a human form, but similarly to how I bond with you and live symbiotically, I can do what Coyote did when he took control of those people and used their bodies as his own."

I can't help the expression that takes over my face.

"Aye, I know it sounds horrific, but back in the early days, there were a great many followers who worshipped us. They were honored to stand as our vessels. Later, when those days passed, I never felt right about takin' over anyone."

"It seems Raven doesn't share that compunction."

"No. I don't suppose she does. Anyway, after we parted ways, I gave up the practice. Standin' on two legs—as well as bein' a drain on my power—did nothin' but make me ache fer my mate. When I gave her up, I gave up that form and focused on bein' my true self."

My mental hamster has fallen out of its wheel and is now being tossed around like a sack of potatoes. "Do you think you could still do it?"

"I don't know. The important point is that I don't *want* to do it. I love this life, Fi. Yer a firecracker and I love who we are both together and apart. I didn't like the man I was when I walked on two legs as her mate. I am Bear, and that is who I want to be."

I get that but hokey doodle...

Bear can take human form.

"Mind blown." I set my empty mug on the nightstand and frown at the picture I'd seen Kaija holding last night. It's a family photo taken of us decked out in wedding finery, and yes, Bear is right there with us.

What did she see when she looked at this?

I don't even care. Even if she is a mythical being, we are a family and will fight to keep Bruin with us. "Where is she now? Did she tell you what she wants?"

"Och, to determine what Raven truly wants would take ten lifetimes. I don't think *she* knows."

"Okay, then what brought her here?"

"Long ago she placed a spell to notify her if ever Coyote and I came to vicious blows. At the time, she was concerned about the well-being of two men vying fer her affections. Over the past couple of days, when the two of us faced off, her spell activated."

I blink. "Talk about a sleeper spell."

Bruin nods. "She said she's kept an eye on us since she sensed my presence when she healed ye a few years back. She's kept tabs on me through her black-feathered spy network, so when she felt Coyote and I collide, she knew right where to find me."

I didn't like her when she was flirting with Sloan as an ex-lover. I like her even less now that I know the whole story. "How do you feel about all this, hotness?"

Sloan looks up from his book, sets his bookmark in place, and sighs. "Honestly, *a ghra*, I don't know what to think. I'm annoyed I was lied to, embarrassed I missed her magical signatures and failed to figure out the truth, and angry I dragged ye into it and yer brother too."

"None of this falls on yer shoulders, lad," Bruin says. "Raven is a great many things, and few are decent and forthright. Maybe she was with ye fer a genuine good time as ye thought or maybe she had a premonition of our future link and used ye fer her gain."

"Aye, but which is it?"

"Ye'll likely never know, and from my experience, it's best not to stew on it because she's as devious as they come when she wants to be."

I run my fingers through the messy morning curls of my hair and exhale. "I really have to pee. The only thing I need to know now is whether the bitch is sitting downstairs at my table or if she cleared out."

Bruin chuckles. "Stand down, Red. She's gone…at least for the moment."

By the time I'm dressed and downstairs, Calum, Dillan, Nikon, Dionysus, and Sloan are milling around, and the energy in the air tells me something is up.

"Okay, what did I miss?" I grab a bowl from the cupboard and two packages of hot cereal. I start the kettle and pour myself some juice.

"You tell us, Red," Nikon says. "Sloan said there's news, but we needed to wait for you before anything was said."

I pour the boiling water into my bowl, toss in some blueberries and raspberries, and stir things up. "He said we have news?"

I glance at Sloan, and he nods. "I think it's best if we tell them about our visitor last night."

I wrinkle my nose at him. "Do we have to?"

"Aye, if we're goin' up against Coyote today and she shows up, or somethin' happens between him and Bruin, it's safest for everyone if all the intel is on the table."

Calum lifts his chin looking alarmed. "Why? What happened last night? She who? Did Coyote make a play for you guys here?"

I wave that away. "No. Nothing like that." *Bruin? Are you okay with this?* I ask inwardly.

Aye. There's nothin' to be done about it now. Sloan's right. If they're riskin' their lives to take down Coyote, they deserve to know the whole story. Besides, they're family, and ye don't keep secrets well from yer family.

With Bruin's blessing, I explain the events of last night starting with finding Kaija in our bedroom and ending with what Bruin explained to us this morning about their mating gone bad.

"Well, shit." Nikon purses his lips as he exhales. "Welcome to the diabolical immortal ex-lover club, Bear. It's been a membership of three for millennia, but we're happy to have you."

I blink and look at him. "Who else is in your club?"

Dionysus raises his hand. "It's how Eros and Nikky first bonded and when I met him back when you first arrived, we realized the three of us had a lot in common."

Nikon laughs. "It's been a brotherhood of survive and thrive ever since."

Well, I'm glad I helped facilitate that in some way.

"So, a bear and a raven," Calum says, sending me a sidelong glance.

"He used to be able to take human form, and we already know Kaija's human form."

"Biblically." Dillan rubs a hand over his mouth.

I finish my cereal and set my bowl into the sink to soak. "It might be awkward for a little while, but the important point is that Coyote has a grudge against Bruin. Now that he knows Bruin's happy and living here in Toronto, he might escalate things."

"Where does Raven factor into the taking down Coyote plans?" Calum asks.

"Consider her a wildcard. From what Bruin said, she has known where he was, but she might or might not have known how to catch up with Coyote. If she's feeling destructive, she might add to the mayhem."

"Oh, goody," Dillan snarks. "Two immortal beings wanting to fuck with not only the human population but also one of our own."

I lift my glass in a toast and smile. "And we're off to an amazing start to our day."

Two hours later, Sloan and I *poof* into the Batcave for the morning meeting, and I take the pan of warm apple crisp I'm carrying to the conference table. "Good morning, all. I brought a treat."

Diesel arches a brow. "I didn't know it was a potluck morning meeting."

Dillan chuckles. "Anxious Fi bakes. It's a thing."

"You're welcome." I grab the serving spoon and dish out portions onto paper plates.

"The real question is, did you bring ice cream?" Diesel has a hopeful gleam in his eyes.

"I've got ye covered, sham." Sloan steps in beside me with a carton of French vanilla and a handful of utensils.

I slide a plate to Sloan for him to dollop the ice cream topper, then rinse and repeat. "Nikon, can you see if Tarzan is coming down? It's almost time to start, and I don't want to derail the meeting with my culinary stress relief."

"On it."

I'm halfway through dishing out second breakfast when Dionysus joins us. He's got a spring in his step, and it seems all the aches and pains of yesterday have worked themselves out.

Dionysus is a happy boy once more.

"Everyone, grab yourself some fresh apple goodness, and we can get down to business."

"I take it there haven't been any Coyote events since last night?" Maxwell comes out of his office to join us. He grabs a plate and a spoon and takes his place at the head of the table.

"Nothing since the Alamo, no. Things are all quiet on that front." I make a plate for Garnet and slide it down the table. "But there is a new development."

Garnet spoons in a bite and grins. "And what's that?"

"Coyote and Bruin have an adversarial history and the female who stood in the center of that hostility is Raven. She's in town too. She paid a visit to our home last night and Bruin thinks she might stir up trouble."

Brody's brow is creased, and he stops eating. "You're talking about the mythical Indigenous gods, right? That makes Bear, *the* Bear?"

He holds up his hands and air quotes, and I nod. "You never put that together, I take it?"

He sits back and exhales. "That went completely over my head. No offense, but he doesn't act like an Indigenous god...and he has an Irish accent. Where did that come from?"

"Ireland." I chuckle.

Nikon and my brothers get a kick out of that one.

I hold up my hand in apology. "No, really, he is *the* Bear, but you're right. He's very unassuming."

"Unless he's in battle," Dillan corrects.

"True story."

When the room settles down, Maxwell grabs hold of the reins again. "So, assuming the hexes in Texas are taken care of, and with no way of knowing how to track Coyote or whether Raven is here to stir up trouble, we'll fall back on a couple of local issues and wait to see what happens."

"Yeah, that was what we figured too," I say.

Maxwell is flipping open his file folder when my phone rings and I pull it out of my pocket. I check the screen and frown.

"What's wrong, Jane?"

"It's Kinu. She hasn't talked to me in two months."

"Maybe she needs a babysitter."

"Maybe." I accept the call and answer. "Hey, Kinu. What can—"

"Fi! They took Jackson!"

Dionysus launches to his feet, and I hit speaker so my brothers can hear this too. "Who took him? What happened?"

"Two people. A couple. They blew in the back door and did something to Aiden. The woman pushed me into the front room with the babies, and the man grabbed Jackson and dragged him off."

"Greek. My back yard, now."

The surge of power that bursts from him is incredible. In a microsecond, we're standing in the shared backyard of the two houses I've lived in my entire life.

Garnet storms off toward Aiden's house without hesitation. It's the rest of them that need direction.

"Sloan, help Aiden if he needs it. Calum and Nikon, check on Meggie and the babies. Dillan, get your cloak and get back here. Bruin, find those two assholes. I want my nephew back."

I meet the worried gazes of Diesel and Brody. "What can we do, Fi?" Diesel asks.

"I don't know."

"What can I do, Jane?" Dionysus asks.

"I need you to find Da and bring him here."

Dionysus squeezes my hand and is gone.

I study the back of my old house and yeah, the door has been blown off the hinges and is hanging at a wonky angle. "Okay, if you two want a job, can you figure out how to get the back door hung again?"

Diesel nods. "We'll take care of it."

Manx comes through the doggy door and trots over. "What's happened? Dillan tore through the house like his arse was on fire."

I explain, and he glances around.

"I can track their scent."

"If they're gods, won't they portal out?" Diesel holds the door while Brody works on untangling the hinges.

I don't think so. "Raven has been inhabiting Kaija's human body for years. I'm guessing she won't give it up to ghost out. Besides, if their powers are the same as Bruin's, they don't portal and couldn't take Jackson with them."

"She was in our house last night. I know her scent," Manx repeats.

"Good, but I don't want you going alone. We're going to buddy up until we know what we're dealing with."

Dillan rushes out of the house, swinging his enchanted Cloak of Knowledge around his shoulders.

"D, go with Manx and see if the two of you can turn up anything. Be careful and let us know if you find anything."

"You know I will."

My mind is buzzing when Dionysus returns with Da and my grandparents. My relief is immediate. For all of my life, there has never been an emergency my father couldn't handle.

"What do ye know, *mo chroí?*" Da slips seamlessly back into being the cop I need.

With everyone here now, I wave for them to follow me as I stride across the back lawn to Aiden's and Kinu's house. I catch him up on the Raven and Coyote situation and how neither of them is happy with Bruin right now.

"Why take the wee lad?" Gran asks.

"That's a helluva good question." Aiden's face is flushed red with fury as we step through the broken doorway into the back of the house. "But they knew who they wanted."

"How so?" Da asks.

"The minute I heard the crash of them breaking in, I rushed them. They immobilized me, and the woman said, 'Get the boy.' The man didn't hesitate. He went from room to room, then upstairs. They grabbed Jackson, and I was helpless to stop them."

"Not yer fault, son." Da grips Aiden's shoulder. "We'll find him, and we'll get him safe home."

"Aye, we will," Granda agrees.

"I'll stay here and help with the wee ones," Gran says. "The rest of ye, do what ye need to do to bring the lad back to us."

Sloan is kneeling in front of the couch, his hands cupping Kinu's jaw, his eyes locked with hers. When he finally breaks the connection, he pats her shoulder and comes into the hall to speak to us. "I ran through the memory to be sure we had all the information."

"And?" My voice cracks and I swallow and try to push down the panic twisting my lungs so I can't breathe.

"It was Raven and a man—no doubt, some innocent chap with no clue he's been possessed by a mythical power. They burst in here, and it seemed they knew exactly who they wanted to snatch."

"The question is why?" I say.

"No!" Kinu shouts. "The question is how we get him back. Don't you see that, Fi? It doesn't matter *why* bad things happen around you. The fact is they do."

"Kinu, stop!" Aiden snaps, whirling on her.

"No! I won't stop! My baby is gone, and we all know who brought this to our door."

"Not now. For fuck's sake, not now."

I can't breathe.

My lungs constrict as her words spear me through the heart. I wave off the sympathetic looks and bolt out the back door.

There's no oxygen, and the world is spinning.

I run...across the yard...into the trees...and collapse in the rattan basket seat Sloan bought me when we first flirted with the idea of dating.

Is this my fault?

Time slows down as my world—my very soul—is fractured into a million pieces. The idea that I let this happen... That Jackson is gone because of me....

Bruin warned me that Coyote and Raven would strike us with something personal. I was too busy playing coonskin cap to pay attention.

My heart is hammering against my ribs, trying to break free of the cage. I feel every painful heartbeat.

So dizzy.

I drop my head between my knees and the seat bounces with my weight. I can't breathe. My hair swings aimlessly toward the forest floor as my breath comes in shallow gusts.

"Fer fuck's sake." Sloan kneels in front of me, his hands warm against my skin. With one palm on my neck and the other under my shirt and pressed against my sternum, he sends his healing warmth through me.

"Yer heart is racin', luv. Focus on breathin' with me, or ye'll pass out. Deep breath in and blow it out."

I try, but I've got nothing.

"Fiona, I'm here. Look into my eyes, listen to my voice, and let go of the anxiety. Try again, *a ghra*. Deep breath in and blow it out."

I don't know how long he stays there, pushing his healing into me. It could be minutes...it could be hours. In the end, my muscles relax, and I can breathe again.

I suck air into my lungs in greedy breaths and swipe at the moisture warming my cheeks.

"That's it, *a ghra*. Come back to us. Let the panic go. None of this is yer fault."

I groan and try to stop the trembling of my legs. I wish that was true. "Shit. I'm really shaking."

"Aye, ye are. It was a panic attack, but it's over. Yer safe and well and I've got ye."

I draw another deep breath and lift my head. Da's there looking panicked, and so are Aiden, Nikon, and Dionysus. "Sorry, guys. I didn't mean to make a scene."

"Don't ye dare apologize," Sloan snaps, straightening to stand at my side. "Aiden, with all due respect, I've been patient with Kinu, and I've tried to stay out of it, but I'll not let her tear Fi down every time something magical happens in our lives. It's not fair, and it's causin' real damage."

My brother looks stricken. "I know. I don't want Fi hurt either. It's just…I've tried to talk sense into her. Kinu's afraid of our world and what that will mean for the kids. I don't know how to reassure her."

"As important as that is, now is not the time." Da meets my gaze. "We need to focus on finding Jackson. The breakdown of family dynamics must wait, I'm afraid."

I wipe my palm against my cheeks and haul my ass out of the chair. "Absolutely. Where do we start?"

CHAPTER NINETEEN

Dillan and Manx come back as we're leaving the forest and I can tell by their downcast expressions they didn't find anything that could help.

"Sorry, brother. The scent ended at the side street." Dillan points at the fence. "They had a car and the minute they drove away the scent vanished."

Aiden swallows. "Fi? What about scrying? You're amazing at that."

"Merlin's better." I pull out my phone and dial.

After the fifth or sixth ring, my heart is falling, but he answers, breathless. "You have terrible timing, girlfriend."

"Sorry. Did I interrupt a private moment?"

He chuckles. "Nothing quite so salacious. I was in the middle of practicing for Saturday's show. What's up?"

"Jackson was taken. We need you. Can you come?"

He mutters a breathy curse, and I hear him on the move. "Give me two minutes to get out of these heels. Send someone to my apartment to pick me up."

"I heart you hard. Thank you."

"Don't worry about it. Let's get him home."

I end the call. "Someone go to Merlin's apartment. Tell him to bring his cards and his scrying tools."

"Bring him to yer Batcave." Da glances around to see who's going. "If the kidnappers left by car, we can use Maxwell's systems to track traffic cams."

"Got it. Meet you there." Nikon holds up his hand and vanishes.

I turn to Sloan. "You and Aiden gather some items of Jackson's that might help scrying and meet us at the Acropolis."

Sloan kisses my forehead. "We'll find him, luv. I swear."

I turn to Dionysus next. "The rest of us need to be at the Batcave."

Dionysus nods and we portal again.

I'm not sure what we look like when we first arrive, but it must be bad because Maxwell runs out and—oh, Garnet is right behind him. I didn't realize he came back.

"What have you learned?" Maxwell asks.

I fill the two of them in on what happened with Jackson. I'm so thankful that for this one, he and Da are taking the lead. I don't mind running the team in battle, and I'm confident when the world is going to hell, but Jackson being taken has cracked my foundation.

He's my buddy...my guy...my joy.

"Aw, come here, baby girl." Calum's arms tighten around me, and I fight not to fall apart. "You have my permission to snot on my shirt. Go ahead."

I choke out a labored laugh. "Isn't this Kevin's shirt?"

"Oh, is it?" He winks at me and squeezes me again. "Love you."

"Love you back."

"Can I get in on this?" Aiden joins us. "I really need to hold you, baby girl. Tell me you don't hate me."

Calum transfers the hugging to our oldest brother, and I press my cheek against his solid chest. "I could never hate you."

He's trembling and squeezes me until I can barely breathe. "We'll fix this, Fi. I swear."

I hear the words floating in the air, but I can't quite seem to grab hold of them and make them real. "I love you all so much. It kills me that Kinu is so angry with me. I thought we were sisters."

Aiden groans. "It's not even so much about you. You know that, right? She needs somewhere to focus her fear, and for whatever reason, she's chosen you as the scapegoat."

"Lucky me."

He squeezes me again. Then Nikon's back with Merlin...oh, nope, they're still in full drag and wearing their Dora persona.

I pat Aiden's shoulder, gain my freedom, and rush over to greet her. "Thanks for coming, girlfriend."

Dora's dazzling in a white bustier, feathers, and net stockings. Without hesitation, she gets right to it, setting her altar cloth and map on the conference table. "No time to switch hats. You get whom you get today."

"I'm thrilled to have you in any persona. I've missed Dora. Is this a new wig?"

She grins. Her purple lipstick is outrageously sparkly. "I have a new number I've been performing on Saturday nights. The regulars love it. You should swing by."

"A night on the town? I don't even know what that looks like anymore."

Dora finishes setting up, and I hold my hand out for Sloan to come to stand with me. I'm still shaking like a leaf in a hurricane, so if he's near me when my strength buckles, I might have a chance at not ending up faceplanted on the floor.

"All righty then, boys and girls, let's see where our little lost sheep has wandered off to."

Sloan hands Dora the dragon figurines Jackson's been obsessed with lately, and we circle the end of the table to watch.

Closing my eyes, I send up a prayer to the goddess, the Fates, or any or all deities that might want to give us a helpful nudge.

Please let us find him and let him be okay.

"Fi, come here to me, *mo chroi*." Da signals me over. "Calum says ye found the bitch in yer house last night, aye?"

"Yeah, she tracked Bruin to us and was snooping through our lives when I found her."

"Where was she? Did she find the portal to the island? Could this be a power play to gain access to Isilon?"

"I don't know. I don't think so. Merlin worked his usual brilliance to ensure the portal door is undetectable to anyone who doesn't have Cumhaill DNA."

"Did she take notice of anythin' in yer home...anythin' that might tell us why she targeted wee Jackson?"

I think about that for a moment. "Downstairs no. We sat at the table and glared at one another. When I found her in our bedroom, she was staring at our picture pretty intently, though."

"What picture?" Sloan asks.

"The wedding group in the silver frame on my side of the bed."

Da looks at Sloan. "Grab it fer me, son. I'd like to look at it. Maybe she saw somethin'."

Sloan is gone and back in the space of a racing heartbeat. He hands Da the frame, and I shift around to look at it with him.

"Sure, it was taken at the island, but I don't see anything that gives that away. Palm trees and—"

"Dragons." Sloan points at the sky in the background.

"Would Raven and Coyote have any desire for dragons?"

Da grunts, still staring at the picture.

I don't see what he's looking for, but then again, I wasn't a cop for forty years.

"I figured she saw Bruin as part of our family and didn't like it. She considers him to be her property."

Da shakes his head. "What if it was Jackson himself?"

"What do ye mean, Niall?" Sloan asks.

Da points at Jackson's image in the photo. He's grinning ear to ear with his arm hanging over Imari's shoulder. "What if she saw their crescent marks and it means somethin' more to her than we know?"

"Got him." Dora straightens, her gaze filled with confused horror. "Myra's Emporium."

I gasp. "They're after the Crescent Marked kids."

Garnet's murderous expression barely registers before he's gone. We're half a beat behind him, my mind stalling out on the horror of this now spilling into the lives of Myra and her family.

The moment we materialize at Myra's Mystical Emporium, Garnet roars, his voice more lion than man. "Myra!"

"Jackson!" Aiden yells.

"Spread out," Da shouts, waving toward the other areas of the enchanted bookshop. "Nikon and Dionysus, check the other section."

There's a mad scramble as everyone races through the aisles, searching for any sign of Myra or the kids.

"I've got Myra!" Nikon shouts in the back.

I race through the opening of the other section, launch down the two steps, and home in on Nikon kneeling before Myra's prone body on the rug. "Nikon, move, now!"

My warning comes a second too late as Garnet backhands him across the room to get to his mate. As he drops to his knees, the only thing I can tell is that she's much too still.

Sloan and Dora race to my bestie lying unconscious underneath Leniya's branches. I can't look. I can't deal with losing Jackson, Imari, *and* Myra.

I shove my fears down and lock my emotions away. To give the emotional barricades I put up a moment to set to stone, I veer off and tend to Nikon. "Are you all right, Greek?"

He's leaning at a steep angle, his arm propping him up against the bookshelf that acted as the end of his flight. He has blood on his lip and looks dazed. "A couple of broken ribs and by the way my head's spinning, probably a concussion."

Shit. "Sloan will fix you up as soon as he's done with Myra, I'm sure."

I glance back, but Sloan, Garnet, and Myra are gone. "What happened? Where'd they go?"

Dora scrambles to her feet and comes over to join us. "Garnet wanted to take her to his medics, but Sloan insisted she go to Wallace."

I swallow. "Well, she's in good hands then. What was wrong with her?"

Dora shakes her head. "I don't know. The magic from Bruin's pantheon is very different from ours."

"Bruin! Shit. We've been rushing around..." I look around and hold my hand out to Dionysus. "Tarzan, I need a power boost. I need to tell Bruin where we are. He got left behind again."

Dionysus jogs over and takes my hand. When he pushes power into me, I brace myself against the spinning world.

Bruin, we're at the Emporium. Myra's hurt and they took Imari. It has something to do with the Crescent Marked kids.

Thank fuck, Red! Ye can't disappear on me like that. Ye'll be the death of me, I swear.

I hear the panic in his gruff grumble and smile. *I love you too, Bear. Now come join us.*

On my way.

Aiden roars and pushes over a display rack, sending tarot cards and angel cards flying. "There's no one here. Now Jackson *and* Imari are gone. What do they want with the two of them?"

Two of them? But there are four of them.

Grabbing my phone, I call Tad. It rings...and rings...and rings. "Dammit."

"What's wrong now, *mo chroi?*"

"Tad's not picking up, and there's one more Crescent Marked

child we're aware of in this realm. If they're rounding up the marked kids, we need to safeguard Bella Tremblay in Montréal."

Da frowns. "Aye, we'll need to secure her until we know what Raven and Coyote are after."

The idea of protecting Bella snaps my mind into clear focus for the first time since Kinu called me with the news. "As soon as Bruin gets here, Dionysus and I will go to Montréal and get Bella. Dora, help Nikon. Garnet broke him, and he needs a magical patch-up. Da, you keep on keeping on. If they took the kids, they had a car at the curb or the back door. Calum knows where the security cameras are in the kitchenette. When Nikon is upright, he can take you back to the Batcave to use the traffic cameras to see if you can track them."

Bruin materializes next to me and curses at the mess and Nikon getting patched up. Both those things were self-inflicted, but there's no time to worry about that. "Bruin, do you want to stay with me to get Bella or work with Da to find the car they used?"

"My answer will always be the same, Red. We're partners. Where life takes ye, there I'll be."

Thank all things wise and wonderful for that.

"Perfect. Then we're off to Montréal. I'll text you when I'm back, and we'll catch up to you then."

Da hugs me, kisses my head, and pegs Dionysus and Bruin with a serious gaze. "Keep her safe, boys."

I roll my eyes. "He says as if I'm still his baby girl and can't take care of myself."

He doesn't seem to care about my opinion. "Ye'll always be my baby girl. Besides, havin' two powerful gods at yer side can't hurt. Ye know how ye are."

I don't respond. Patting my chest, I invite Bruin to take his place within me, and I lace my fingers with Dionysus'. "Montréal, Tarzan. Mayor Tremblay's outer office, please."

It's been months since I stood in this office. Montréal was under siege from a vampire insurgence, and it was my first mission as the Toronto Fae Liaison to help sort it out. It took a while to figure out who the bad guys were, and people died.

History won't repeat itself. Not this time.

Our sudden appearance has the woman behind the desk staring wide-eyed and her hand sliding under the surface.

"You don't need to hit the panic button." I hold up my hands. "I need to speak to Mayor Tremblay immediately. Tell her it's Fiona Cumhaill and it's about Bella's safety."

The woman's gaze is scrutinizing as she looks me over.

"Tick-tock." Dionysus taps his bare wrist. "We could've materialized into her office, but out of respect, we came here. Tell Mayor Tremblay Fiona Cumhaill is here and needs to speak about Bella."

I hear the push of persuasion in his voice, and I won't even scold him for it.

The woman succumbs, either because she believes us or because of Dionysus' divine influence. I don't care which. She picks up the phone receiver, and a moment later, she's hustling her beige wedges to usher us into the mayor's office.

Mayor Clarissa Tremblay stands behind her desk looking alarmed. She's a sleek businesswoman, and I know from working with her last time she's resilient and smart. "Fiona, what is it? What's happened?"

"We'll get to that. First, where's Bella?"

Mayor Tremblay gestures at the room off her office, and I exhale a sigh of relief. At least one thing is going our way today. "Dionysus, check on her while I explain."

Clarissa looks alarmed, but there's not much to be done about that. She'll likely be more alarmed when I explain what's going on.

Gabriel Lauden turns in the chair opposite the mayor's desk. Lauden is a snazzy silver fox who uses fancy suits and pocket squares to hide the fact that he's the ruthless Vampire King of Montréal.

We had more than one run-in during my time here, but as much as I don't like the guy, I trust that he loves the city and wants to work with Mayor Clarissa to keep its citizens safe. "Would you like me to leave, or can I be of help?"

I meet Clarissa's gaze and shrug. "That's up to you. So far, this doesn't involve Montréal, but there have been several things happening in Toronto."

Clarissa nods. "You can stay, Gabriel."

He sinks back into his seat, and I take the empty chair beside him and opposite the mayor. "This morning, my nephew Jackson was kidnapped from my brother's home. We didn't know why at first, but when Imari was taken a short time later it seemed pretty clear that it might be something to do with—"

"Their marks." Clarissa gasps.

"We believe so, yes."

The vampire stiffens beside me and pulls out his phone. "I can have an army of men protecting her inside twenty minutes."

I shake my head. "I don't think that will be enough. Not with who is behind it."

Clarissa's mouth tightens. "You know who took them?"

"It was the Indigenous gods Raven and Coyote."

Clarissa reels back in her chair. "Gods? How do we protect our children against gods? They are powerful and I assume immortal."

"Unfortunately, yes." I point at the open door of the next room. "We can assign her an immortal god as her security and take her to a place where Coyote and Raven have no access."

"Take her? Take her where?"

I hear the panic straining her words and debate how much to tell her. "There is a place. A haven inaccessible from the realms. We can take the two of you there until we negate the threat."

"How do you negate the threat of immortal gods? Even if you recover Jackson and Imari—"

"It's not if we recover them. It's *when*." I push that outcome more aggressively than I intended.

"Of course, my apologies. *When* we recover them, there's still no way to eliminate them from our lives."

I draw a deep breath. "Your concerns are valid, but with all due respect, Madam Mayor, our first step is to get your daughter somewhere safe. We'll worry about the long-term repercussions once we have more information."

She scratches her head, looking stricken. "I can't leave with no idea when I might be able to return. I'm hosting a summit next week and have dinner engagements and responsibilities on municipal, provincial, and federal levels."

"Then we'll play it the same way we did last time. We'll assume responsibility for Bella's care and update you on her situation. You can be portaled to her each night or whenever you're free to spend time with her. Nikon and Dionysus will be at your disposal."

She exhales and runs her fingers through her brunette waves. "Who will care for her? I'm assuming if Imari's gone, Myra and Garnet will be in no shape to take care of her this time."

"That's likely true. No, I'll have my family take care of her. My two older brothers live on the island and so does a fourth child with the mark. Binx and his family already live there, and I'm sure Bella will be welcome to play with them and keep herself amused until we know more."

"And Dionysus will stay with her?"

I nod. "Absolutely."

Until this point, Gabriel has listened without comment, but he shakes his head and holds up a finger. "When you say Dionysus and refer to him being a god, you mean—"

I meet his gaze and grin. "Yes, Dionysus, son of Zeus, God of Fertility and Wine."

"No offense, but why would he sequester himself with a child he barely knows for an uncertain amount of time?"

"Because I'm family." Dionysus frowns as he and Bella join us in the office. "Jackson and Imari are my family. Bella's my friend. I'm not going to let anything happen to her."

He presses a kiss against her cheek and wrinkles his nose at her.

Bella has long dark hair and brown and beige ram horns that come from the front of her skull and curl back to hang freely by her ears. They are delicate and ribbed. Between them, on the crest of her forehead, sits what looks like a birthmark of a crescent moon.

I wink at him, applauding his timing, and swing my attention back to Mayor Tremblay. "I wouldn't raise the alarm unless I truly believed there was cause for concern. Please, until we know what the marks mean and why they matter to Raven and Coyote, it's important we take a proactive stance."

Clarissa opens her arms, and Dionysus sets the little girl on her lap. "Remember when you went to stay with Imari while *Maman* sorted out some business a few months ago?"

"*Oui, Maman.*"

"Well, we're going to do that again, this time with Dionysus and Fi's brothers. And you know what?"

"What?"

"You're going to meet another special boy with a mark like yours."

Bella raises her fingers to touch the crescent moon on her forehead. "What's his name?"

I lean forward in my chair. "His name is Binx, and he has five brothers and sisters. They all love to play and make new friends."

"You know what else?" Dionysus adds.

"What?"

"They have fur. They're feline folk, and they look like big kitty cats."

Bella blinks at Dionysus. "Big kitties?"

"Yep."

"Are you coming to see the big kitties too?" she asks him.

Dionysus nods. "Absolutely. In fact, if your mommy says yes, you and I will take this adventure together."

I wait, watching Clarissa as her decision takes hold. She squeezes Bella tight and nods. "Take her now, and I'll put together a bag tonight after work and will bring it with me when I come to see that she's settled."

She smothers Bella with a dozen kisses and hands her daughter off to Dionysus. She looks lost and a little bereft and clamps her arms across her stomach. "I'm trusting the two of you with my entire reason to be. Please make sure she's safe and happy."

I press my hand over my heart. "We will. And I'll keep you posted on things, I promise."

"Give Garnet and Myra my best. I can't imagine..."

"I will." Stepping over to Dionysus, I take his free hand. "Take us to the island, Tarzan."

CHAPTER TWENTY

"Hello, the house!" We materialize in the Great Hall, and there's no one here. "Let's try the top floor, Tarzan. They've been working on the penthouse."

We portal again and this time when we reappear, we find my brothers. "Hey, guys."

Brenny and Emmet are lounging on the sectional, video game controllers in hand, and the unmistakable rapid-fire of a shoot 'em up game echoing through the apartment. It's no wonder they didn't hear me. "Guys!"

They jump and pause the game, the sudden silence deafening.

"Fi, what the fu—dgecicle are you doing here?" Emmet smiles at the little faun in Dionysus' arms. "Hello, sweetie. What's your name?"

"Bella."

"Hello, Bella. I'm Emmet, and this is Brendan."

"These are two of my brothers," I say. "I have four."

Brendan looks at me with raised brows, and I can see all the questions he wants to ask. "Tarzan? Will you take Bella onto the balcony and show her how pretty the island is?"

He grins. "Sure. Guess what you're going to see flying in the air outside?"

"Birds?" she guesses.

"Yes, probably birds but also dragons. We have dragon friends who live here with us."

She squishes Dionysus' cheeks between her palms. "Don't let dragons get me."

He laughs and makes fish lips at her. "I won't. There's no need to be afraid. They are our friends."

When they're out on the balcony that runs the entire circumference of the golden dildo, Emmet and Brendan turn and wait for the explanation. "I take it you haven't heard from anyone from the family in the past hour or two?"

Brendan straightens. "No. Why?"

I start from the beginning and get them caught up on Raven, Coyote, and Bruin, the hexes in Texas, the home invasion, Jackson and Imari getting taken, and Myra getting hurt.

"Fucking hell." Brendan storms around the massive open area, pacing like he's crawling out of his skin. "I hate this. I feel so tethered and useless here. I want to be home, helping you guys find Jackson."

"I know you do and I'm sorry you can't be. That said, I need you to bring Binx up to one of the suites and have him and Bella here where the two of you and Dionysus can watch over them...at least until we figure out what Raven and Coyote are after."

"Do you think they'll be able to get here?" Emmet asks.

I draw a deep breath. "The Boundary Gate accesses many realms, and Coyote and Raven can inhabit the bodies of others. It's plausible they could possess someone and gain entry as a refugee coming into the city."

Emmet finds that as alarming as I do. "Astrid. Can you come here, please?"

The fairy AI interface with the island appears directly in front of him. "I can."

"Thank you. Can you please halt all immigration until further notice? There's been an incident, and we're going to lock down until I'm confident the wrong people aren't coming through."

Her head tilts to the side, and she nods. "All immigration is halted. Shall I speak to Kidok?"

He nods. "Ask him to bring Binx to the palace with a bag of personal belongings. We're securing him here where we can watch over him. Kidok is welcome to stay as his guard. HaiLe and the kids are welcome too. I'll explain everything when they get here."

"Understood. It shall be done."

When she leaves, I smile. "She's a lot more agreeable now than that first day."

Emmet chuckles. "With us, yeah. She still hates you, though."

Rude.

"Okay, I need you two to show Bella into one of these rooms while Dionysus portals me home. I'll send him right back, but I don't want her to panic that he's gone and she's been left behind. Oh, and he'll be bringing her mother in the evenings to stay with her."

Brendan nods. "That's fine. We'll take care of everything on our end. It goes without saying, but the minute you know something about Jackson and Imari, we want to know too."

I hug each of my brothers and ease back, anxious to catch up with the rest of the team. "Count on it."

Dionysus drops me back at the Batcave and leaves as soon as he sees Team Trouble milling around. Nikon is back on his feet, Garnet and Sloan are still absent, and Da and my brothers are busy working on laptops and monitors tracking down our kids.

"Hey, I'm back. What did I miss?"

Da straightens from where he's perched against the edge of

the conference table watching the monitor wall. "Calum, back up that car in the intersection and see if we can get a look at the driver and the license plate."

Dillan gathers me in a hug, and I'm thankful for the strength he lends me.

"Where's Aiden?"

"Nikon snapped him home to check on Kinu and the kids."

"I'm sure Gran and Granda have them covered."

He nods. "For sure they do, but he was making us all crazy, and we couldn't focus. I've never seen him like this. He's losing his mind."

"I suppose that's to be expected."

"Yeah, but it's not helpful when there are no leads for us to follow and nothing for him to do about it."

My heart sinks. "No leads? Nothing?"

"I'm hopin' Bear might stir up some possibilities." Da joins us. "Can ye let him out so I can talk with him a bit?"

"Of course." I release Bruin, and my battle bear appears in the open space beside me a moment later.

Da runs his fingers through his wild russet hair, and I wonder how many times he's done that today. It's longer now in his retirement than it's been my whole life. He looks like Einstein after working on an exceptionally challenging math question. "Hey, Bear. Let's go over this again and see if we can shake somethin' loose."

Da and Bruin begin at the beginning and go over everything again. What happened in Texas. What was said between him and Raven last night. What Raven and Coyote were like individually and together back in the day.

I know Bruin hates every moment of the interrogation, but he endures it for Jackson's and Imari's sake. Still, at the end, I can tell that nothing shook loose for any of us.

"What about Jackson portaling out?" Nikon asks.

I sigh. "He only portaled the one time, and it was involuntary because he did it in his sleep. Kinu wouldn't allow Sloan to encourage him or work with him."

Da doesn't look pleased about that. Still, being mad about that now doesn't change a thing.

"What about scrying for him again?" I ask.

Dora frowns. "I've tried, girlfriend. Nothing is registering. Either they've got a privacy spell on them to repel my intentions or—"

"Don't say it." I hold up my hand, my resolve about to crumble.

"Or they're outside the city, and I don't have the right maps." She grabs my wrist and pulls me into her embrace. "Don't go there, Fi. It's way too early to give up hope."

I suck in an unsteady breath and hug her tighter. "Yeah. You're right. We're not out of this yet."

"It would help if we knew where the mark came from and what it means," Da moves on to the next idea.

I ease back from Dora and exhale. "Agreed, but we've been trying."

Da nods. "I don't doubt it fer a second, but maybe havin' a couple of different minds workin' on it will spin yer ideas off in a different direction. Go over what ye know and what we don't."

I draw a deep breath. "We know there have been episodes of children marked several times over many centuries here in our realm and other realms. We know the children are supposed to guide us through troubled times. We don't know if they are simply lighting the way or if they are supposed to grow up and become warriors themselves."

Calum cracks the tab of a can of soda and chimes in. "We know there is a connection of some kind with the four of them. They all came into our lives and were marked within a three-month timeframe."

I reach over to steal a swig and let the bubbles wake me up a little. "We know there is an actual power behind the crescent. I felt it when I pressed my lips against Bella's forehead. The same thing happens with Jackson and Imari."

That surprises the men.

"You haven't experienced that?"

They all shake their heads.

"I'm a snuggler, so yeah, when I kiss their marks, I can feel the strength of the power behind it."

Dora gathers her scrying set and tarot cards. "Nikon, take me home for five minutes. I need to get this bustier off so I can breathe and think. Then, when we come back, I want you to take me to the island. I want to examine Binx and Bella."

"Examine them for what?" I ask.

"I wonder if there's a link between them I can trace. If their marks hold power, maybe there's a signature I can locate."

That surprises me. "You think there could be a bond between them you could track?"

She shrugs. "When magic is involved, anything is possible."

Less than ten minutes later, Merlin returns with Nikon, and we portal to the new Cumhaill condo on the top floor of the palace on Isilon.

"Look, we have company!" Dionysus waves at us from where he's sitting on the sofa with Binx and Bella playing Spyro. "Welcome to the fun zone. We've got pizza, ice cream, and video games. Later, we're going to play Mario Kart. We've got costumes."

Brendan and Emmet rush over and I shake my head. "Nothing yet. We've been so focused on what the crescents mean and what happened in history that we might have missed something important."

"What's that?" Dionysus asks.

"Merlin wonders if the power behind the marks might link

the kids somehow and maybe he can trace it to the location of the other two."

"Oh, that's an idea," Brendan says.

Emmet's brow is creased, and he doesn't comment.

"What is it, Em?" I ask. "What are you thinking?"

"I was just wondering about the power behind the marks. Is there a way Sloan could gauge the power signature to give us an idea of the source? If we knew if it was Wiccan or a goddess or sorcery, maybe we could figure it out that way."

Dammit. "We were so focused on the meaning and the history of the marks we totally missed the idea of tracking it."

"We don't even know if it's possible," Merlin cautions, moving in. "Don't berate yourself over an idea. Let's see if there's anything to it."

I nod and let him move into position between the kids on the sofa and the massive game system set up on the wall behind him. "Hi, kids. Would you mind if I touch your moon marks?"

"Will it hurt?" Binx asks.

"Not at all. I want to feel the magic and see if I recognize it."

Neither kid objects, so he brushes a gentle finger over the moon marks.

I wait, my pulse thundering in my ears with a solid, booming rush.

When he eases back and stands, he shakes his head. "I agree there's power there, but I don't sense the signature or know how I could trace it. Let me think about it for a bit. I'm sure there's a way."

Dionysus moves in next. "Can I try too?"

The kids shrug and Dionysus gives it a shot. He takes a page out of my book and presses a kiss against the crescent moon on Bella's forehead. Then he repeats the process with Binx.

When he pulls back, he snaps his fingers, and both kids are holding a bunny. "For being so brave, I award you, Fun Bun and

Cinna Bun. Can the two of you take them over to the kitchen and see if they're hungry?"

The kids beam at the tiny black balls of fur in their palms. Binx helps Bella scootch off the couch, and the two of them take their rabbits to the kitchen.

Dionysus is all grins. "They like them."

"Yes, they do, but maybe we shouldn't give other people's children pets as presents."

He waves my concern away. "Bella won't be going anywhere anytime soon, and Binx lives here. It'll be good to keep their minds off things. I'll make them a little rabbit habitat—Oh! It'll be a *rabbitat*. Get it?"

I hate to break up his joy in making up a great new word, but we need to focus. "Tarzan, did you learn anything by touching their marks?"

Dionysus waggles his brows and grins. "I know who marked them and how to get Jackson and Imari back."

Seriously? My entire body starts to do a little shake, rattle, and roll. "You're sure?"

He winks and holds up his finger to stop the flood of questions he must know are about to tsunami on him. "I need to focus to access a line for a person-to-person call to Mount Olympus. Hold please."

CHAPTER TWENTY-ONE

Dionysus finishes his mental conversation with Olympus, and I'm not sure whether to kiss him or strangle him. He's so pleased and calm, and we still have no idea what he knows or thinks he knows. "Please, you're killing me. Stop holding out on us."

He grins. "If I had a dollar for every time I've heard those words."

Da clears his throat. "Try to focus, son. We're all worried about the kids. Tell us what ye figured out."

His smile dims as he becomes more serious. "It's obvious now that I'm thinking about it. I would've figured it out sooner if I hadn't whisked Sloan away during the Montréal mission and missed all the Crescent Marked drama. When I was allowed to return, I had no powers. And this is the first time—"

"Dude," Dillan snaps. "Less words, more talking."

Okay, that doesn't make a lot of sense, but I know where Dillan's coming from. "Tarzan. Explain."

"Who from my pantheon is the goddess of the moon and children?"

Nikon groans. "You think Artemis is behind this?"

"I know she is. Now that I've got my powers back and touched their marks, I feel her presence."

Da frowns. "Artemis, goddess of the hunt and wilderness?"

Dionysus nods. "That's her."

"All right, so how does knowing this get our kids back?" Da asks.

"I would think that's obvious. She's the goddess of the hunt, and two other gods have dared to take what she has marked as her own. She's not going to let that stand."

"No. I will not." The air shimmers as a tall woman with long mahogany brown hair appears. Her green eyes flash with a promise of bloodshed, and I'm suddenly glad she's on our side.

She's wearing a sleeveless green leather vest, tight hide pants laced across her belly, and soft-soled leather boots that come to her knees. A strip of green rawhide wraps her left forearm, and I assume it protects her skin from the lash of her bowstring.

Calum's eyeing the bow nestled against her shoulder with unveiled lust and appreciation. I don't blame him. It's a magnificent weapon.

The goddess is truly impressive, especially when flanked by two enormous gray wolfhounds. Lifting her chin, she scans our group, and her gaze stills on Dionysus. "Brother."

Dionysus drops his gaze to the floor at her feet. "Greetings, sister."

I don't like him submitting to her. Maybe he does it to keep things cordial and in our best interest. He sweeps his hand toward the kitchen where Binx and Bella feed carrots to their bunnies.

Artemis studies them for a moment and returns her attention to us. "Which of the others were taken?"

The others? Are there more than four?

"Jackson mac Cumhaill and Imari Grant," Dionysus answers.

Her gaze narrows. "We shall find them, and when we do, blood shall flow like wine."

"It seems blood has flowed freely already this day, sister." He gestures at the scarlet stains on her hands and wetting the front of her vest. The muzzles of the two hounds are damp and matted with it too.

"Poachers. They lacked the understanding of a true hunt so I availed myself upon them to correct their misconceptions."

"I am certain you did."

The cruel smile curving her lips makes my shield flare. "Now, to the children. You said Fionn's kin and the young bear cub."

"That's right. They were taken several hours ago from their mothers."

"You are certain you know by whom?"

"We are certain. It was Raven and Coyote. Confirmed by one of our own."

She raises a hand and strokes the top of one of her hounds. "Then let the hunt begin."

"Just when I think I've got a handle on your life, things get weirder."

I chuckle at Brendan's comment, spoken so only he and I can hear. I don't think he realizes Artemis and Dionysus have god senses and likely not only hear everything spoken around them but also what's thought.

That must be difficult, especially for Dionysus growing up among a pantheon that despised him.

"I will return when the children are found and reclaimed," Artemis says.

"We're coming with you." I leave Brenny and stride toward the goddess.

The glare she pegs me with makes me wish invisibility is one of my gifts. Still, I fight beyond the danger bells going off inside my mind and take a page out of Dionysus' book. Dropping my gaze to the floor, I convey as much respect as I can. "The children are my family. Raven and Coyote targeted them because of me."

"How so?" she asks.

"They are angry and jealous. Raven chose Bear over Coyote, and Bear has chosen my family and me over her."

Artemis frowns. "A woman vexed and rejected can be dangerous indeed."

"Yes. Bear and I need to help find them and make this right."

"We all do," Da snaps, stepping forward. "Clan Cumhaill stands together in all things."

Artemis huffs and waves her hand.

My head spins, and I fight the sudden urge to vomit. When my surroundings settle, Dionysus stands behind me, holding me up with an arm braced around my waist. The rush of wind in my face is a balm to my unease, and I focus on what's happened.

Dionysus and I are standing behind Artemis in a large golden chariot. Her wolfhounds are sitting beside her, and we're being pulled through the sky by four massive stags.

I glance over my shoulder at Dionysus, and he leans down to rub his nose against mine. *I've got you, Jane. What she lacks in manners she more than makes up for in efficiency. She'll get us to the kids, and we'll make sure they're safe.*

Still a little woozy, I press my cheek against his shoulder and let him bear the weight of control for the moment. *Thank you, sweetie. I'm so thankful for you.*

He squeezes me tighter, and I try my best to strengthen my stance and be ready for what's coming. *Bruin? Are you ready to face them and get this done? I know you're still bound to her and love her in some way.*

Don't worry about me, Red. She forfeited any chance of my sympathy the moment she came after our family. I'll not hesitate to do what needs to be done.

The harsh resolve in his words makes me sad. *I'm sorry it came to this, buddy. You deserve so much better.*

It's hard to gauge travel by magical chariot so I give up trying. I retreat into my thoughts, thankful for the stalwart presence of Bruin and Dionysus, and send Myra all the positive vibes I can.

Sloan wouldn't have left me without a word unless he had to, and he wouldn't have overruled Garnet's wishes about where to take her unless he was certain it was the right course.

I have faith in Sloan, and therefore, I have to believe he won't let Myra down.

The trip seems endless, but with the way time travels near gods and goddesses, it could've taken only the briefest moment. Pantheon magic is mind-bendy like that.

The important thing is, when we land in a rich green forest with water flowing and the CN Tower peeking above the canopy in the distance, I know she's on the right trail.

We never told her they went missing in Toronto.

The moment the chariot comes to a complete stop, Artemis grips the helm of the golden cart and launches over the front to the forest floor. Her dogs follow her, and the three run through the trees in a graceful rush.

Bruin. Don't lose her. I release him as quickly as possible and jump down to chase them. "Tarzan. Get the others and hurry back."

Dionysus snaps out in a flash, and I take off after the goddess of the hunt.

I navigate the spotty shade of trees beginning to turn color for the winter. Goosebumps raise my skin, and it has less to do with the temperature and more to do with my anxiety about this situation.

Running without direction only gets me so far. I pause to listen. Where did they go? Did Bruin catch up with Artemis?

Jane, talk to me, and I'll find you, Dionysus says in my mind.

I'm here. I lost the trail and am trying to figure out where they are.

We're coming. We'll put Dillan to work.

Hurry, sweetie. Bruin's gone off to follow, and I don't want to leave him against Raven and Coyote, especially if the kids are in the mix.

Artemis will keep them busy enough.

Putting Dillan to work tracking Artemis is an idea, but maybe I've got a better one. Calling my druid power forward, I scan the forest around me. *"Animal Friendship."*

There's a couple of raccoons sleeping in the hollow of a tree nearby, skunks, muskrats...there!

I reach out to the red fox watching me from beneath a mass of fallen branches. "I need your help, little one."

With our connection made, I show him images of Artemis and her dogs. "I need to find them. It's very important."

He stretches and ambles out, glancing around as he approaches.

"Will you help me?" Movement in the trees behind me has him shrinking back, but I send him reassurance. "That's my family coming to help find our lost kits. Help us find them, please."

"Your kits? You've lost your little ones?"

"Taken from us by them." I send him images of Coyote and Raven.

"I've seen them." The little fox bounds off, racing past me with a swish of his bushy tail and his ears pulled back. "Those gray beasts smell of blood and death. There's no missing the scent."

"Excellent. Thank you so much."

Dionysus, Da, Dillan, Calum, and Nikon catch up with me as I push off and we're off again.

Leaves rustle and twigs snap underfoot as we race after the fox. While I was focused and driven when it was me alone in this race, it is much less overwhelming now with my peeps there with me.

Artemis underestimated the force we are when united and set

on a course...especially in a natural environment like the Don Valley.

"Not far now," my furry guide says, scurrying over the scrub with speed and agility.

"He's so cute." Dionysus races beside me. "Can we keep him?"

I'm about to respond when the fox slows and crouches low to the forest floor. His ears press back, and he stops. "There. The gray beasts are there."

The wolfhounds are snarling and engaged, fighting against the man Coyote possesses. Even though the man himself is innocent, I don't think we'll be able to save him. Those bloodhounds are mauling him too violently.

Artemis is fighting Raven, the two of them locked in a brutal and dangerous dance. Raven may not be in her true form, but her familiarity with Kaija's body is obvious in the way she moves.

Bruin is standing off to the side protecting the kids. He's reared up on his back legs snarling and creating a wall between the battle and the little boy huddled around a bear cub.

"Nikon, snap in behind Bruin. Take the kids to Wallace's clinic and get Aiden and Kinu to them."

He portals behind the wall of my bear, gathers the kids, and is gone.

A huge weight lifts off my chest knowing they're safe with Garnet and Sloan.

Wallace will take care of them.

My mind catches up with the moment, and I try to remember if the kids moved or responded to Nikon when he got them.

A sinking feeling in my gut tells me they didn't.

I can't go there right now. For this moment, I must believe they are healthy and well.

Bruin roars when he realizes his guard duty is over, and he's free to fight. He charges into the fray with claws and fangs bared.

I'm not sure what Raven and Coyote had in mind when they stole our kids, but I can see by the looks on their faces that being charged by three gods, two warrior beasts, and a family of pissed off druids is more than they bargained for.

It's also more than they can defend against.

When Bruin goes after Raven, she splits her attention, and Artemis takes advantage of her momentary mistake. The goddess of the hunt lunges forward and draws her dagger across Kaija's belly, spilling her insides onto the forest floor.

The woman falls to the ground like a marionette with her strings cut.

I exhale a sigh of relief. Then I'm bombarded by a magical presence.

My thoughts, my cells, my very sense of being shatters...then I realize why.

Raven has taken over my body.

CHAPTER TWENTY-TWO

It's been a long time since I was in my private sanctuary deep within my core. Over the past two years, it manifested as Shenanigans, then my sacred grove. The last time I was here, it was the Shenanigan's bar located within my sacred grove with Brendan tending bar. Today, it's neither of those places.

I walk the quiet space, studying the colorful fish swimming beneath the glass floor. The tropical breeze blows the gossamer drapes into the living room, and I breathe the salty mist of the turquoise waters into the depths of my lungs.

I'm not surprised this is my new safe place.

It's the overwater bungalow Sloan rented us in the Maldives. It's our honeymoon home.

While every sight and scent around me brings warm memories of love, peace, and reflection, I can't give in to the illusion.

I'm not here of my free will.

I've been forced here with nothing to say about it.

Clenching my fists, I stare at the vast waters and gather my strength. *Get out of me you bitch!*

I scream with everything I've got, but it does no good. Raven has possessed me and locked me away in my mind.

Have they noticed?

They'd notice right away, wouldn't they?

When nothing happens, I turn inward and focus.

My bare feet pad silently across the section of the glass floor in the living room to the rich, polished wood of our bedroom.

It's all exactly as I remember.

The four-poster bed draped with lush vines and velvety white flowers…the bottle of wine chilling…the glass wall open to let the magnificence of nature into our celebration.

It's perfection.

Even though I told Sloan I could stay there with him forever and never want for a thing, this isn't truly that. This is a dreamscape.

Sloan's not here.

I'm not on my honeymoon.

I'm trapped.

Lying on the crisp white coverlet, I fold my hands onto my stomach and close my eyes. Even if Raven stuffed me in here, this is my body, and I don't have to stay here.

At least…I don't think I do.

Meditation hasn't always come easily, but Sloan is a master and has taught me all I need to know. I'm present and mindful. I'm aware of my body and my breathing. I am in control of my destiny.

All right, that last one might not be technically true right now, but manifesting has power too.

I can do this.

My body. My senses. My power.

I'm not sure how long it takes to break through the veil of her exile, but when I open my eyes, at least I see the world around me.

Da and Dillan are kneeling over the human bodies Raven and Coyote possessed, and I fight with all I have to make my situation known.

My arms don't flail.

My words don't break free.

Nothing I say or do gets their attention.

At first, the world outside my body is like a distant void, and I can barely make out what's said. As I dig in and fight Raven's control, I become fully aware.

"Dionysus, take me to the children." I hear my voice, but everything about it sounds wrong to my ears. "I need to make sure they aren't hurt."

Nonononono...don't take us to the monkeys.

"Sure, Jane. Let me check in with Artemis first, and we'll go. You don't want me leaving her in your city if she's still in a mood."

Damn, I hate this. I have so many questions for his half-sister, and I can't ask any of them.

While he jogs off to speak to Artemis, my family gathers around.

Da runs a hand over the red and gray scruff on his jaw. "The humans are dead. Calum will stay behind and take care of identification and notification of the next of kin fer the man."

"What about Kaija?" Dillan asks. "From what she said, it sounded like Raven inhabited her body for a long time."

"Aye, I'd say a very long time. Did ye not see what became of her?"

Dillan frowns, and we both follow Da's pointed finger to the mound of ash where Kaija fell. "That's her?"

"What's left of her, aye."

"That's messed up."

You will pay for that. Raven's thoughts echo in the air around me.

How is you losing that body our fault? You kidnapped our kids, and Artemis cut you down. We had nothing to do with any of this.

You have everything to do with this, and you know it.

Why, because Bruin loves me? The charged silence tells me I'm right about that. *From what Bruin told me, you and he ended things thousands of years ago. I'm not sure what the statute of limitations is on being a jealous ex, but I'm pretty sure it's not millennia.*

You know nothing of Bear's love.

Not his romantic love but I know his heart. Speaking of Bruin. What's your plan?

My plan about what?

About Bruin. He lives within me. We're bound. I'm guessing the two of you can't both occupy my body at the same time, and if you can, he'll know you're here.

You are a nosy child who knows nothing.

I chuckle. *If you say so.*

Dionysus returns and holds out his hand.

I struggle against the tether of her hold, my anxiety spiking at the idea of this vindictive bitch getting anywhere near those kids again.

Raven stares down at his palm and hesitates. It's only after he holds his free hand out and my family starts stacking hands that she accepts the gesture.

When everyone's ready, Dionysus looks at me. "Jane? Are you going to invite Bruin to join you?"

My gaze turns to my Bear sitting among the group. "He's filthy. Perhaps after he's clean."

That raises quite a few eyebrows and I chuckle.

You find something funny, girl?

Nope. Just minding my own. Carry on. You do you.

In truth, I was worried she might fool them long enough to get another run at the kids, but she won't. She might have the upper hand now, but it won't take long for my fam jam to figure out what happened.

Then the only question is, how will they pry her out of me? It didn't work out well for Kaija, and I'd rather not wind up as a heap of dust on the floor.

Wallace's clinic is buzzing when we arrive, and the knot of anxiety in my stomach twists. It's maddening looking out the windows of my eyes and not being able to move my head or try to find Sloan.

He'll know it's not me.

In the aftermath of the battle, Da and the others had split focus, but as soon as conversations strike up and Raven pretends to be me, they'll figure it out.

"Lady Druid, there you are." Garnet rushes out of the hall to the recovery rooms and straight at me. His long, ebony hair flows behind his shoulders as his stride cuts the distance between us.

I sense Raven's unease and wait for her to shoot herself in the foot.

Garnet snatches me off the floor, his arms tight around me as he presses his cheek against my head. "You never cease to amaze me. I won't forget this, Fi."

"I'm glad everything worked out," Raven says.

He nods. "Myra's awake and is asking for you. Come, it'll make her feel better to thank you herself."

Raven's annoyance ratchets as we're swept into the wake of the alpha lion. "Where are the children?"

He stops at the open door of a recovery room and smiles. "Wallace checked them over and other than that fucking bitch forcing them to sleep, they were unharmed. Nikon took them to the island for safekeeping."

"Then we need to go there."

"We will, but first, I know how anxious you must be to say hi to Myra."

I am. And even if Garnet doesn't realize it, delaying Raven and removing her access to the kids is a win for all of us. Also, Garnet can smell lies, so the longer he's around, the better the chance the jig will be up.

"Hey, girlfriend." Myra is lying down, looking pale but alert. She lifts her hands to me and wiggles her fingers.

With a gentle nudge against my back from Garnet, we shuffle forward. "You look much better than the last time I saw you."

All right. That's probably true.

Knowing Myra, she wouldn't have sat idly on the couch in a panic while her child was being kidnapped as Kinu did. She fought with everything in her and needed to be rushed in for medical intervention.

"Thank you for finding our baby girl and getting her back safe. Before you say it, I know it was a team effort, but I also know that you would never have given up or slowed down until you found them."

"They are incredibly important to me."

She squeezes my hand. "I know. When I woke up and Garnet was here, I knew you were on the case because he wouldn't trust anyone else to fight as hard as he would to bring our baby home."

"She is a special child."

"Absolutely."

"I should let you rest. I want to check in on—"

"Och, there ye are, *a ghra*. I heard ye were here."

Sloan's voice has my heart tripping in my chest. My gaze lifts to my handsome hubby striding through the doorway, and he pulls me to my feet. With a hand cupped under my jaw, he studies me from head to foot. "Yer all right then?"

"Never better."

"Nikon said when he left yer group was elbow deep in the battle against Raven and Coyote."

"It's over now."

"Yer Da said Raven escaped when Kaija was killed."

"That's the way it seemed, yes."

Sloan tilts his head as he looks into my eyes, and I see him questioning something. *Come on, hotness. You know me. I know you'll figure this out.* "Are ye sure yer all right, luv? Ye seem...off."

"I'm very worried about the children. I think we should go to them and make sure they are all right."

"They are." Nikon strides up the corridor and ducks into Myra's room. "Glad you're feeling better, Myra. I wanted to let you know that Dionysus relieved me and has Artemis checking on them."

Myra frowns. "Do we have any idea why Artemis marked them in the first place?"

"Not yet. That's still a mystery," Nikon says.

Garnet runs a gentle caress down Myra's arm. "I'm sure between Dionysus and Clan Cumhaill there with her they'll find out."

"Are you heading back there?" Raven asks.

"Not if I can help it. Hecate, Artemis, and Selene are the Greek triad of sisters. Needless to say, Artemis and I have crossed paths a few times over the centuries, and it's never been pleasant. She thinks Hecate was too good for me in the first place and me trying to get as far away from her as possible is insolent and insulting."

"So, yer avoidin' the palace at all costs?" Sloan asks.

Nikon waggles his brow. "Pretty much, yeah. I thought if everyone is cool with it, I'd head home, sort my sock drawer, and catch up on my knitting."

Garnet, Sloan, and Myra all laugh. Raven misses the humor altogether.

Sloan rubs a hand against my back, and I stiffen.

"Thanks for letting us know, Greek," Garnet says. "As soon as Wallace gives Myra one last once-over, we're leaving too."

"When we all get home, you can expect a barbeque blowout in the oasis in all of your honor," Myra says.

Nikon waggles his brows. "Sweet. Fi could use a little sun on her skin. She looks like Casper."

I glance from him to Sloan. "Casper, ruler of the Mayan city of Palenque?"

Sloan's brows shoot up, and I laugh. *Good one, Raven. Yeah, that's exactly who he means.*

Silence! I can't help it that your insipid life is too mundane for me to comprehend.

Sure. We'll go with that.

"Anyhoo." Nikon looks me over with a scrutinizing gaze. "I'm off. Laters."

"Thanks again, Greek," Garnet says.

"Not a problem. Happy to help with the happily ever after."

Sloan and I leave Garnet to help Myra get dressed and meet Wallace in the corridor. He moves in to say hello and Raven tenses before realizing he's about to kiss my cheek. "There's my favorite daughter-in-law. Congratulations on gettin' Jackson and Imari back where they belong. Ye must be so chuffed."

"It's been a day of unexpected highs and lows, for certain."

A blonde elf with kind eyes comes by with a clipboard, and he reads the top page of whatever she's showing him. He nods and then hands it back. "That's fine, Willow. Send him home but ask that he come back if the symptoms return."

His attention falls back on me, and he smiles. "Yer whole after the battle? None of the usual Fiona catastrophes that we're all much too accustomed to?"

If he only knew.

"Nothing worth mentioning."

"I'm relieved to hear it. Hey, before ye go, could I give ye a book I've been meanin' to send to Lugh? We got to talkin' at yer weddin', and I think he'll enjoy it."

I feel Raven's reluctance to get involved, but I nod. "Of course."

"Perfect. I set it on the table in yer room upstairs."

Sloan slides his hand into mine and *poofs* us into the far wing of Stonecrest Castle and his childhood bedroom. Raven glances around the room, and I'm not sure what she's looking for. Doesn't matter. The more disoriented she looks, the better.

"Are ye truly all right, Mrs. Mackenzie?" He steps in front of me and studies me with a warm gaze.

"Don't I seem all right?"

He brushes a gentle finger down the side of my cheek and under my chin. "I'm not sure. That's why I asked."

"Don't concern yourself. I'm fine."

"Yer my bride. I'll always concern myself with yer well-bein', luv. That's my job." He grins and leans down to brush a kiss across my lips. "If I haven't proven it often enough, I love my job."

I'm not sure what her plan is, but Raven takes his act of tenderness and amps things up. My hands slide around him, pulling him closer, one hand on his lower back and the other on the back of his neck.

I'm honestly not sure how I feel about this. I want the bitch out of my body, but technically, Sloan's kissing me...but it's not me...

It's very confusing.

Wait...tongue? Seriously? We're picking up a book for my grandfather and heading to meet up with my family, and she's testing his gag reflex?

Not the time or place.

Sloan doesn't seem bothered by the sudden groping. And I do mean groping. I'm clinging to him like a desperate koala bear suckerfished to his face.

Come on, hotness. You gotta know something's off, right? I haven't seen Jackson or Imari to make sure they're safe. Garnet and Myra are downstairs waiting to go to the island. You know me. I wouldn't get carried away like this while people are waiting on us and so many balls are in the air.

It's Sloan who breaks the kiss and comes up for air. He eases back and can't look at me. "We should get back downstairs. Myra and Garnet are anxious to get back to Imari."

Raven isn't the least bit worked up. That says a lot because Sloan's an amazeballs kisser and a kiss like that would steal anyone's breath.

"If ye'll excuse me fer one second, I need to pop into the ensuite. I'll be right with ye."

Sloan strides off to the washroom, and I sigh. He didn't figure it out. How will I get out of here if no one is figuring this out?

A moment later, the toilet flushes, the faucet runs water into the sink, and Sloan is back. "All set, luv. Shall we go back downstairs to get Bruin and the others?"

I hold my hand out. "Absolutely."

We pop back down to the clinic where Bruin is milling around and chatting with Garnet. When they register our return, their conversation ends, and Garnet straightens. "Wallace wants to keep Myra in bed for a few more hours, but I'm anxious to check in with Imari. I would still like to join you if that works."

Sloan nods. "Absolutely. I'm sure Imari is anxious to see her father."

Sloan takes my hand and grips Garnet's shoulder. Garnet has his hand on Bruin's muscled shoulder, so the moment the connection is complete, we portal out of Stonecrest Castle.

I expect the warmth of Isilon but am surprised to be standing on the open lawn of Gran and Granda's backyard. Then I remember the book. Sloan probably wants to drop off the book before we go and—

I feel the signature of Sloan's powers rush over my skin and a spell takes hold. Whatever he did, it's immediate. He *poofs* ten feet away and holds his palms out. "Get out of my wife, ye wily bitch.

I'll give ye one chance to leave peacefully. Then it won't go as well fer ye."

He did it! He knew I'm not me!

Dionysus snaps in on my left beside Bruin, and Nikon appears on my right. Artemis joins the circle, and with Garnet behind me, I'm well and truly surrounded.

"Hello again, Raven," Artemis says. "I've just spent an illuminating time with my marked children. It seems you didn't get what you wanted from them after all."

"What I wanted was to knock you to your knees."

Artemis laughs, and the peal of her amusement rings through the clearing. "What you wanted was to ruin my plans and try to absorb my power in the process. What's the matter, old girl, not feeling as dangerous as you once were?"

Raven's possession already immobilized *me*, but now with Sloan's spell, she's immobilized too.

Ha! Sucks to be you.

Silence. If you think your pathetic friends can hold me, you are sorely mistaken.

Oh, they can hold you. And I'm quite sure they can eject your pompous ass out of me. Buh-bye, bitch.

Gloat all you want, but if I go down, I'll take you with me. Bear is mine. You had no right to bond with him.

I didn't even know you existed until a few days ago. How is this on me?

I don't think logic will help me. Whatever Raven has in mind it's taking hold.

A wave of bitterness coats my tongue as a dark, icy dread spreads through my system. It consumes the warmth in my body at a mind-numbing rate.

I fight against the plague infecting my system, but it's no use. She's too strong.

The poisoning of my system is vile, and I choke...spitting froth as my lungs burn. What is she doing to me? I try to call my powers forward to protect me from the bombardment, but my cells won't ignite.

None of my power is coming online.

I drop to the ground, heaving…

Then convulsions set in.

The moment Raven releases me, I'm free from her grasp, but I'm blacking out.

Sloan *poofs* forward and drops to his knees.

Scooping me into his arms, we *poof* again.

CHAPTER TWENTY-THREE

I wake to the sun's warmth on my skin and the sound of powerful wings beating in the air. My body feels heavy, and my limbs aren't responding to my commands.

In the distance, I hear children playing wildly, and I want to sit up and see where I am and what fun I'm missing out on.

From the smell of the air and the sound of that deep and rhythmic *whump, whump* of wings, I figure I'm recuperating in Isilon. Fog still blankets my mind, and my eyes are too heavy to open.

Whatever Raven did to me, it took its toll. Still, encased in the warmth of the sun, I feel the healing strength of nature all around me.

Bruin? Are you here?

My bear doesn't answer, and I can't feel his strength inside me. That more than anything makes me worry.

Or at least I would be worried if I could think clearly...or move...or open my eyes....

"Internal Warmth."

I sigh as a rush of heat suffuses my body, chasing away the chill.

"Och, yer frozen, *a ghra*. I'm sorry. I didn't realize Meg stole yer blanket until I found it on the sectional in the living room."

He's right. I'm shivering, and my skin feels like that dark, icy plague is still inside me.

The weight of several blankets presses down on my body, and he rubs my arms. "Is that better?"

Much better. Thanks.

Sloan keeps his hands on me, rubbing my arms and reaching under the blanket to press his palm on my chest. The infusion of heat from his spell is incredible.

My teeth stop chattering and my muscles unlock from their hypothermic spasms.

I want to groan, but nothing I do makes any impact.

Whatever Raven did to lock me out of my body is still in full effect.

Warm lips touch mine and I wish I could kiss him back. "Ye need to fight this, *a ghra*. Don't give up. Ye need to fight her hold."

Her hold? I thought she left.

Is Raven still possessing me? I search within myself, seeking out any hint of the bitch still residing in even the darkest recesses of my body.

I don't find any trace of her.

If she's still got a hold on me, I don't think it's from possession. It has to be from poisoning my system when she abandoned me.

Sloan snuggles in, curling around me. He slides one arm under my neck and rests the other across my stomach. "Good night, *a ghra*. Sleep well. If ye can hear me, know that I'll be dreamin' of the day ye open yer eyes again."

"Hold her up, Em. Don't let her tip."

"Dude. There's no way I'd let her tip. I've got her."

I chuckle as Emmet and Dionysus bicker about whether I'm secure. From the decadence of being surrounded by water, I'm guessing the boys have flashed me over to the hot tub on the rooftop of the tavern garden.

"Pass her to me."

There's a shift in my world as they pass me over to sit on Dionysus' lap. His arms wrap around me, and he brushes his warm, wet fingers against my cheek.

"Hey, Jane. It's hot tubbing day. Don't tell Irish. He'll lose his mind if he finds out. That boy's wound tighter than a camel's ass in a sandstorm."

"It's not his fault," Em says. "He loves her so damned much."

"True, but she still deserves a change of scenery. Don't you, Jane?"

"Hells, yeah, she does. I think she looks better already. At least there's some color in her cheeks."

Dionysus presses a kiss on my cheek. "I *agape* you, Jane. I miss you."

I'm right here, boys. I hear you. I just can't respond.

Dionysus adjusts me on his lap. "So, let's catch you up. Today Irish is meeting some crazy witch doctor in the jungles of the Amazon. Nikon and I have been portaling him all over the world, trying to find something to break you out of this curse."

Seriously? The bitch cursed me?

"You'll love this. Jonah and I celebrated our one-month anniversary together last night. He sends his love, by the way."

A month? My heart races. *I've missed a month of my life? No wonder Sloan's wound up.*

"Yeah, my sweet Texas cowboy is staying at the loft, and it's going really well. He gets me, Jane. Like you do."

I'm so happy you're happy, Tarzan.

"So, even though I teased him about keeping him prisoner as

my plaything, for our anniversary, I extended the elevator up to my floor so he can get in and out of the building."

That's very thoughtful, sweetie.

"You gotta wake up, Jane. It's almost Halloween, and I need help with my joint costume with Jonah. I need it to be mind-blowing. Eros always tries to outdo me, and I want us to shine as a couple."

I want that too. I'm trying.

The crackle of flames and the scent of burning logs accompany the toasty warmth of my insides. Someone is fussing with the fireplace and adjusting me on the couch. "Are you ready for our movie marathon, sista?"

Ready, Em.

"We've got *While You Were Sleeping, Just Like Heaven, Coma,* and *Return of the Jedi*. Technically, Han didn't wake from a coma, but he missed out on a gap of time and had to wake up, so I counted it."

He adjusts us on the couch and...

I smell the popcorn.

"Here you go, baby girl." Brendan sets the bowl on my lap, and I smile. Yep, if the popcorn is to be shared, I always hold the bowl. "You gotta try to come back to us, Fi. I know you're in there."

I'm trying, Brenny. I am.

"He's right, Fi. Just try to wake up, 'kay?"

I would if I could, Em.

"When I said I wanted you to live here and spend more time with me, this isn't what I meant. I need you to laugh and tease me and give Dillan the finger when he's being an ass."

When isn't Dillan being an ass?

"When isn't Dillan an ass?" Brendan says.

Exactly.

"The thing is...without you here to call him on it, Dillan's gotten creepy quiet. Calum too. It's been too long, Fi. Nobody's giving up, but we don't know what to do for you."

I don't know either, Em. I wish I did.

The sun is warm on my skin again, and I breathe the heat deep into my lungs. Wings flap close by, and I know it's Dart. I feel him across our bond. *I miss you, blue boy.*

Fi? Is that you?

Dart! You can hear me?

I feel the explosion of relief that bursts across our bond. *Yes, I can. Finally! Dionysus, Nikon, Bruin, and I have all been trying to reach you, but none of us have been able to get through.*

Does that mean I'm getting better?

How could it not? Listen, I'm not sure how aware you are, but Raven cursed you.

Yeah. I take it I'm a bit of a wreck.

Sloan, Wallace, and Merlin worked on you for ages. They almost didn't get you back.

Back? I died?

A couple of times. Eva wouldn't let the reapers take you. She battled hard to keep you with us. She got into a lot of trouble about that but doesn't care. She's claiming that being your guardian angel doesn't end with the human world. You need a champion on all fronts.

True story. Why can't I wake up?

No one knows. Sloan's been researching, traveling, and trying, but you're still stuck in the curse.

My heart aches for what he's going through. I lived through the same thing last year during the Culling. Tell him I love him, buddy. I'm trying. It's just so cold. Whatever she did to me is like a dark chasm of ice freezing me from the inside. The only time I seem to rise to the surface is when I'm toasty warm.

I'll tell him. Maybe that's important.

I love you, buddy. Please don't give up on me.

Never. Not in a thousand lifetimes.

Light pierces my eyes, and I groan as searing pain spears through my head. "Holy hell, that's bright."

"Emmet, pull the curtain," Sloan barks.

Wait, did he hear me? I squint and turn my head. I feel like the Tin Man when he's all seized up. "I need a quart of oil on my joints."

Sloan grins at me and shakes his head. "I don't even know what that means, but I'll take whatever crazy yer dishin' out."

"Wait. Who are you?"

The panic that rocks him is way too shattering, and I reach up and touch his face. "Just messing with you, hotness. Bad joke."

He drops his head and exhales. "Feckin' hell, Fi. Ye just robbed years from my life."

"Sorry. But really, how could you believe I could ever forget this face? My God, you're gorgeous."

The dim room rumbles with male chuckles, and I glance around at Da, my brothers, the Greeks... "Jonah! Welcome. Congrats on the anniversary."

Jonah blinks, and Dionysus wraps his arms around him from behind. "You *did* hear me. I knew it."

"I did. How could I not wake up for hot tubbing?"

"Hot tubbing?" Sloan snaps, turning to glare at Dionysus.

"Jane! I told you not to tell him. That was supposed to be our secret."

"Sorry, Tarzan. Forgive me. I was in a coma and forgot that part."

"You're forgiven. I *agape* you, Jane."

"I *agape* all of you." I shift my legs under the mountain of blankets bringing me close to a broil. Everything seems to be working. I can feel my legs and wiggle my toes. "So, is the curse broken? Aurora isn't going to go back to sleep, is she?"

"You shouldn't, Sleeping Beauty." Merlin smiles at me from the end of the bed. "Once Dart told us about how the curse felt to you, we were able to narrow down our course of treatment. Basically, we needed to reignite your fae pilot light."

I chuckle. "Oh, is that all?"

"Yeah. All in a day's work."

Even with the lighthearted kidding around, I see the strain and exhaustion on all their faces. "How long has it been? Am I in time to help with the Halloween costumes?"

Dionysus' smile falls. "Not this year, Jane. But the good news is, you're in time for egg nog."

"Egg nog? It's December?" My voice comes out a lot more screechy and panicked than I meant.

Da sits on the edge of the bed opposite Sloan. "A few months lost is a small price fer gettin' ye back, *mo chroi*. At least this time when ye were taken from us, we knew ye were safe, and we could keep watch over ye."

The loss of time feels like a dark, icy, gaping vortex. Three months…I swipe at the hot tears burning down my cheeks. "It's our first year of marriage, and I missed a quarter of it."

Sloan pulls me up to sit and wraps me in a hug. "In a lifetime together, three months will seem like nothin', *a ghra.* I promise."

I squeeze him tight and the fear and frustration I've been suffering under rush to the surface. "I'm so sorry. I know how sad and lonely you were. How you never stopped researching. How you traveled the world, searching for a way to wake me. You were doing everything, and I left you alone in your grief."

I know this without a doubt because it's how I felt when he wouldn't wake up last Christmas.

Grief takes over, and silent tears turn to sobs. I close my eyes and hug him, holding on as if he's the anchor to my existence.

Which he is.

There's a soft shuffle of footsteps, and the bed lifts as Da gets up and leaves with the others. Yeah, they know I need a minute.

My fam jam is good like that.

I'm not sure how long it takes me to cry myself dry, but I'm a hot mess, and his shirt isn't much better. Easing back, I accept the tissues he pulls from the box and regroup. "Sorry. I snotted all over you."

He shrugs and pulls out a couple of tissues for himself. "I'll never complain about havin' ye need me as ye do, luv. It's the only thing that can balance how much I need ye right back."

I pull the hem of his shirt and lift it off him before tossing it to the floor.

He chuckles and arches a brow. "I like where yer mind's goin' but we've got a dozen people outside the door waitin' fer their turn to hold ye."

"We're not getting sexy, Mackenzie. I want to lay with you for a minute and don't want your grody shirt touching me."

Leaning back onto my pillow, I hold my arms open. "Just for a few minutes."

My snuggle time with Sloan is over too soon, but I want to hug everyone else too. The fact that it's been three months since I've showered is a hit to my feminine ego.

Although somehow I'm not gross.

Somebody spelled me somehow on that one.

Still, I'm a hugger, and I want people to want to hug me too, so I take a shower, brush my teeth twice, and towel-dry my hair. When I step back into the bedroom I woke up in, I'm shocked and stop dead in my tracks.

Kinu is sitting on the edge of the bed, worrying her fingers in her lap. "Hey, Fi."

"Hey."

When she looks up at me, my emotions war between anger, hurt, and sorrow.

"We used to be as close as sisters," she says.

"Yeah, then something broke, and you refused to talk to me so we could fix it."

That reality strikes a blow. I can tell by the guilt in her gaze that she finally sees the damage she caused. "I'm sorry, Fi."

I lean back against the dresser and cross my arms. There's a lot I want to say but... "I'm not going to make it easy on you. You can suffer a little of the emotional frustration and rejection that you've been putting me through for months."

She flinches under the bite of my tone, but I don't care. Being a protective parent worried about her kids doesn't give her *carte blanche* to trash our relationship when I did nothing wrong.

"I know you know my reasons. I was afraid for Aiden, I worried about the kids' future, and there are so many dangers and unknowns in the magical world that it's terrifying. One minute Jackson is playing in his room and the next he's been abducted by two gods."

Yeah. That is the one incident I *do* blame myself for.

Bruin warned me what could happen, and I didn't anticipate that it could hit my family. Not that I had any indications it would. Still...I'll own that one.

"Then you did what you always do. You threw yourself in front of the danger to shield us. In the moment, I've seen only the horrors of your injuries—the stabbings, the possessions, the poisonings, the beatings. I saw only the violence."

She stands and straightens. "I missed the part where this happened to you. Fionn marked you as his successor, and you had no say. You took up the druid mantle to save Lugh's life, and there was really no choice in that, either. Your shield draws danger to you, and as much as that scares me, it's you who lands in the crosshairs time and again."

"I don't deny there is collateral damage." I take ownership of what I know is because of me. "Liam was shot. Sloan, Calum, Emmet, Dillan...they've all suffered injuries because of the Pandora's Box I opened. I get that. I don't deny that."

"That's where I got tunnel vision. From the outside looking in, I only saw the people we love coming home bloody, and I put that on you. That wasn't fair."

I shrug. "So, what changed?"

"A few things. Aiden showed me the news coverage of what you did at the Alamo. It kills him that he wasn't there to help you and I know he didn't go because of me. And yet...I saw the footage of you, Dillan, Calum, and Sloan putting yourselves between the danger and all those people and it dawned on me that if you weren't there, they would've all died."

She shrugs and exhales a long breath. "As much as I hate the violence, I know you're all heroes. What you do matters as much as what they did as cops mattered. I also know you love the kids as your own and you fight even harder than me to keep them safe."

The sting of emotion burns the rims of my eyes, and I look up and blink to stop the tears.

"You brought Imari and Jackson home. You safeguarded Bella and Binx. No matter what the situation, you stand as the shield to protect the innocent at all costs. I should have seen that sooner."

Hope pushes at my lungs and my breath flutters. "And now that you do?"

She lifts her chin and smiles. "I'm truly, genuinely, terribly sorry for everything I put you through. You've been lying here for months after saving my son. You died, and everything we've shared lately has been anger. I realized bad stuff happens to good people all the time in the human world and there's no one to blame. It's how we handle it that matters."

"Yeah? You're sure?"

She nods. "I want to ask you two favors."

"All right. What are they?"

"I want you and Sloan to oversee Jackson's training and one day do the same for Meg and the twins. I don't understand what they can be, but I want them to embrace their heritage. They need to know how to defend themselves and the people around them. I want them to learn from the best."

Relief washes through me. Jackson has gifts, and he needs to start developing them, especially if people are targeting him. "We'd be happy to train them. And the second favor?"

She pegs me with a pleading gaze and opens her arms. "I'd really like to fix this and have my sister back in my life."

I move without hesitation and just like that, I have my sister back again. Love is magic.

CHAPTER TWENTY-FOUR

The next hour is filled with hugs and happiness as the She's Out of Her Curse Coma celebration rages on. Jonah showed Dionysus pictures of event decorations, and the Cumhaill condo at the top of the palace tower is decked out in streamers, stars, balloons, and glitter.

There's even a giant sign that says, Awake at Last.

Thankfully, Dionysus is a god and can clean this all up with the snap of his fingers.

"You gotta stop doing this shit, Fi." Liam stands behind me on the balcony, wraps an arm across my shoulders, and rests his cheek on the back of my head. "You're a hard woman to love, you know that?"

I chuckle, drinking in the sight of Dart and Saxa racing through the message, We missed you, Jane! written in the clouds.

"If I could be easier on everyone's nerves, you know I would be."

"Yeah, I know."

"Sorry I missed the grand opening of the tavern. I was really looking forward to us getting our groove on."

"Meh, there's plenty of time to make it up to me now. It was a good time, though...well, as good as it could be with you lying up here."

"Have I been here the whole three months?"

Sloan comes out to join us. "Aye, ye have." He's carrying two flutes of pink champagne, each one blessed with a couple of raspberries bobbing on the surface. He thinks this is a fruit abomination, but I think it's fun and festive.

Like all things, he indulges me.

"Raven intended to tear ye from Bruin's life. We weren't about to let her take another run at ye by leavin' ye unconscious where she could get ye."

"Speaking of Bruin. Where is he? I miss him, and he's not at my party. I've had visions all afternoon of him off somewhere getting drunk out of some self-sabotaging guilt."

Liam's expression makes my heart ache.

"Oh, no."

Liam waves away the champagne offered and shows Sloan he has a beer. "No. That phase came and went. We lost him to the tavern for a few long, dark weeks, but your dad stepped in and set him straight with one of his more aggressive 'Pull yer shite together' speeches."

I chuckle. "I know exactly the ones you mean. So, where is he now?"

Sloan swallows a sip of champagne and gives his raspberry a dirty look. "He felt helpless here, so Dionysus hooked him up with Artemis, and they've been on the great hunt."

"They're going after Raven?"

"Aye, they are."

"What about Coyote?"

"Bruin doesn't know if they're together, so there's no way to guess if he's goin' after just her or them both. It's clear that she's the bigger threat to you and the kids."

"I don't like him chasing her down alone."

Dionysus comes out to join us and snorts. "He's not alone, Jane. Artie is with him. Trust me, Raven will run, but she can't hide from the goddess of the hunt."

Sloan grins. "Once they find her, Artemis has a special place in the core of Mount Olympus where she locks down empowered problems."

"If Coyote is there too, they can have a communal cell."

I draw a deep breath and exhale. "I like the sound of that, but does Bruin need to be there? I'm sure Artemis and the hounds have minions to hunt with her, don't they? It doesn't have to be Bruin."

Dionysus leans forward and kisses my forehead. "He'll be fine, Jane. Artemis is a lot of things, but first and foremost she's a cunning huntress. Raven made a huge mistake going after the Crescent Marked."

I squeeze Sloan's arm. "What about the kids? Are they safe?"

"Aye, luv. Binx is back in the house with his family. Bella is home in Montréal with her new pet rabbit."

"Cinna Bun," Dionysus corrects.

Sloan nods. "Jackson is enjoying every minute of his new empowered life."

I meet his coy smile, and my curiosity piques. "What's this now? Have you all been holding out on me?"

He steps toward the balcony's stone wall and points down at a sprawling blue house with phosphorescent moss growing on the roof. "Kinu and Aiden decided to move here. They have twice as much space, and it eases Kinu's mind to live here where the kids won't be targeted. Besides, he and Binx have become thick as thieves."

I take in the cul de sac below. It backs onto a long, forested area and has a pond at the end of the street. "Wow, that's awesome. Bizzy's going to miss them like crazy, though."

Liam grins. "Not really. Do you see the yellow house across

the little courtyard from them? That's Kev and Calum. They moved here too."

"What?" I blink, staring at the golden two-story directly opposite Aiden's blue house.

I see where this is going, and my heart is hammering. Turning to Sloan, I squeeze his wrists. "Which one is ours, hotness? You picked one for us too, didn't you?"

The coy smile he flashes me tells me I'm right. "Which one do ye think?"

I look at the little community around the cobbled courtyard. There are five houses around the lightbulb of the street, and four more on either side as the road leads deeper into the city.

Now that I'm looking, it's as obvious as his love for me. "Oh, we have our own little stone castle. Cute."

Liam snorts. "It's not so little, Fi. Remember we're way up here on the golden dildo."

I wave that away. "It's not Stonecrest Castle big, is all I was saying. And, no, I don't want huge. It's location, location, location, for me…and, of course, making sure we have good neighbors."

Sloan smiles and points. "Then ye'll like to know Dillan and Eva chose the pink one and—"

I snort. "Seriously, Dillan is living in a pink house?"

"Until he convinces Eva to paint it."

"Which he won't." Liam laughs. "She loves her pink house. There's no way she'll let him change it."

I laugh at that. "Can we go down and see them?"

Sloan *tinks* my glass with his. "Garnet and Myra just got here with Imari, and ye need to give Dillan a few minutes alone with ye. This one hit him hard, luv."

He's right. I know he's right.

"Yeah, okay. First, we spread the love. Then we'll explore the home base for our new lives. Honestly, I don't care if it's a cardboard box. If it brings everyone back together, it'll be perfect."

Dionysus rolls his eyes. "And here we worked hard to give her the home of her dreams. We could've given her a cardboard box."

Sloan laughs. "Och, well, I think we could still find her a box if she prefers."

"I have some boxes back at the tavern," Liam offers.

I laugh. "Har-har. You boys are *soooo* funny."

ENDNOTE

Thank you for reading *Hexes in Texas*, book five in the Case Files of an Urban Druid series. While the story is fresh in your mind, and as a favor to Michael and me, please click HERE and tell other readers what you thought.

A quick star rating and/or even one sentence can mean so much to readers deciding whether or not to try a book, series, or a new-to-them author.

Thank you.

If you want more of the Cumhaill adventures, you can find book six in the series, *Wendigos in Washington,* on Amazon.

AUTHOR NOTES - AUBURN TEMPEST

WRITTEN OCTOBER 11, 2022

I finished this book on Canadian Thanksgiving Monday. (Obviously I wasn't using a detailed calendar when I gave Michael my proposed submission dates because really? I made my book due on Turkey Day? What the hell was I thinking?)

Anyhoo...it's done, and I am thankful for that.

I spent a few fun hours with my fam jam carving turkey, laughing at how cute my three-year-old granddaughter is, and eating too much raspberry trifle.

Hexes in Texas will be coming to you soon after American Thanksgiving, so there's a theme I thought I'd embrace.

I'm thankful for Michael and LMBPN for all they do to take my stories and make them great. The support and encouragement within that group make it a pleasure to produce every book.

I'm also hugely thankful for all of you who read my words

and continue to love and support Fiona and the Cumhaill Fam Jam.

Sincerely, I thank you.

The Urban Druid books are always fun to write, and it's a privilege to be able to love what I do every day.

I really enjoyed this one.

Sometimes Dionysus gets away from me, and I'm sitting in front of my computer laughing and worrying I need to rein him in. I try not to.

As Fi said, I don't love him *despite* the way he is. I love him *because of* the way he is. I *agape* him.

I love them all, but Dionysus is special.

On another note, I did something kind of crazy this week. I signed up for an author signing/masquerade ball/dinner dance in Liverpool, England, in March 2023. I've never been to England, and I have no idea if Auburn Tempest or JL Madore have any fans who will show up.

I envision mine being the only author table with no one there. *What? She's a Canadian? Never heard of her.*

Oh well, I did it anyway.

Don't tell my hubby, but it's sort of an excuse to hop the pond. So, yeah, Fiction, Fans, and Ballgowns 2023. I'll put info about that into the series Facebook page as we get closer to the date.

Okay, I'm going to sneak another half a piece of key lime pie now. Thanks for reading. I *agape* you.

Blessed be,
Auburn Tempest

Facebook page: https://www.facebook.com/groups/167165864237006

Or feel free to drop us a line: UrbanDruid@lmbpn.com

AUTHOR NOTES - MICHAEL ANDERLE

WRITTEN DECEMBER 5, 2022

Thank you for not only reading this story but these authors' notes as well.

AGAPE ...

When you ask Alfonse the Idiot AI™* what 'Agape' is, here is his response:

Agape is a Greek term that refers to selfless, unconditional love. It is a love that is not based on any personal gain or benefit but rather is a love that is given freely and without any expectation of return. In Christian theology, agape is considered the highest form of love, as it reflects God's love for all of humanity.

Ok, I agree that as authors, we often put our book 'out there.'

Then, I thought to myself, 'I feel love for my readers in that I do not expect any love in return. The fact that you read my books and care to read another is the most I can hope for.'

However, curious Mike wanted to know what Alfonse thought a good reason for an author to feel Agape love would be. I hope you are interested as well, because here it comes:

An author might have agape love for his readers because he genuinely cares about their well-being and wants to make a positive impact on their lives. This type of love is not motivated by a desire for personal gain or recognition, but rather is driven by a desire to serve and help others. An author with agape love for his readers may be motivated to write books that are thought-provoking, inspiring, and educational, in order to enrich the lives of his readers and make the world a better place.

Now, I hope that ALL of you are in a good place in your life, and I'd love to know if I made a positive impact. However, can I really expect that to have happened? I write and am involved in Sci-Fi and Urban Fantasy / Paranormal books.

Not exactly life-changing subjects where I could hope to change a life or two.

However, I've been heartened in the past to get fan stories where humor helped a reader through sickness, depression, the loss of a loved one and other things. Perhaps a character going through their own turmoil helped a reader know their personal experience is felt (and understood) by others, and they took something good out of it.

So, from the perspective that I want to entertain and support my readers, I have Agape love for you, our fans.

Wishing you the best for your life, and should you be going through a tough time (quite possible at the end of 2022 with recessions, inflation, wars, and other sh#t going around), I hope you find a little peace, prosperity and pleasure with family, friends, and frivolity as we head into the new year!

Have a fantastic week or weekend, whichever it is for you, and I look forward to chatting with you in the next book.

Ad Aeternitatem,

Michael Anderle

Alfonse the Idiot AI™* - my name for all things A.I. that I

mess with. Over the last 24 months the tools to communicate with Alfonse have gotten better and better. He's pretty damned smart now!

MORE STORIES with Michael newsletter HERE:
https://michael.beehiiv.com/

BOOKS BY AUBURN TEMPEST

Join us on the Facebook page: https://www.facebook.com/groups/167165864237006
Or feel free to drop us a line: UrbanDruid@lmbpn.com
Find Me
Amazon, Facebook, Newsletter,
Web page – www.auburntempest.com
Email – AuburnTempestWrites@gmail.com

Auburn Tempest - Urban Fantasy Action/Adventure
Chronicles of an Urban Druid
Book 1 – A Gilded Cage
Book 2 – A Sacred Grove
Book 3 – A Family Oath
Book 4 – A Witch's Revenge
Book 5 – A Broken Vow
Book 6 – A Druid Hexed
Book 7 – An Immortal's Pain
Book 8 – A Shaman's Power
Book 9 – A Fated Bond
Book 10 – A Dragon's Dare

Book 11 – A God's Mistake
Book 12 – A Destiny Unlocked
Book 13 – A United Front
Book 14 – A Culling Tide
Book 15 – A Danger Destroyed

Case Files of an Urban Druid
Book 1 – Mayhem in Montreal
Book 2 – Sorcery in San Francisco
Book 3 – Necromancy in New Orleans
Book 4 – Hazards in the Hidden City
Book 5 - Hexes in Texas
Book 6 - Wendigos in Washington

Chronicles of an Urban Elemental
Book 1 – Incendio: Fire Born
Book 2 – Magicae: Powers Dawning

If you enjoy my writing and read sexy/steamy romance, my pen name for the books I write in Paranormal and Fantasy Romance is JL Madore.

You can find me on Amazon.

BOOKS BY MICHAEL ANDERLE

Sign up for the LMBPN email list to be notified of new releases and special deals!

https://lmbpn.com/email/

For a complete list of books by Michael Anderle, please visit:

www.lmbpn.com/ma-books/

CONNECT WITH THE AUTHORS

Connect with Auburn

Amazon, Facebook, Newsletter

Web page – www.jlmadore.com

Email – AuburnTempestWrites@gmail.com

Connect with Michael Anderle and sign up for his email list here:

Website: http://lmbpn.com

Email List: http://lmbpn.com/email/

https://www.facebook.com/LMBPNPublishing

https://twitter.com/lmbpn

https://www.instagram.com/lmbpn_publishing/

https://www.bookbub.com/authors/michael-anderle

www.ingramcontent.com/pod-product-compliance
Lightning Source LLC
LaVergne TN
LVHW041909070526
838199LV00051BA/2555